# HomeComing

# HomeComing

## A MISTER PUSS MYSTERY

## MICHAEL CRAFT

QUESTOVER PRESS

Design and typography: M.C. Johnson
Cover images: Adobe Stock
Author's photo: TimCourtneyPhotography.com

Library of Congress Cataloging-in-Publication Data

Craft, Michael, 1950–
HomeComing : a Mister Puss mystery / Michael Craft
    ISBN:   978-0-578-72143-9 (hardcover)
    ISBN:   978-0-578-72162-0 (paperback)
    BISAC:  FIC011000   Fiction / LGBT / Gay
            FIC022110   Fiction / Mystery & Detective / Cozy / Cats & Dogs
            FIC022100   Fiction / Mystery & Detective / Amateur Sleuth

First hardcover and paperback editions: November 2020
Questover Press
    California • Since 2011

**A sentimental journey. A shot at stardom. A talking cat.
What could possibly go wrong?**

The idyllic little town of Dumont, Wisconsin, is atwitter with the news that its favorite son, actor Thad Manning, is returning from Hollywood to try his hand as director of a film recalling his youth. A test scene is scheduled, right there on the town commons, with a cast and crew from Tinseltown. Locals are needed as extras. And there's even a role for a cat. Enter Mister Puss.

When the big day arrives, though, something goes terribly haywire. The test footage looks fabulous, but in a shocking development, someone ends up dead. It was murder, all right, and suspects abound.

Architect Brody Norris and his husband, Marson Miles, have been busy preparing to move into a new house they are building. But now Brody is called to reprise his role as amateur sleuth and sidekick to Sheriff Thomas Simms.

And once again, Brody himself gets a bit of help—from that chatty Abyssinian, Mister Puss.

## HOMECOMING
### Mister Puss Mystery #3

"In this third installment of a series, a Midwestern architect and a clever cat are pulled back into the detective game when a Hollywood movie—and a Hollywood murder—comes to town ... Craft writes in typically polished prose, illustrating his characters with precision and humor ... Fans of Mister Puss will likely enjoy this personality-filled and altogether pleasant sojourn in Dumont."
— *Kirkus Reviews*

"The delight of Michael Craft's 'Mister Puss' adventures lies in his ongoing ability to capture the nuances of architect Brody Norris's life, those he encounters, and small-town living ... The result is a fine mystery that successfully integrates the evolving relationship and lives of a gay couple, a talking cat, and the conundrums they face in trying to reconcile past, present, and future worlds. Readers of LGBT fiction who love cozy mystery styles with a bit of supernatural cat action will relish the setting, approach, and delightful twists and turns of *Home-Coming*, where Mister Puss truly shines."

— *D. Donovan, Senior Reviewer,*
*Midwest Book Review*

## FLABBERGASSED
### Mister Puss Mystery #1

"What an elegant mystery. What an absurd idea made irresistible and almost mystical at the hands of a gifted writer. A talking cat? Yes ... Mister Puss. The best cat in all of modern fiction."
— *Ulysses Dietz, Backlot Gay Book Forum*

"Crisp, lively prose ... an exuberant murder mystery ... delightfully offbeat."    — *Kirkus Reviews*

"*FlabberGassed* is quirky, original, and a delightful read."    — *D. Donovan, Midwest Book Review*

## CHOIRMASTER
### Mister Puss Mystery #2

*Gold Winner:* IBPA Benjamin Franklin Award.
*Finalist:* Lambda Literary Award, Gay Mystery.
*Finalist:* Muse Medallion, Cat Writers Asscociation.

"The reader is breathless from possibilities and flipping pages briskly to find out what's really going on."
— *Andrew J. Peters, Out in Print*

"Compellingly odd ... a lovely place to spend a few hours trying to figure out whodunit and why. A satisfying mystery, pleasantly told."    — *Kirkus Reviews*

*Home*

Sphinx-like he waits
at the door, then slips
through its openness,
a damp of paws,
cold shedding from his coat

Inside, the soft warmth
of cooking smells
and a window seat where
he stares at a hush of falling snow
in blue-gray dusk,

primal purr misting the glass.

— *Lynn DeTurk*

# CONTENTS

PART ONE: *October* . . . . . . . . . . . . . . 1

    Chapter 1              2
    Chapter 2            17
    Chapter 3            34
    Chapter 4            50

PART TWO: *November* . . . . . . . . . . . . 69

    Chapter 5            70
    Chapter 6            88
    Chapter 7          102
    Chapter 8          115
    Chapter 9          124
    Chapter 10        136
    Chapter 11        152
    Chapter 12        164
    Chapter 13        176
    Chapter 14        186
    Chapter 15        201

PART THREE: *December* . . . . . . . . . . . 211

    Chapter 16        212
    Chapter 17        228
    Chapter 18        239
    Chapter 19        250
    Chapter 20        264

Acknowledgments        274
Author's note        275
About the author        276
About the type        277

PART ONE

# OCTOBER

CHAPTER

1

Mister Puss awaited my arrival, and I was running late. If annoyed by my tardiness, he would let me know—in no uncertain words.

Ten years earlier, when I was still in my late twenties, when I was still a young man with far-flung dreams, I could never have guessed that the dual forces of career and love would lead me to settle in Dumont. Against all odds, this idyllic little town in central Wisconsin now felt like home.

Odder still, my calling as an architect had flourished here, in spite of the scandal that rocked the town and titillated the local gentry some three years ago—shortly after my move from California—when my new employer left his wife for me. Twenty-four years my senior, architect Marson Miles had been married for three decades to Prucilla Miles, née Norris. Tongues were wagging not so much because Marson had switched teams, but because Prucilla was the sister of Inez Norris, my proudly single lesbian mother. In other words, Marson had dumped his wife for his nephew.

(Nephew by marriage, that is. Fortunately, when Marson and Prucilla divorced—which didn't take long—Marson ceased to be my uncle.)

Odd circumstances, indeed.

Oddest of all, though, was the cat.

One bright May morning about a year and a half ago, Mary Questman, a wealthy widow who enjoyed her later-life role as

Dumont's leading philanthropist, took in a beguiling Abyssinian that had landed on her doorstep. She named him Mister Puss, and forging what she described as a "special bond" with the mysterious stray, she began confiding to friends that she and Mister Puss had achieved an inexplicable level of communication, verging on the transcendental.

Word on the street: Mary claimed to have a talking cat.

In private, most snickered. In her presence, they humored her. But no one contradicted her. Mary's cheery disposition and loving nature—coupled with her deep pockets and boundless largesse to the community—assured that she was cut some slack.

"Good *morning*, Brody," warbled Mary, stepping out from her front door as I approached the house from my car at the curb.

I waved. "Morning, Mary. Beautiful day." The sky radiated an intense, impossible blue. Since moving to Wisconsin, I had come to favor October over any other month. The dry air was cool that Tuesday, but brilliant sunshine warmed my face. A whisper of a breeze jiggled the turning leaves on stately oaks and elms along Prairie Street, where, in generations past, members of Dumont's upper crust had staked out their turf.

The grand old houses were set well back from the street, with vast front lawns. Mary's home—two stories, classically white, with tall, elegant windows and a deep front porch—sat foursquare atop a gentle rise of the property. While strolling up the boxwood-edged walkway, I glanced to the left, across Mary's long driveway, where I noted the distinctive neighboring house, designed some eighty years earlier by a student of Frank Lloyd Wright, trained at Taliesin in Spring Green.

"Someone's been expecting you," said Mary as I approached.

"Busy morning at the office. My apologies to Mister Puss."

At the mention of his name, the cat emerged from the doorway to join Mary on the porch. Lithe and statuesque with a gleaming ruddy coat and the flecked markings of a wild, much bigger feline—a cougar or bobcat—Mister Puss bore an unmistakable resemblance to the regal domestic cats of ancient Egypt. He wore the jaunty little harness of tanned leather straps that permitted excursions beyond the house, but his matching leash was not yet attached. Mary swooped him up into her arms.

Handing him over to me, she said, "He's been *so* looking forward to his stay with you boys."

"And we've been looking forward to the patter of little feet." As I spoke, Mister Puss reached his paws to the shoulder of my sport coat and stretched his snout toward my ear. His purr rumbled.

*You're late.*

So. Here's the thing. Everyone talks to their pets. Some even indulge in ongoing conversations, responding to imagined dialogue from a fawned-upon furbaby. But when Mary started telling people that her cat sometimes lulled her into a waking trance with his purr—and when she further explained that words clearly emerged from the depths of the purring—even Mary's closest, most loving friends were forced to conclude that her years were catching up with her. If she'd lost a marble or two in her early seventies, so what? Her "talking cat" was merely a benign eccentricity. Still, that didn't stop them from wondering, with a good measure of trepidation: What's next? Had Mary begun an addled, slippery slide to befuddlement and diapers and conservatorship?

I shared those worries—or did, that is, until my skepticism was blown away one afternoon while looking after Mister Puss in Mary's absence. Exactly as Mary had described, the cat lulled me into a waking trance with his purr, and then I, too, began to hear words. On other occasions, snippets of conversation. Later, Mary would repeat some of this back to me, verbatim, having also heard it from the cat.

What sense could I make of this? None at all.

Could I deny that it had happened—and continued to happen? No, I couldn't.

Mary asked, "Come in for a few minutes? Berta's putting His Majesty's things together." Berta was Mary's housekeeper. His Majesty was the cat.

"With pleasure." Stepping inside with Mary, I nudged the door closed and set Mister Puss on the parquet floor. The graceful front hall had been pressed into service as a staging area for the trip that Mary would embark upon that afternoon.

A few months earlier, that past spring, Mary had gone to a weeklong literary conference in Chicago, accompanied by Berta. Mary hadn't ventured much farther than Green Bay in many years, but the junket to Chicago proved so stimulating, she claimed to have been bitten by the travel bug, and now she and Berta were heading out to Arizona for two weeks, to join a tour of Sedona.

Mary's matched set of vintage Hartmann luggage was arranged in two rows near the foot of the wide walnut staircase. Nearby, Berta had stacked a few of her own mismatched, unpedigreed bags. Closer to the front door, Mister Puss's supplies and necessaries were gathered—canned and dry food, litter and box, toys and whatnot—awaiting his departure with me. He had stayed with Marson and me during Mary's last trip, and to my surprise, Marson enjoyed the cat's visit.

Berta, a sturdy woman with a brusque manner and a gray uniform, now appeared from the back of the house and lugged a few garment bags into the entry hall, plopping them on the floor. She was perhaps ten years younger than Mary. They had both been widowed in recent years, and Berta's role in the household, that of a servant, had evolved to include duties that would more aptly describe her as a caretaker and companion.

Every inch a lady, Mary was dressed for travel in kitten-heeled Ferragamo pumps and a smart, matronly skirt and jacket, nubby silk for autumn, probably Chanel. Berta's drab uniform included her usual black service shoes. I couldn't help thinking they would make quite the odd couple in dusty, rustic Sedona.

Berta asked me, "Can I take His Majesty's things out to your car?"

"Nice of you, Berta, but I can handle it. You've already got plenty to deal with."

"Suit yourself." With a shrug, she turned to tend to something.

"Nonsense," Mary piped in.

Berta turned back to me, palm extended. I gave her my keys.

Mary bubbled, "It's going to be just *thrilling*. Some of the ladies were telling me the weather in Sedona will be *perfect*. And the energy vortexes are supposed to be *splendid* this time of year. We might even catch a ... what's it called?"

"Harmonic convergence," said Berta, deadpan, as she schlepped a first load of cat-things out the door.

"Shall we sit down?" suggested Mary, fatigued by the excitement.

I followed her into the parlor adjacent to the front hall. Mister Puss followed me. The tidy room had tall windows looking out toward the street, framed by white enamel trim and floor-to-ceiling drapery of bone-colored silk. A comfy loveseat and two plump armchairs were upholstered in tufted floral chintz. Mary alighted softly on a cushion of the loveseat, crossing her legs at the ankles; Mister Puss hopped up to sit next to her. I sat across from them in one of the chairs. To my right, I could see Berta through a window, rummaging in the trunk of my car. To my left, on a cigarette table between the chairs, I noticed a folded copy of that morning's *Dumont Daily Register*.

As I leaned to take a closer look at the paper, Mary asked, "Did you read Glee's column today?" She was referring to Glee Savage, a close friend of ours who had worked at the *Register* for decades, rising through the ranks from beat reporter to her current position as features editor, covering arts, fashion, society, and gossip. Among her many bylined stories were occasional columns titled "Inside Dumont," introducing readers to someone worth knowing.

I told Mary, "I was rushed this morning—meeting with clients —didn't even have time to open the paper."

Mary leaned forward with a twinkle in her eye. Then she turned her head in the direction of the house next door, the Taliesin house.

I asked, "Thad Manning?" A few months earlier, in June, while attending a cookout at Mary's, I was surprised to meet the popular film actor, who had popped into town for a visit. He had grown up in Dumont and, during his high-school years, had lived in the house next door. I told Mary, "I *wondered* what he was doing here. He seemed sorta tight-lipped about it—nice guy, though."

Mary gestured to the newspaper. "Read all about it."

Mister Puss moved from the settee to my chair, hopping into my lap as I reached for the paper, which had been folded open to Glee's column.

## Inside Dumont

### Hollywood heartthrob with local roots comes home with some big surprises

By Glee Savage

•

OCTOBER 15, DUMONT, WI — If, gentle reader, your years in our fair city measure twenty or more, you already know the background to this story.

Born and raised here, Thad Quatrain suffered the untimely grief of losing his mother, Suzanne Quatrain, under tragic circumstances shortly after starting his sophomore year of high school. Thad's only able living relative, Mark Manning, a famed reporter for the *Chicago Journal*, had recently arrived in town as the new owner and publisher of the *Dumont Daily Register*, taking up residence in a Prairie Street home built by his forebears.

Acting as guardian, Mr. Manning took Thad in as a foster son or nephew (they are technically second cousins). Manning and his life partner, Neil Waite, raised Thad during the formative years of his adolescence, when he developed a passion for theater. Upon graduating from Dumont Central High, Thad left for California to study acting with renowned director Claire Gray, now deceased. During those college years, he met and eventually married fellow theater student Paige Yeats, an accomplished actress in her own right who also happens to be the daughter of software titan Glenn Yeats.

When Thad Quatrain signed on for the film role that would launch a stellar career—that of dashing young Ed Bax in the Spencer Wallace epic, *Crossing a Fluvial Plain*—Thad changed his last name to Manning as a tribute to his adoptive uncle's side of the family.

Fifteen years passed. And now, since early summer, with increasing frequency, Dumont locals have been spotting Thad and Paige about town. Given that Mark Manning moved away more than ten years ago (after ownership of the *Register* once again changed hands), you may well have been wondering: What gives?

And here, gentle reader, is the scoop.

Thad Manning, now 38, has grown restless with his career and wants to explore other aspects of filmmaking—behind the camera. What's more, he and Paige have long wanted to start a family.

"We're not getting any younger," Thad told this reporter, "so it's now or never. We love the energy of LA, but it can be frantic, too. What better place to raise a kid than Dumont? And here we are."

The plan is for Thad to divide his time between Wisconsin and California, while Paige intends to anchor their future homestead here. At present, they are making do with temporary housing, but the search is on for a permanent home.

Meanwhile—and remember, you heard it here first—Thad Manning has already developed solid plans for his first turn behind the camera, as director and executive producer of an independent film to be titled *Home Sweet Humford*, starring none other than Miranda Lemarr.

"Humford," he explained, "is a pseudonym for Dumont. The film will be a loving, fictionalized memoir of growing up in Hometown, USA."

Why not simply title it *Home Sweet Dumont?*

"Because I wanted to give myself the creative liberty to shape the setting in ways that complement the film's narrative arc. It's not a travelogue, not a documentary of the real Dumont, although this town was definitely the story's inspiration."

Even though the town in the movie will not be named Dumont, portions of the film will be shot on location—right here—with test scenes to be scheduled soon, before winter weather sets in.

Everyone ready for their close-ups? Extras will be needed. Keep watching this space for updates.

I set the newspaper aside and rubbed Mister Puss behind his ears. He looked up from my lap, purring. I said to Mary, "Unusual for Glee to keep a story like that under wraps for so long—it's huge."

"She told me she didn't want to waste it during the summer. I guess readership falls off during the dog days."

"Aha," I said. "You've known this all along."

Mary chuckled. "Of course. I heard it from Thad, too. Ever since he lived next door, we've been close. I saw his first school play."

"Do you know Paige Yeats?"

"I didn't meet her till this summer." Obliquely, Mary added, "Since then, we've spoken from time to time—in fact, often."

"Thad and Paige," I thought aloud. "Talk about a worldly couple—settling in Dumont? Thad, maybe, since he's *from* here. For Paige, it must be a total culture shock. She's a fine actress, but I can't see her playing a stay-at-home hausfrau."

Mary gave me a sly look. "There's a little more to it than that."

I grinned. "I'm listening…"

"Hint," said Mary. "Two words: Questman Center."

"Do tell. Now, *that's* intriguing."

Questman Center for the Performing Arts had opened about four years prior, with significant funding from Mary Questman, the childless heir to a fortune that was rooted in the timber dynasty built by her husband's family during Dumont's early days. When Mary became the driving force behind the dream to construct a state-of-the-art theater complex, she also wrote the checks to help get it off the ground, so she had plenty to say about the project's design. She insisted that local talent be given first consideration when awarding the contract—which ended up going to Marson Miles, now my husband and business partner.

There had been skeptics, but Marson delivered. Questman Center wowed critics and public alike, not only landing Dumont squarely on the cultural map, but also bringing a flood of important commissions to Marson's architectural firm. More help was needed—fresh blood—which is why, about a year later, I came to Dumont, where I found much more than a job.

As a result, Marson and I felt a tremendous debt of gratitude to Mary. She was our most important client; she was also a loving friend.

I asked her, "Questman Center—and Paige Yeats?"

She nodded. "Basil Hutchins is retiring. In fact, he's gone. Friday was his last day. Caught a plane on Sunday—off to the Canary Islands. His family has owned an estate there for generations, a sunny getaway, but Basil is staying there for good. He told me he wants to be as far from Wisconsin winters as possible."

Mary was talking about the executive director of Questman Center, an aging impresario of scattered European ancestry who had been lured to central Wisconsin as a swan song for his illustrious career. His name on the Questman Center letterhead had endowed the fledgling arts complex with immediate gravitas, but the board came to feel snookered by his job performance. The position of executive director required not only sterling credentials and artful leadership, but also a constant, hungry focus on funding.

Basil Hutchins, however, had simply rested on his laurels, spending too few hours at his desk, sipping tea from a delicate cup and saucer—Royal Copenhagen, Flora Danica. In the evenings, after changing into his finery, he dawdled about the vast teak-floored lobby shared by the three theaters. During intermission, he hobnobbed with the better-heeled patrons, sopping up their adulation, but never bothering to squeeze them for a nickel.

"Bye-bye, Basil," I said. "And good riddance." Mister Puss arose from my lap, where he'd been curled, and stretched to rest his paws on my shoulder, purring.

*What a fruitcake.*

I asked Mary, "Why do I get the feeling Paige Yeats is interested in that job?"

Mary winked. "Because you're every bit as clever as you are adorable."

Mister Puss gave me a look, rolled his eyes, and hopped down to the floor.

Mary continued, "Basil informed the board six months ago that he'd be leaving, and we established a search committee at once. But Basil kept trying to edge himself into the process, so the board kept it low-key till he was out of the way."

I laughed. "And now it's open season."

"You bet it is. We've collected a file of informal queries from candidates who got word of the opening, including Paige Yeats."

"How'd she find out about it?"

Mary flipped her hands. "I *told* her. I encouraged her to apply. She has plenty of dazzle. She can learn the management skills. And when it comes to fundraising potential, well … need I spell it out?"

Mary didn't need to spell it out: Paige had a direct line to her father, Glenn Yeats, a billionaire many times over who had a taste for philanthropy and a soft spot for the arts.

On a practical note, Mary added, "I won't be around forever."

Gently, I said to her, "Stop that."

Berta stepped into the parlor from the front hall. "All set, Mr. Norris." She handed me the car keys and Mister Puss's leash.

Mary and I rose. Mister Puss stepped to my feet. I clipped the leash to his harness, which I had taught him to use the last time he stayed with Marson and me.

Mary picked up the cat and cooed some parting farewells. He responded with a loud purr and a nose bump. Mary asked me, "Now, you're *sure* he won't be any trouble?"

"Of course not."

"I mean, with the move and all…"

Marson and I were building a new house on the outskirts of town. In spite of many delays, it now seemed we'd be able to move from our downtown loft by the end of the year. I told Mary, "You'll be back before things turn crazy."

In truth, though, the final stages of construction had already taken that turn.

Stepping away from Mary's front porch, I heard the click of the door as she closed it behind us. Mister Puss pranced smartly at my heel as we paraded down the walkway to the street.

When I reached to open the door of my car, I noticed that two other cars were now parked some twenty yards ahead, in front of the neighboring Taliesin house. Standing on the sidewalk was none other than Thad Manning, engaged in a spirited discussion with another man. Though I was tempted to walk over and greet Thad, his conversation appeared not only spirited, but heated, so I decided not to interrupt.

Just as I was about to get into the car, however, Thad glanced in my direction and broke into a smile of recognition. "Brody?" he called. "Brody, right?"

I must have blushed. He was Hollywood handsome, with fans around the world. I'd met him only once, months earlier. And now, he remembered my name. Gosh.

He began moving in my direction, followed at some distance by the other man. I walked to meet him halfway, followed by Mister Puss on his leash. We stopped face-to-face, standing in the driveway of the house where he'd once lived. Offering a warm handshake, he leaned in for a subtle hug, a pat on the back. Double gosh.

I told him, "I think you've already met Mary's cat."

"Sure—hi there, Mister Puss."

While I explained that Marson and I would be cat-sitting during Mary's travels, Mister Puss rubbed the length of his body across Thad's shins. Thad stooped to pat the cat's flank.

When the other man joined us, Thad introduced him as Conrad Houghes, one of the principal investors in Thad's film project.

"*Home Sweet Humford*," I said brightly. "Big news for Dumont."

"Yeah"—Thad laughed—"the cat's out of the bag."

Mister Puss turned to me with a dull look.

I said, "And you'll be shooting parts of it right *here*—what a great idea."

"It's a lousy idea," said Conrad Houghes, scowling, arms crossed.

Thad told me, "Connie's never been accused of sugarcoating his opinions."

"I call 'em like I see 'em," said Houghes. "And the way I see it, it's nuts to do location shooting out here in the middle of nowhere. No support services. We'd need to bring *everything* in. Way too expensive. If you want a little town, we can get one closer to home—in New Mexico. They have an aggressive film office with plenty of incentives."

"For the umpteenth time," said Thad, "that just won't work. For the artistic integrity of the project, it needs to be filmed *here*. And it *will* be."

Houghes tossed his arms. "I hauled my ass all the way out here to talk some sense into you. Budget sense. Profit sense. But *you* don't seem to give a damn."

"It's my film."

I tuned out. This conversation was all too familiar. As an architect, I often found myself in the crosshairs of the inherent conflict between aesthetics and costs.

Watching them wrangle, I noticed that despite their disagreement on production details, they shared a similar look, an LA style that had also been mine before I left the coast for the heartland. Their pants had skinny, stretchy legs. Their wispy calfskin loafers had no socks. While I generally wore a jacket and tie to the office, their workday equivalent on that cool autumn morning consisted of cashmere sweaters with protruding shirttails.

The trendy, casual attire fit Thad to a tee, at thirty-eight (a year younger than I). Houghes, however, was well into his fifties, and by clinging to a look not natural to him—forever young, forever hip, forever tan—he came across as sad and frustrated. Perhaps even desperate.

"Look," Thad told him, "I can't get into this right now; I have a meeting. But if you want to hash it out—*again*—I'll catch up with you later at the Manor House."

A primo bed-and-breakfast, the Manor House had been converted from a sprawling old mansion, a few blocks away on Prairie Street. I assumed Thad and his wife had been staying there for some time, now joined by Conrad Houghes, just in from LA.

"Count on it," said Houghes, who turned on his heel, stomped off to his car, and then made a show of roaring away.

I said to Thad, "Your day isn't getting off to a good start. Sorry."

"Thanks," he said with a warm smile, "but I can handle Connie. He needs this film more than I need his backing. When it comes to artistic differences—I win."

"I like your confidence."

"I wish I had a little more confidence about ... *that*." Thad turned to give a wistful look at the Taliesin house formerly owned by Mark Manning. The architect's training by Frank Lloyd Wright was readily apparent—the strong horizontals of the brown brick exterior; the wide, shallow bowl-shaped planters adorning the entrance; the limestone lintels over the doors and windows; the low pitch of the roof, which appeared flat from the street, with its broad, overhanging eaves. *Not* typical of Wright, however, was a conspicuous Palladian window, a half-circle of glass centered on the third floor, which resembled a gargantuan eye peering out from under the eave.

Thad explained, "I want to buy it back. I want it back in the family. I want it for *us*—Paige and me—to start *our* family here."

I grinned. "Just turn on the charm. I'll bet you can be *very* persuasive."

"Trust me, Brody—I've tried that. And generous offers. But they won't budge. So I need to give it another whirl." He checked his watch. "The Gerbers are expecting me."

"Then I won't keep you." I picked up Mister Puss while telling Thad, "Good luck in there."

"Hey," he said, stopping me as I turned to leave, "maybe we could all, uh ... get together sometime?"

I beamed. Mister Puss purred. "As a m'm'matter of fact," I stammered, "Marson and I have wanted to invite you and Paige over for dinner some night. Any chance you're free this Saturday?"

Thad drew a sharp breath. "This weekend? That's kinda short notice…"

Mister Puss abruptly stopped purring. I choked. I'd been crazy to ask. Of *course* they were busy.

With a soft laugh, Thad assured me, "We'd love to."

2

Truth be told, Marson and I had never discussed inviting Thad Manning and Paige Yeats to dinner. So my husband was more than a little surprised when I told him that the movie star and the multibillionaire's daughter would arrive on our doorstep that Saturday.

Surprised, yes. Perturbed, no. He was always up for a challenge—especially if it involved entertaining at home.

"T-minus twelve hours," Marson said with comic foreboding as he reached to fill my coffee mug that morning. Our guests would arrive that evening at seven.

I was barely awake—the sun still lolled below the horizon of a chilly gray sky—but Marson was as chipper as a suburban housewife on uppers. He had already fed Mister Puss, who now sat on the kitchen island, staring at me as I leaned to blow across the top of my coffee before taking the first sip. Perched on a barstool in my heavy terry bathrobe, I must have looked like hell, but Marson always said he found me huggable when scruffy. He, of course, was dressed and groomed and perfectly presentable. Bacon crackled in a skillet as he buttered toast. Mister Puss sniffed and purred. I stared across the island into the main room of our loft, with its twenty-foot ceiling and its front wall of windows looking out onto First Avenue, downtown Dumont's main drag, dead quiet at dawn. The steaming black coffee warmed my face, smelling as rich and mellow as chocolate. Swallowing some, I felt my body awaken. I felt the day begin. I felt the cat's velvety chin bump mine with a greeting of good morning.

Marson kissed the top of my head as he slid a plate of toast in front of me on the granite countertop. The toast's golden hue was intensified by a glimmering layer of apricot jam; though Marson couldn't stand the stuff, he knew it was my favorite. I broke off a buttery corner for Mister Puss, who politely nipped it from my fingers.

"The paper ought to be here," said Marson, crossing the loft to the street door.

A moment later, he thumped the door closed against a cold breeze and returned to the kitchen, unrolling the *Dumont Daily Register* and fingering through the sections. "Well, now," he said, "this looks timely." He set one of the pages next to my toast, then stood behind me, looking over my shoulder while we read it together.

## Inside Dumont

### *Paige Yeats to take the reins as new director of Questman Center*

By Glee Savage

•

OCTOBER 19, DUMONT, WI — When Questman Center for the Performing Arts opened its doors for its inaugural season only four short years ago, the entire community sensed that big things lay ahead. Surely, the world-class performance complex would bring to Dumont a level of cultural enrichment not previously possible. Just as important, many hoped that the Center's stunning architecture would "put Dumont on the map," drawing the attention of arts patrons far and wide to our quiet little city. All of those aspirations have been met.

Now, however, Questman Center finds itself at an important, defining juncture. With the recent retirement of executive director Basil Hutchins, the Questman board was faced with the challenge—some might say, the opportunity—to build on the organization's initial success. In its search for new leadership, the board asked itself, Who? Who might step in to steer Questman Center in a bold new direction toward financial and artistic growth?

Enter Paige Yeats.

As chronicled in these pages on Tuesday, Ms. Yeats has recently arrived in Dumont with her husband, Thad Manning. The Hollywood glamour couple has decided to settle here in Mr. Manning's hometown while starting a family, far removed from the hustles and hassles of La La Land.

Mary Questman, the Center's honorary life chair and principal benefactor, had encouraged Ms. Yeats to apply for the open position. Earlier this week, before departing for travels, Mrs. Questman sent her written recommendation of Ms. Yeats to the Center's search committee and board of directors, who then met with Ms. Yeats on Thursday evening and offered the position, which she accepted.

Ms. Yeats later told the *Register*, "I'm honored beyond measure to be entrusted with the duties of executive director of Questman Center—what a remarkable welcome to Dumont. I still have so much to learn about the Center and this charming little town. I can't wait to begin."

Mrs. Questman, responding by email to our request for comment, wrote from Arizona, "Paige is ideal for the Center. She'll bring a vigorous new sense of drive and creativity to the executive offices, not to mention a much needed breath of fresh air."

At press time, we were still unable to reach Basil Hutchins, the former director, for comment. He is believed to be in transit from the European mainland to the Canary Islands, where severe autumn storms in the Atlantic off northwestern Africa have disrupted communications.

Marson plucked the sheet of newsprint from the counter and dangled it in front of Mister Puss, who leapt to grab it, tumbling to the floor, where he pounced and rolled with it, tearing the paper to shreds.

I handed Marson my napkin, who fastidiously wiped imaginary smudges of ink from his fingers.

While refolding the napkin and setting it next to my coffee, he said, "Good thing we asked Glee to join us tonight. She never lets the conversation lag—and it seems there's plenty to talk about."

He had a point. I still couldn't fathom how I'd been brazen enough to invite Thad and Paige to our home. Although both Marson and I had the self-assurance to acquit ourselves in almost any social setting, the "Hollywood glamour couple" (as Glee had described them) were in another league altogether. Perhaps it was Glee's journalistic instincts that would never, ever allow her to feel cowed, that would guarantee she could fill any awkward silence, any lapse in a discussion, with a probing question or a scintillating comment. She would be a valuable addition to our foursome.

A table for five, however, was anathema to Marson's somewhat … *particular* standards of symmetry, balance, and decorum. "We need someone else," he'd said flatly while planning the meal earlier that week. "But who?"

I suggested at once, "Yevgeny."

"Brilliant," he agreed.

Yevgeny Krymov, the world-renowned ballet dancer, had recently retired from the stage and accepted a faculty appointment as artist-in-residence at the conservatory in nearby Appleton. It was a temporary position, so Yevgeny was staying at the Manor House in Dumont, just a half-hour's drive from his thrice-weekly teaching duties. More to the point, he was doubtless already acquainted with Thad and Paige, who were also staying at the Manor House—and in terms of star power, he was very much in their league.

Bonus point: for a man of fifty-six (or of any age, for that matter), Yevgeny was hotter than hell. Glee Savage adored him, and the admiration was mutual, so they would make a good pairing at the table, but not as a couple—not as "dates"—because Yevgeny was decidedly gay, with a flirtatious nature, and he had made no secret of his attraction to *moi*.

So it was dinner for six, and it was bound to be ... interesting.

G*rrring.*

Mere seconds after seven o'clock that evening, the sputtering old twist bell on our loft's street door announced that the party had begun. We were ready.

The table was set, the bar was stocked, and unobtrusive cocktail tunes played gently in the background. The meal was under control, with the open kitchen spiffed for the roving eyes of guests. And we were dressed—blazers, flannel slacks, no ties—Marson in black and gray, myself in earth tones.

Mister Puss perched on a turn of the spiral stairs, observing the scene from above. As Marson stepped across the room to answer the door and greet our first arrival, I checked the table and gave the flowers a final primp. Through the windows looking out to the street, the last dusky hues of twilight faded into an inky night sky.

"*Marson,* love!" said Glee Savage, bounding through the open door. She was never shy about being first—she had a nose for news, an eye for detail, and no desire to miss *anything*. With a fearless sense of style, she was the self-anointed fashionista of our remote little burg, a missionary of pizazz in the wilderness. Although she was a few years older than Marson, well into her sixties, she always wore spike heels and ruby-red lipstick. Whenever venturing out, she finished her ensemble with a splashy hat and an oversize purse chosen from a vast collection that ranged from kitsch to couture. That night, she dazzled in an autumnal palette of pumpkin and mustard and rust. Her steel-tipped heels snapped on the loft's concrete floor as she strutted toward me, rattling a necklace with beads the size of golf balls. "And *Brody*—good evening, sweets."

We smooched.

She stage-whispered, "Is the bar open?"

Marson whisked her to the kitchen island. "Of course, milady."

I followed, offering, "Martini?"

"I'd *kill* for one," she said with a sigh, "but the night is young, so I'd better take it down a notch."

"Good idea," said Marson. "How about a champagne cocktail?"

"Lovely."

I told Marson, "Make it two."

"I'll make it three," he said, lining up the glasses. As I set about opening a bottle of Veuve, he dropped a sugar cube into each flute and added a dash of bitters, a splash of cognac. I removed the wire *muselet* from the bottle and flicked it toward the spiral stairs. Mister Puss soared after it as it skittered across the polished floor. Glee laughed at the cat's antics while I removed the cork with a sturdy pop. Marson filled each of the glasses. We skoaled and sipped. Mister Puss, purring, trotted toward us with the wire cage dangling from his mouth. He deposited it at Glee's feet, then watched, on high alert, as she stooped, snatched it, and tossed it underhand across the room, toward the door. And he darted off, chasing it.

*Grrring.*

I set my glass on the counter. "I'll get it." Moving to the door, I swooped up the cat—with the retrieved *muselet* again dangling from his mouth—and held him in one arm as I reached with the other to admit our next arrival.

It was Yevgeny Krymov.

He wore a bulky gray turtleneck, accessorized with a delicate silvery scarf to ward off the chill of the night. From the waist down, his tight black slacks left little to the imagination. Those muscled loins had thrilled legions of the cultural elite during his legendary career of dancing on the greatest stages in the world.

Beading me with his gray Muscovy eyes, he leaned to kiss the edge of my mouth. "Good evening, Brody."

Aroused, I stammered, "Great to see you. Welcome back, Yevgeny."

"Uh-uh-uh," he corrected with a playful wag of his finger, tapping it on my cheek. "To you, I am Zhenya."

He had previously invited me to use the Russian diminutive of his name, but I could never remember it.

Cradled in my arm, Mister Puss was purring loudly—ever the little glutton for attention. Gazing up at Yevgeny, the cat displayed a sudden interest in one of ballet's most shining luminaries.

Yevgeny twiddled the cat's chin. "You have a gift for me, *koshechka*? Thank you, kit-cat," he said as Mister Puss dropped the wire *muselet* into his palm. Yevgeny cupped and rolled both hands while mumbling some hocus-pocus, then splayed them open, empty. I was no less amazed than Mister Puss, whose purring abruptly stopped.

Marson called over to us, "Champagne cocktail, Yevgeny? Or vodka?"

"*Shampanskoye*, thank you." Yevgeny moved into the room, greeting Marson and Glee.

I closed the door and set Mister Puss on the floor. He followed as I joined the others at the kitchen island.

We gabbed as Marson arranged a tray of appetizers and checked the oven. (Much of the meal had been prepared in advance by

Nancy Sanderson, a local restaurateur who often helped when we entertained, especially on short notice.) Glee complimented the table setting, in which Marson always took justifiable pride. I glanced at my watch—ten past seven. Our chitchat petered out as we awaited the arrival of the Hollywood glamour couple.

*Grrring.*

Mister Puss, ever curious, shot to the door and sat, switching his tail.

Marson and I quickly followed, straightening our lapels, sprucing our hair. I swung the door open.

And *there* they were. "Well, well," said Marson with a soft laugh. "Look who's landed on our stoop."

I introduced Thad Manning to my husband, and Thad, in turn, introduced us to his wife, Paige Yeats. I had expected her to be pretty in person—she was a movie star—but I now realized that the camera had never really done her justice. She was markedly beautiful, a match made in heaven (or at least in Tinseltown) for Thad. Good grief, the babies *they* could make.

We ushered them in, joining Yevgeny and Glee, who were already on a first-name basis with Thad and Paige (Yevgeny was staying at the Manor House with them, and Glee had interviewed each of them for the *Register*). Marson's champagne cocktails had two more takers—"But just a splash for me," said Paige—so we opened a second bottle of Veuve and made a fresh round of six. After a few perfunctory toasts, we took the appetizers to the seating area of the main room, where three loveseats surrounded a low, square stone-topped table.

The fourth side of the table was open toward the front wall, where a section of exposed brick rose from floor to ceiling, resembling a chimney between the windows to the street. Marson had designed a minimalist mantel and surround of feathered slate, suggestive of a fireplace, which contained several tiered rows of fluttering pillar candles, a theatrical nod to the onset of colder weather. From the ceiling, a huge Mexican chandelier of punched tin hung squarely over the conversation area, casting playful starlight about the room.

When Thad and Paige hesitated to be seated first, Marson suggested, "Let's get acquainted—no couples—shall we?" With a bit of jockeying, Marson sat with Paige on one side of the table, and Glee sat with Thad, opposite them. Which left the middle loveseat, facing the fireplace, to Yevgeny and me. He gently bumped knees with me and turned to ask with a wry smile, "Cozy, yes?"

Plenty cozy.

Mister Puss hopped up from the floor and climbed to my shoulder. Walking along the back of the sofa, he moved over to Yevgeny, then dropped into his lap, where the cat curled and nested.

Plenty cozy, indeed.

Everyone settled into amiable conversation, which focused mainly on Thad and Paige. Having read about Paige's new job in that morning's paper, Marson asked her, "Have you moved into your office at Questman Center yet?"

Paige reminded him, "I wasn't offered the position till Thursday night. Friday, the board's executive committee gave me the grand tour and introduced the staff. I *saw* my office, but won't be moving in till next week. Oh!" She laughed, as if recalling something, then told Marson, "*You're* the architect. What a magnificent facility—you must be *so* proud of it."

Marson replied with a modest nod.

I spoke up. "He deserves to be proud. And we're proud of *him*."

Glee offered dainty applause as Yevgeny raised his glass with a "Hear, hear."

Thad said, "I was worried the Questman Center job might be too much too soon for Paige, but she's a very determined woman."

Paige laughed, setting aside her drink. "I think what he's trying to say is that I'm a very *determined* woman—as well as a moderately *pregnant* woman."

Predictably, this pronouncement evoked a moment of silent surprise, followed by an energetic hoo-ha of well-wishes. Glee asked her, "When...?"

"I'm thirteen weeks along, and—"

Thad interrupted. "Moving here this summer proved quite relaxing." He twitched his brows.

Paige smirked. "So this is a new adventure. A few days ago, I noticed the first signs of a baby bump."

To my eye, she looked Hollywood thin. Then again, I had an unreliable perspective regarding her bumps—baby or otherwise.

She said, "Within a month or so, as soon as Thanksgiving, we'll know the sex."

I was distracted by Mister Puss. Next to me, in Yevgeny's lap, the cat was purring again—and kneading his paws into Yevgeny's thigh, where I noticed a distinct lump beneath the fabric of his pants.

Marson was saying something about Thanksgiving, about the house we were building...

Breaking into a sweat, I considered plucking Mister Puss from Yevgeny's lap and putting him on the floor, but that would only draw attention to the situation.

Yevgeny asked, "Find something, *koshechka*? What do you want, kit-cat? Is it... this?" Yevgeny shoved his hand into his pocket and whipped out the wire *muselet*, apparently hidden there by sleight of hand when he arrived.

Mister Puss froze, eyeing it.

Yevgeny flicked it over the back of the sofa. The cat sprang after it, disappearing behind us.

The six of us listened, amused, while the cat tussled with it on the concrete floor, where it skittered and ticked. Then Mister

Puss pranced out into our midst with his wire prey dangling from his mouth.

Thad Manning made a kissy sound, tapping his knee. "Here, Mister Puss. Whatcha got?" The cat stepped over to Thad and dropped the *muselet* into his palm. Then Mister Puss hopped up into his lap, purring.

While stroking the cat's back, which intensified the purring, Thad asked his wife, across the low table, "Know what I'm thinking?"

Paige nodded, telling the rest of us, "Just the other night, Thad and I were talking about his screenplay, wondering if *Home Sweet Humford* might need a dog or cat in the cast—a pet for Miranda Lemarr's character."

Thad added, "And Mister Puss is a natural. He's smart, takes direction, walks on a leash. Plus, he's flat-out gorgeous—the camera will love him.

"Careful," said Paige with a low laugh. "You don't want Miranda feeling upstaged."

Glee Savage, sitting next to Thad, said with mock gravity, "You wouldn't want a cat fight."

Mister Puss stretched to Thad's shoulder and nuzzled his ear, purring.

Thad turned his head to face the cat, nose to nose. "You drive a hard bargain, Mister Puss, but you have my word. You'll get a close-up."

Everyone laughed, except me. I was wondering: Was Thad just "acting," pretending to have a playful conversation with the cat?

Or was he responding to an actual question from the little ham?

The casting call didn't end with Mister Puss. Thad invited Yevgeny to appear in a walk-on role as himself; since the test scenes would be shot on a Thursday, when Yevgeny had no teaching commitments, he accepted. Thad also invited Glee, Marson, and me to appear as extras, but we all declined. Marson, though flattered to be asked, just wasn't interested; Glee would be busy reporting on the activity that day; I would be there to look after Mister Puss.

I asked Thad, "What about Paige? I assume she has a role in *Humford*."

Paige answered for her husband. "I wasn't joking when I said Miranda Lemarr might feel upstaged by a cat. She's terribly insecure. So I need to stay well removed from this project."

Glee said, "How exciting. A bit of Hollywood—with all its intrigues and infighting—right here in Dumont."

Thad laughed.

I said to him, "It seems your investor, Conrad Houghes, was overruled. No more talk about moving the location shots to New Mexico?"

"Connie's not happy about it," said Thad. "In fact, he was mad as hell when he flew home to LA. But he'll be back. He can't afford *not* to invest in *Home Sweet Humford*."

Our oblong Parsons dining table separated the kitchen area at the back of the loft from the main living area in front. When we ushered our guests to the table, Marson seated Paige and Thad in the two prime spots, along the side of the table facing out toward the street windows. As hosts, Marson and I would anchor the two short ends of the table. Which left Glee and Yevgeny seated facing Paige and Thad, who were backdropped by the kitchen. Marson delivered artfully arranged plates to our guests while I poured wine (but Perrier for Paige). Played low, a piano recording from the heyday at Chicago's Pump Room featured gentle, stylish renderings of Gershwin, Porter, Berlin. Circling with interest, tail erect, nose on full alert, was Mister Puss.

When Marson and I sat, we offered a toast to our guests, who in turn toasted their hosts, complimenting the wine, the food, and our efforts to stage such an enjoyable evening.

With the niceties out of the way, I said to Thad, "When I saw you Tuesday morning, you were about to meet with the current owners of your uncle's house on Prairie Street. Any luck?"

"They wouldn't budge. I think Gerber was interested, but his wife shot him down."

"Sorry to hear that."

Yevgeny looked confused. Glee explained to him, "Thad's uncle, Mark Manning, lived next door to Mary Questman in that striking house, designed by a student of Frank Lloyd Wright. Now Thad would like to buy the house back."

Paige said with a soft laugh, "We can't stay at the Manor House forever—especially with a baby on the way."

"The house on Prairie Street would be perfect," said Thad. "Plus, the sentimental value."

I said, "Hope you work it out. I'd *love* to get a look inside."

Marson assured me, "It's spectacular. Over the years, I've seen it several times."

"Hey!" said Thad, setting down his fork. "Suppose I tell the Gerbers that my architect friend—Brody—has a purely academic interest in touring the house. That would be a good excuse for another meeting, without making them feel pressured to sell, even though that's exactly the point. This time, I'll bring Paige along, too. The woman's touch—the needs of a pregnant woman, no less. That could help sway Mrs. Gerber, who seems to be the holdout."

"Fine," said Paige, cutting off an asparagus tip and swiping it through a puddle of hollandaise.

"Sounds *great*," I told Thad. "Whenever you can set it up, just let me know."

The conversation lapsed only briefly before Marson asked Yevgeny, "The teaching gig in Appleton—is that working out to your liking?"

"Very much so, yes. The plan is, this first year, I am 'visiting' as artist-in-residence. But I know already, it will become permanent."

"How *wonderful*," said Glee. I watched the twitch of her right hand and assumed she would rather be taking notes than eating. She continued, "Will you be looking for permanent housing soon?"

Yevgeny echoed Paige's earlier comment: "One cannot stay at the Manor House forever."

Glee looked a tad forlorn. "And you'll settle in Appleton?"

"No. I stay in Dumont. I like it here." Under the table, he bumped knees with me—again. I thought I should probably inch mine away.

"Marvelous." Glee lifted her wineglass and touched it to his.

"Well, then," said Marson, "it seems we're *all* on the move."

"I'm not," Glee reminded him. "But when do you boys think you'll make the move from the loft?"

I was still considering the position of my knee.

Marson whirled a hand. "December maybe? Before you know it, we'll be packing. It comes at a busy time—Brody's library commission is gearing up, and I've got that *church* to build, if you can believe it." Marson took a dim view of religion, but that was outweighed by his zeal for improving the aesthetics of Dumont's downtown commons, to be fronted prominently by a new Episcopal church.

"In any event," said Marson, "we ought to be settled in the house—the perfect house, Brody's masterpiece—by Christmas, no later than New Year's. This might be pushing things, but I think a party will be in order. A housewarming for the holidays. What do you think, kiddo?"

I moved my knee. "Sure. Why not?"

Glee turned to me, studying my face. "Do you think Inez would come?"

Whoa. My mother might indeed pay a visit from California, as she had heard plenty from me about "the perfect house" and was curious to see it, but there was a history of bad blood between Inez Norris and Glee Savage, who had grown up together in Dumont and, later, were college roommates in Madison—until their bitter and sudden estrangement. They had not spoken in more than forty years.

I told Glee, "Hard to tell. You know Inez—she has a mind of her own."

Glee agreed, "That's *one* way of putting it."

I turned to Paige. "How about your father? Any chance the great and powerful Glenn Yeats might drop into town?"

She shrugged. "New job, new home, new *baby*—he might want to check on me."

Marson asked Thad, "And how about your uncle? Does he ever talk about coming home to Dumont? A lot of us would love to see Mark Manning again."

"Amen," said Glee.

Beneath the table, I dangled a scrap of something from my plate and felt Mister Puss nip it from my fingers. He hopped into my lap, purring.

Everyone waited for Thad to answer Marson's question, but he hesitated, taking a sip of wine. He set the glass aside. "I doubt that Mark will ever leave Molokai."

Molokai? I gave Marson a quizzical look. "Didn't Uncle Ted …?"

Ted Norris, my mother's brother, was Marson's original business partner, the original "Norris" in the Miles & Norris architecture firm. Three years ago, however, shortly after I moved to Dumont to join the firm, Ted's wife, Renée, died under bizarre circumstances (a highly publicized amnesia case) that sent Ted into an emotional tailspin. He needed some time off, to grieve and heal, and went to Hawaii, ending up on remote, isolated Molokai, where he decided to stay.

Marson told me, "It's not pure coincidence that Ted went to

Molokai. He knew Mark Manning—we both did—while Mark owned the *Register*. More to the point, Mark's 'other half' was an architect, Neil Waite. So there was a professional connection. When Mark lost Neil, he went to Molokai. When Ted lost Renée, he must've taken a degree of inspiration from Mark's 'escape.'"

I thought aloud, "Molokai's not very big…"

"Right," said Thad. "Mark bumps into your uncle Ted now and then. In fact, Paige and I saw Ted last time we visited. He seems better now; he met a woman there who's good for him. But Mark—still alone."

Paige nodded. "Still brooding—about Neil."

I had to ask: "What *happened*?"

Thad reminded Glee, "I was in California when Mark sold the paper."

"Sad times for the *Register*," Glee said with a sigh, "but Mark saw it as a fresh beginning. About ten years ago—he'd bought the paper eleven years earlier—the digital age was snuffing out small-town dailies left and right. Things weren't looking good for the *Register*, but Mark lucked out with a generous offer that would merge the paper into a multi-platform media deal, ensuring its survival, at least for a while. Sold."

Thad picked up the story. "By that time, my career had taken off—Paige was landing some killer roles, too—so we asked the guys, 'What are you waiting for? Palm trees, swimming pools. Move!' And they did."

"But…," said Glee.

Thad explained, "Mark was in his mid-fifties, financially set, and comfortable with the idea of semi-retirement, maybe writing a book. But Neil was younger and not ready to hang up his career. He'd already moved his architecture practice from Phoenix to Chicago when he met Mark, and later to Dumont, again to be with Mark. They became my 'two dads.' Neil encouraged me to try out for my first school play. And now, he was ready to follow Mark, once again, this time to the West Coast, so they could be closer to Paige and me.

"They moved to the LA area, joking about grandkids. Mark started his book. Neil reestablished his design practice. Then, one afternoon, driving home after meeting a new client, he was rear-ended by a semi in a freeway pileup. Killed on the spot."

"Jesus," I said, "I'm so sorry."

"Mark blamed himself. Said it never would've happened if he hadn't dragged Neil away from the safety of Dumont. Crazy, huh?"

I agreed with a sad nod. Sadder still, I sensed—and suspected that Thad also sensed—there was a kernel of logic at the core of Mark's nagging guilt.

Thad slowly swirled the wine in his glass, repeating his earlier comment: "I doubt that Mark will ever leave Molokai."

Mister Puss lay fast asleep in my lap.

Stroking a tiny paw, I marveled at the fragility of life.

Cringeworthy. Marson and I routinely referred to the new home we were building as "the perfect house"—outlandish hyperbole from two architects, not to mention gross immodesty.

Originally, the "perfect" designation had been strictly *entre nous*. When Marson acquired the land on the outskirts of town two years ago, he challenged me to design the perfect house to build there as our permanent home. I worked at a feverish pitch to deliver the plans to him on our first Christmas Eve together. We were at home in the loft, dressed in tuxes, just the two of us, preparing to join Mary Questman for a festive dinner party at her home. He unrolled the bundle of prints, secured by a floppy red ribbon. I held my breath while he paged through the plans. He then proclaimed the house "perfect," and I was inclined to agree with him—it was the perfect house *for us*. (While spontaneity is not in Marson's nature, we then made love. Tardiness is not in Marson's nature, either, but we arrived twenty minutes late for Mary's party.)

Somehow, our private description of the house slipped out. I might have mentioned it to Glee; Marson might have leaked it to Mary. By now, Clem Carter, our builder, was crowing to the world that he was wrapping up his work on the perfect house, and despite our efforts to tamp down that phraseology, it had become everyone's shorthand reference to the remarkable structure that was taking shape among the birches in a ravine overlooking native prairie at the edge of Dumont.

On Friday morning, six days after entertaining Thad Manning and Paige Yeats at the loft, I was in my car with Mister Puss, driving out to check progress on the new house. The cat had grown accustomed to riding in our vehicles and was well behaved, so I no longer bothered caging him in a pet carrier for our excursions. He was in his harness, secured by his leash, content to watch from the passenger seat as the twisted branches of colorful fall foliage zipped over the windshield, blurring the view of a hyper-blue sky. Bouncing and swaying, we sped along the rural road that took us out to the countryside.

I tapped the brakes as we approached the huge sign, consisting of burly black letters against shocking yellow: CARTER CONSTRUCTION. A smaller sign had been added to one of the posts after the structure began to take shape: *PROUD BUILDERS OF DUMONT'S PERFECT HOUSE, BRODY NORRIS, ARCHITECT.* Carter's trucks lined the roadway, with tradesmen's pickups parked to one side of the steep driveway leading up to the house—electricians, plumbers, plasterers, painters.

Parking on the road, I got out of the car with Mister Puss and walked him up the drive. Clem Carter, who must have spotted my arrival, stood waiting at the top, giving me a wave. As both architect and co-owner of the project, I would be accorded his full attention, despite the frenzy of workers rushing to meet a tangle of interdependent deadlines.

"Brody!" he said with a cheery laugh as I climbed the last few yards. "I see you brought the inspection crew." He scooched down to twiddle the cat's chin, then stood to shake my hand.

Surveying the activity with an approving nod, I asked, "Everything under control?"

"Sure is. Come on in."

I picked up Mister Puss and followed Clem as he led us into

the fray. We paused every few feet to answer workers' questions or to decide between options A and B. Some of the contractors offered me congratulations on the outcome of the project; most of them took a moment to pet Mister Puss, who lapped up their attention. His purr rumbled beneath the ruckus of voices and tools and activity.

When Clem was called away to help assemble the painters' scaffolding, I carried Mister Puss to the glass wall at the front of the main room. From there, we looked back at the interior, and I saw with instant clarity that my notion of the space—an idea spun out of nothing but creative invention—had now been transformed into a tangible reality. And it worked. It clicked. It seemed so right, as if it had been inevitable.

Then I turned to look beyond the windows. A small stream that sluiced underneath the building emerged from the front, cascading as a gentle waterfall where the ravine opened up to the prairie.

Mister Puss had pawed his way to my shoulder, nuzzling my ear. I asked, "What do you think?"

*The purr-fect house.*

"Comedian."

On our way back into town, I planned to stop at Questman Center before returning to the office. The performing-arts center, designed by Marson, anchored an area that was to become Dumont's "cultural campus," where construction of the new county museum, also designed by Marson, was now well along. The next project, still in the planning stages, was a new main library, which I myself was commissioned to design. I needed to take another look at the building site and check its relation to the existing structures before moving forward with my library concept.

Just as I parked at Questman Center, however, my phone rang. The readout identified the caller as THAD MANNING.

"Hey, Brody," he said, "I know this is crazy short notice, but I just got the Gerbers to agree to another meeting at the house on Prairie Street. They'd be happy to show you around—like, right now."

"I'm already in the car," I said. "On my way." Mister Puss hunkered down as I shifted into drive and took off toward downtown.

A few minutes later, I slowed the car as we approached the town commons, a quadrangle of parkland that served as a buffer between Dumont's main business street, First Avenue, and the more genteel streets of the historic residential district. Circling the green, I passed by the site that would eventually be occupied by the Episcopal church Marson was designing. On the opposite side of the green, I passed the handsome old Carnegie library. Then I left the commons and drove the few blocks to Prairie Street.

Mister Puss took notice of Mary Questman's house and gave me an inquisitive look, perhaps wondering if he was being taken home. But no. The car drifted past Mary's, and we parked next door, behind an SUV that I recognized as Thad's.

I would not normally bring a cat when visiting a stranger's home, but the invitation had come unexpectedly, and Mister Puss was already with me. I wasn't willing to lock him in the car, so he stood at my heel, leashed, when we arrived at the door of the distinctive—and somewhat mysterious—Taliesin house that had once been owned by Thad's uncle, Mark Manning. The porch was decked out with a few pumpkins and cornstalks in anticipation of Halloween, less than a week away.

*Ding-dong.*

"Yes?" said a man as he cracked the door open. He appeared to be in his sixties, bland but pleasant enough, wearing a cardigan sweater the color of creamy cocoa. Spotting Mister Puss at my feet, he smiled.

"Mr. Gerber?" I asked.

"Yes, yes," he said with a chuckle, swinging the door wide.

"I'm Harlan. And you must be Brody." He leaned down, hands to knees, saying, "Hello there, Mister Puss. Where's your mistress hanging out these days?"

I doubted that Harlan expected Mister Puss to speak for himself (gossip notwithstanding), so I answered, "Mary's in Arizona for a couple of weeks. My husband and I are cat-sitting."

Harlan waved me down the hall. "Come on in, Brody, and bring the livestock. Thad's here already." Harlan grasped my elbow and leaned near to whisper, nearly giddy, "And guess who he brought—*Paige Yeats*. She's a hottie."

Different strokes, I reminded myself.

When we entered the living room, Thad, Paige, and Mrs. Gerber dropped their conversation and stood to acknowledge my arrival. Thad and Paige were bright and chatty and happily surprised to see Mister Puss. Mrs. Gerber, on the other hand, stiffened upon seeing the cat follow me into the room.

"Bettina," said Harlan Gerber, "this is Brody Norris."

"The architect," she said dryly, stepping over to offer a perfunctory handshake, ignoring the cat. "I understand you have an interest in seeing the house." Pointedly, she added, "*Our* house."

Bettina Gerber shared none of her husband's natural warmth, his down-home candor. Her manner was guarded and reserved, tinged with haughtiness. While Harlan looked as comfortable as an old shoe, Bettina, who seemed a few years younger, no older than sixty, looked stiff and prim in a mannish suit, a white silk blouse, and black patent pumps. Her graying hair was worn in a style that looked as stiff as a wig.

"As you may know," she lectured me, "the house was built in the early 1940s. It has an interior space of approximately four thousand square feet, including the third-floor studio, but excluding the basement. The general style of the house is Prairie School, except for its unique aberration of the Palladian window upstairs."

Facts and figures. Fine, I thought. But this house had a *story*, a provenance—not only the Taliesin angle, the Frank Lloyd Wright influence, but more important, the history of how it came to be built, of the people who had lived there, of the people who (I would learn) had died there.

From where I stood near the entrance to the living room, which sported a heavy, sumptuous decor at odds with the style of the house, I could look back into the center hall. A main stairway led to the upper floors from the front of the hall, with service stairs to the rear. Doorways from the hall opened into a study, near the front door, and a dining room, which apparently led back to the kitchen. From my vantage point, I counted three fireplaces. Even at a glimpse, they echoed the distinctive masonry and design motifs found in many of Wright's landmark homes. All the rooms were flooded with light from high-set ribbon windows.

I asked Thad, "When you lived here with your uncle, did you understand the significance of the house?"

"I was a kid." He shrugged. "Sure, I'd heard that the house had 'history' and a 'design pedigree,' but when you're sixteen, what does *that* mean?"

Paige reminded him, "Your mother's family had roots here—in this very house. That's what 'history' means." Paige then turned to Bettina Gerber with a warm smile. "It's not public knowledge yet, but I'm pregnant. Thad's interest in this house goes way beyond real estate. We'd love to raise our child here."

While Paige's performance wasn't quite Oscar-worthy, it was sufficient to affect Harlan Gerber, who choked up while telling his wife, "Oh, *Bettina*. They've made *such* a generous offer."

But Bettina didn't bite. "That's not on today's agenda. We welcomed you here to satisfy Mr. Norris's professional interest in seeing the house. This way, please." And she whisked us out of the living room, leading the way.

Harlan gave us an apologetic look before following her into the hall.

Hangdog, Thad slung an arm around Paige's waist while leaving the room.

Bringing up the rear with Mister Puss, I felt sympathy for Thad's disappointment, but in truth, I was in dandy spirits, eager to get on with the tour.

The design of the ground floor was precisely articulated, but the formality of these spaces sprang from an organic modulation of forms, as opposed to the more traditional reliance on symmetry and repetition. The house "grew" from room to room.

The study was anchored by an enormous partners desk that had been used by Mark Manning and earlier by his uncle, Edwin Quatrain. The dining room was outfitted with its original wooden built-ins, beautifully crafted and maintained, but the furniture supplied by the Gerbers was dead wrong. The kitchen, as was typical in houses of that era, seemed like an afterthought of the design process. Though large and functional, it was meant for the help, and although it had undergone some necessary updates over the years, it was ripe to be reimagined for contemporary living.

Despite the Taliesin roots of the house, the second floor struck me as uninspired, a succession of boxy rooms—bedrooms, storerooms, a children's playroom, whatever—lining both sides of a hall. Unexpected, however, were the two spacious master suites across from each other at the front of the house. At first I thought this might have been a recent alteration, but I learned that the rooms had been configured that way from the start. Eighty years ago? Why?

Traipsing up to the third floor, recalling the giant Palladian window visible from the street, I expected more surprises— idiosyncrasies from a student architect who had studied with, but had not quite nailed the lessons of, the master. What I found at the top of the stairs was indeed astonishing, but not because of its anticipated design failings. Rather, I emerged into a fabulous space, soaring and imaginative, a studio quarters that left me thinking: He nailed it. I wouldn't change a thing.

Wood and brick and leather. Beams and gables. And books. Loads of books, with ladders to climb the high cases built around both sides of yet another fireplace, this one big enough to roast an ox. And of course, that window—a great semicircle of glass, an eye under the eaves peering out through the treetops, looking across most of the town to the fields and moraines and countryside that stretched to open prairie, where a different sort of house was being built, though I could not see it across the miles.

Paige followed me up the last few stairs, and her reaction to the space was even more pronounced than mine—she squealed with delight as she took it all in, laughing while twirling to the middle of the room, where she dropped into the buttery leather cushions of a big brown chesterfield sofa.

I picked up Mister Puss to give him a better look.

Thad stopped near the top of the stairs, where the Gerbers passed him to join Paige and me.

Harlan chuckled (he did that a lot), telling us, "Everyone reacts that way, like they never would've *dreamed* this was up here. Fine place to read a book, that's for sure."

Mister Puss purred.

Not sharing our enthusiasm, Bettina explained dryly, "This room occupies the entire third floor." She pointed. "A small kitchen and bath are tucked in near the service stairs in back. Someone could actually *live* up here. It reminds me of a mother-in-law apartment—except, well, it seems rather *masculine*, doesn't it?"

I said, "Some lace curtains might fix that."

Bettina gave me a wry look. If she suspected I was being facetious, she was right.

Thad still had one foot planted in the front stairwell, which rose gracefully from below the huge window. Oddly, he appeared reluctant to enter the room.

"Hey, hon," said Paige, "this is *great* up here. You act like you've never seen it."

He reminded her, "I lived here for three years—of *course* I've seen it." His testy tone surprised all of us.

Concerned, she asked, "Did I say something wrong?"

He took a deep breath. "Not at all. Sorry." He stepped over to us. "It's just that... someone died up here."

Mister Puss stopped purring and looked up at me.

Bettina turned to tell her husband, under her breath, "I knew it."

Harlan winced. "I've heard rumors."

Paige said to Thad, "It's an old house." Her voice was soothing. "Good times and bad—there must have been many."

"My mother died here," said Thad. "She was murdered. I found her."

We listened in silence as Thad filled in the crucial details:

His mother, Suzanne Quatrain, had grown up in the house. Many years later, her cousin, Mark Manning, moved to Dumont, bought the local paper, and just before Christmas, moved into the house, which he had visited as a child.

Christmas dinner did double duty as Mark's reunion with Suzanne and an introduction to her sixteen-year-old son, Thad. Because Thad's father had long been estranged from Suzanne, she had recently named Mark the boy's guardian, just in case. That first encounter between Mark and Thad went badly. Very badly. Then, during the commotion of a houseful of friends getting dinner on the table, tragedy struck—upstairs on Prairie Street.

"Who did it?" we asked. "Why?"

When Thad explained, not one of us dared to ask more. Thad joined Paige, sitting on the chesterfield. Mister Puss hopped up from the floor and nestled next to Thad, who stroked the cat's neck.

The Gerbers and I settled in armchairs angled toward the sofa, forming a circle in the middle of the vast room.

"Thad"—I cleared my throat—"I'm so sorry. I didn't know any of this."

He gave me a gentle smile. "You weren't here."

Paige touched his arm. "This is a wonderful house, but—come on. If you'd be living with nightmares…"

He assured her, "I'm a big boy now. I can handle it. And I want to raise our family here. That is, if you're okay with it. Okay?"

She pecked his lips. "Okay."

"*Not* okay," Bettina reminded them. "The house isn't for sale."

Harlan asked her, "Am I allowed *any* say in this?"

"No."

"Do you think that's fair? Do you think—"

"I think I've heard *enough* about this." Bettina turned to Thad and Paige. "You're both in a highly competitive field, so you know what it means to dream and struggle. And you've made it big. Congratulations. You deserve to enjoy that. But *I've* dreamed and struggled, too. Do you have any idea how difficult it is for a woman to get a foothold in electrical engineering? In college, I was the only 'girl' in the department. Even now, in the profession, it's still damn unusual."

Harlan reminded her, "But you've *succeeded*. Gerber Consulting is thriving, doing gangbusters. In all of Dumont County, Gerber is the *only* name in electrical engineering."

Bettina nodded. "And Gerber is *your* name, *your* company. I married you."

"Awww, Betty, let's not go through *that* again, not now. We've been together since grad school. We went into business together and built it from the ground up. It's yours as much as mine. It's *ours*."

"And I'm not giving it up." She crossed her arms.

With a weary sigh, her husband asked, "What about Florida? We've talked about Florida."

"Someday, maybe, sure. But I'm not *ready*. There's still *work* to be done. And I don't appreciate anyone's efforts to force me out of my home—to run me out of town."

Thad spoke up. "Mrs. Gerber, that was *not* our intention, and I apologize if we seemed insensitive. I hope we didn't come across as ... entitled."

"Well"—Bettina's head wobbled—"a little."

(I covered my mouth with my hand as if to stifle a cough, which was in fact a reflexive laugh. Bettina's reaction was apt. Dumont had never dealt with Hollywood royalty.)

Paige leaned forward from the edge of the sofa, elbows to knees. "We don't want you feeling pressured, Mrs. Gerber. Please accept our apologies. I wish we could make amends."

"That won't be necessary," said Bettina. "Main thing is, Harlan and I need to get back to the office, back to *work*. So"—she rose—"if you'll excuse us?"

"Hey!" said Thad as we all stood. "We're shooting a test scene for *Home Sweet Humford* next week, on Thursday, the thirty-first. Harlan? Bettina? Would you like to be in it? I still have slots for walk-ons and extras. It won't pay much, but it ought to be fun, and I bet you'll find it interesting—if you've never been in a film."

Harlan chuckled. "Well, that's a safe bet, Thad—we've never been in a movie." He pondered this with a trace of a scowl, then brightened. "Will *you* be in the movie, Paige?"

She shook her head. "I'll be around for the shoot—moral support for the new director—but no, I won't be in it." She gave me a wink.

I recalled her comments at dinner the prior weekend regarding the insecurities of the featured starlet, Miranda Lemarr. "Besides," I said to Paige, "you'll be busy enough with your new job."

"Oh, *that*," she said with a tone of understatement. "My contract at Questman Center begins November first, but I'm using this time to settle into my office. I've been meeting with staff, getting up to speed on finances, making plans—it's exciting."

Harlan said to me, "How about you, Brody? Handsome guy like you—you *must* be in the movie."

"Nope. But I'll play the stage mom—to a cat. Mister Puss is making his film debut."

Still lolling on the sofa, Mister Puss finally rose, stretched, licked a paw, and preened. He was ready for his star turn. But I still hadn't heard back from Mary Questman, whom I'd emailed in Arizona to confirm she had no objection.

Harlan hemmed. Then he hawed. "I dunno. You folks are sure to have a ball with this, but Betty and I, well, we're just not *that* sorta people, if you know what I mean."

Genuinely curious, I asked, "What sort of people?"

"Well," he said, "we're, uh, you know ... *engineers*."

Thad laughed. "No problem."

"So," said Harlan, "it's nice of you to offer, but I'm afraid we're not interested."

"Speak for yourself," said Bettina.

All heads turned to her.

She told Thad, "Count me in."


Downtown on First Avenue, at our Miles & Norris architecture offices, I spent several hours that afternoon revising preliminary drawings for the new main library. Taking Mister Puss to the office had begun as a now-and-then novelty, to the surprise and considerable delight of our clients as well as the staff, but now Marson and I habitually brought the cat with us. Earlier that week, our accountant had quipped, "Should we put him on the payroll?"

Today the office was quiet, with Marson away for meetings.

Gertie, our receptionist, wasn't bothering me with phone calls, and I could focus on my project, which was shaping up nicely. Mister Puss snoozed in a shaft of sunlight that angled in from a side window and sliced across the carpet.

Busy at my computer, I barely noticed the arrival of occasional emails. *Ping.* But I happened to glance at that one. "Well, guess who," I said to the cat.

Ever curious, Mister Puss arose from his nap and hopped up to my desktop. I said, "Listen to this," and he purred as I read the message aloud.

From: Mary Questman
To: Brody Norris, A.I.A.

Brody, love, I apologize for not getting back to you sooner, but my time in Sedona has been an absolute whirlwind. The tours, the parties, the lectures, the vortexes—it's all been too much! But perfectly splendid, of course. Now that we're into the second week of our trip, I admit that I've grown a bit despondent over the prospect of leaving. That said, I am more than eager to see you and Marson and His Majesty again. So my emotions have been topsy-turvy.

Then, just this morning, one of the ladies on our tour told me that she has taken a large house (with servants) in San Miguel de Allende for the entire month of November. She asked if Berta and I could join her little group there!

At first I thought: I couldn't possibly. What would I wear?

And then I thought: One can buy clothes in Mexico, you ninny. Just go!

Dearest Brody, could I possibly impose upon you and Marson to look after Mister Puss for a month longer than planned? If it's any trouble whatever, please say so, and I shall make other arrangements.

Oh—silly me, I almost forgot—if Mister Puss wants to appear in Thad's movie and you are willing to supervise, I have no objection at all.

Meanwhile, do give the little one a kiss for me.

All my love,
Mary

"What do you think of that?" I said to the cat, lifting him from the desk. He stretched his snout to my ear, purring.

*Pucker up.*

Late that night, at home in our loft, Marson tinkered in the kitchen, setting up the coffeemaker for the morning and arranging two place settings for breakfast on the countertop of the island. His compulsive promptness had led to a proactive corollary: Why put off till tomorrow what you can do tonight?

I sat in the living room, catching up with some reading, with Mister Puss nesting next to me on one of the loveseats. If he felt at all abandoned by Mary's decision to delay her return by a month, he didn't show it, looking right at home.

I had assured Mary that we were happy to extend her cat's stay with us, and when I informed Marson of the protracted visit, he said with a grin, "Then we'll need to stock up on clotted cream." (We had never served the cat clotted cream, and although Marson's tone was jocular, I had a hunch he might give it a try.)

The phone in the kitchen rang. I checked my watch—nearly midnight.

Though Marson stood within inches of the phone, he always waited to answer on the second ring. "Well, my God, what a surprise—hello there, stranger."

I closed my book.

"Too late? *Heavens,* no."

Mister Puss looked up at me with bleary eyes.

Marson was switching off the lights in the kitchen while he talked. "He's right here. Hold on."

The cat stretched himself awake on the cushion, quivering all four legs.

Marson walked over to me with the phone and kissed the top of my head. While handing me the receiver, he silently mouthed, "Inez."

"*Mom?*" I said into the phone. "What's wrong?"

She laughed. "Nothing, Brody."

Marson stepped over to the spiral stairs, turning off a few more lights, leaving me huddled in the warm glow of a single reading lamp.

Inez asked, "How are things in Dumont? How's the weather?"

I held the phone at arm's length and stared at it briefly—this idle chitchat did *not* sound like the freethinking, no-bullshit lesbian activist who'd raised me. A tiny voice squawked from the earpiece, "Are you there?"

Returning the phone to my ear, I said, "Yeah, Mom. The weather's … great."

"That's how I remember it. Fall was my favorite time of year."

Marson had disappeared on the mezzanine, ready for bed.

Inez continued, "And I was thinking: I haven't been back to Dumont for *so* many years, and I haven't seen you and Marson since you were married, and now you're building the new house, and—well, it seems we're overdue for some catching up. So I thought I might pop out for a visit. Before winter sets in. Soon." She paused. "Are you there?"

"Uh … sure, Mom. When do you think you'll arrive?"

"Don't know yet. Just wanted to sound you out. And, Brody, I will *not* impose on you and Marson. I don't know how big your loft is, but I assume there's no guest room, and more to the point,

I want my privacy as much as you'll want yours. Where do you think I should stay?"

I answered mechanically, "The Manor House. It's a nice bed-and-breakfast, converted from one of those monster mansions on Prairie Street."

"Thanks, I'll look into it. You get some rest now. Bye, sweetie."

We rang off. My mind was spinning.

Mister Puss stretched his paws up to my shoulders, purring. He reached his chin to my ear.

*Pleasant dreams.*

## 4

Six days later, a circus. A carnival, it seemed, had rolled into Dumont and taken over the town commons. The idyllic green quadrangle now teemed with the vans and trailers, the cables and lights and porta-potties, the cast and crew of a professional film company preparing to shoot a test scene. Adjacent streets were closed off with police vehicles, and scores of onlookers milled and gabbed beyond a barricade of temporary fencing.

On that Thursday morning, the day of Halloween, I walked Mister Puss on his leash through the crowd and found Thad Manning mobbed in the middle of the action—answering questions, checking over lists, giving orders, appearing affable, but clearly strained. When I caught his eye, he nodded and stepped over to me.

"Hey, Brody. Morning," he said. "If you want to wait with the rest of the cast"—he motioned toward another clump of people— "I'll be with you in a bit. Lots of hurry-up-and-wait, I'm afraid. Just the nature of the business. Plenty of food. Help yourself." And he was pulled away to address other pressing concerns.

Walking toward the cast, I recognized Yevgeny Krymov, who would appear in this test scene as himself, recruited by Thad on the night when they dined at our loft. Spotting me as I approached with Mister Puss, Yevgeny came over to greet us—a slow hug for me and a quick hello for the cat.

Slyly, he asked me, "And where is your husband?"

"Marson's at the office. He was afraid it might be a zoo over here." I glanced about. "Silly, huh?"

"Come, come, come," said Yevgeny, skittering me toward the cast. "I want you to meet someone."

And there, seated in a canvas chair, having her hair styled, was Miranda Lemarr, a rising star known not only for her high-wattage beauty, but also for her innocent vulnerability. I thought of Marilyn Monroe. I also thought of Paige Yeats, Thad Manning's wife, who had told me Miranda was plagued by insecurities. Looking around, I caught sight of Paige hanging out with some of the crew, well removed from Miranda's immediate orbit.

Miranda winced. "Careful, Darnell," she told the hot young Hispanic hairdresser, whose swishy manner made me grin.

He whirled a styling brush. "Hush now, bitch princess, or Darnell won't make you fabulous." His accent sounded Puerto Rican—with a slight lisp.

Yevgeny leaned close to ask me, "Cute? Yes?"

I had assumed he dragged me over to meet Miranda.

"He does makeup, too," said Yevgeny.

"Yevgeny," said Miranda, breaking into her signature wide-screen smile, "who *is* this adorable creature?" She was looking in my direction, but focused on my feet.

Yevgeny asked her, "My adorable friend Brody? Or his adorable cat?"

"Well, *both*." She giggled.

When we were properly introduced, I set Mister Puss in her lap so they could get acquainted before the shoot. Miranda cooed. The cat purred.

Darnell extended his hand to me in a manner suggesting I should kiss it rather than shake it, but I shook it anyway. "Darnell Passalacqua," he said with a wink. "The best in the business."

"Brody Norris," I said. "Architect."

"No, bitch princess, *you* should be in pictures."

"Thanks, but I'll leave that to the professionals—and Mister Puss. He's looking forward to his close-up."

Darnell flung his hands in laughter, as if I was joking.

"Oh, Jane?" called Miranda. "Can you bring Seth over?"

A middle-aged woman, pleasant looking but by no means glamorous, approached with a boy who looked like the typical all-American kid next door. He wore makeup that included a few subtle freckles. His sandy hair had been streaked and feathered. He was about the height of a ten-year-old, but I sensed he was older than he looked.

He was introduced as Seth Douglas, the child star I would *surely* remember from his roles in this and that (but I had seen neither this nor that, so as far as I was concerned, he was just some kid—with a great haircut). He would be playing Miranda's son in today's shoot, and the starlet wanted him to meet Mister Puss.

Seth's real mother was introduced to me as Jane Douglas. She quipped, "I'm one of those dreaded stage moms."

I shook her hand. "Then that makes two of us."

She gave me a puzzled look.

"The cat," I said. "He's not mine, but I'm looking after him."

Our conversation was interrupted by the arrival of a woman who wore tight camo pants with open-toed red huaraches. Athletic looking, in her forties, she wore an orange hunting vest, its pockets stuffed with tools and electrical tape and possibly ammunition. Strapped to her shoulder was an assault rifle. I didn't know whether to laugh or to panic and run. No one else seemed to find her—or the gun—remarkable, so I stayed put, though cautious. She yelled to an Asian man following her, "Move your ass, Wes. Jesus, we don't have all day."

We watched as she barreled through our midst, leading Wes as he unspooled a heavy black cable.

When they were out of earshot, I asked Jane Douglas, "What the hell?"

She laughed. "That's Ellen Locke, our gaffer—chief electrician.

Wesley Sugita is best boy, Ellen's assistant, even though he's at least ten years older."

"But," I stammered, "but that … *gun.*"

Jane tossed her hands. "Ellen's a gun nut, for sure. She can't pull that shit in California, but whenever we travel to an open-carry state, she's like a pig in mud."

"Hot mama." Angelic little Seth Douglas stepped into our conversation. "Yowza, that Ellen's one hot mama," he said in a deep, leering voice that truly creeped me out. He licked his lips as he watched the heat-packing gaffer strut across the green.

His mother said, "Enough of that, Seth." She explained to me, "He's sixteen now—what else can I say? He's feeling his oats."

"Oats?" said the kid with a low laugh. "You think I'm feeling my *oats?*"

A man in black hurried past us, approaching Miranda Lemarr, who still sat with Mister Puss while Darnell now worked on her makeup. Without saying a word, the man in black whipped out a gadget—a light meter, I guessed—and held it first to her face, then to the cat's.

Jane Douglas told me, "That's Zeiss Shotwell, director of photography." In a la-di-da accent, she added, "He's *terribly* British, don't cha know. And a wee bit prickly."

As if proving Jane's point, Shotwell told Miranda, "Your coloring is marvelous, darling, but the lashes are a tad whorish."

Darnell bristled—"Okay, bitch princess, you leave now"—and shooed Shotwell away.

As Shotwell was leaving, he encountered Conrad Houghes, the disagreeable investor I'd seen arguing with Thad Manning two weeks earlier. He hadn't wanted to do any of the location shooting in Dumont, preferring cheaper arrangements in New Mexico. But Thad had overruled Houghes, and now he was back from LA—and looking steamed about it. He carried a sheaf of papers.

Zeiss Shotwell said to him, "Well now, Connie, playing script girl, are we?"

Houghes shoved a page at Shotwell, who wandered off.

Houghes then joined us, announcing gruffly, "Listen up, people: here are the sides. Let's try to make this quick, huh?"

Like the others, I got a "side," the screenplay excerpt we'd be shooting. Despite all the equipment and staff and paid hours that would be expended on that day's efforts, the script consisted of a single page, and the finished, edited scene would run about a minute. We all stopped what we were doing to study it.

I noticed that Miranda Lemarr's character was named Suzanne, same as Thad Manning's mother. The little boy's role, to be played by Seth Douglas, was named Thane, a thinly veiled reference to Thad himself.

```
EXT. CITY PARK - DAY

YEVGENY KRYMOV, renowned ballet dancer, sits on
a park bench reading a newspaper, enjoying a
beautiful fall day in Humford. In background,
security guards hold back some dozen fans and
autograph hounds who wave and call to him.

He glances up to the path in foreground and
watches pretty SUZANNE, 32, and her son THANE,
12, strolling past. Suzanne is walking an
exotic CAT on a leash.

                    YEVGENY
          (Russian accent, calling to Suzanne)
     How you teach him to do that?


                    SUZANNE
          (confused, accusingly to Thane)
     What were you up to, young man?


                    THANE
     Nothin, Mom!
```

                    YEVGENY
                (laughing)
      No, the cat. How did you teach
      him to walk on a leash? I have
      not seen such a thing.

Suzanne, Thane, and Cat step over to bench.
Yevgeny puts paper aside and stands.

                    SUZANNE
      He just sorta took to it. He's
      a clever little guy.

Suzanne lifts the Cat, and Yevgeny leans close
to pet it.

                    YEVGENY
      Hello, kit-cat.

                    CAT
      Meow.

                    YEVGENY
      And what is your name?

                    THANE
      I'm Thane. I'm twelve.

                    SUZANNE
      Sweetie, I think the nice man
      was asking about the cat.
          (to Yevgeny)
      His name is Oolong.

                    CAT
      Meow.

The fans continue to wave and yoo-hoo in the
distance.

I now took notice of the group of extras gathered nearby, who would play the adoring fans. I had assumed they were merely part of the growing crowd of local onlookers assembled along the street, many of whom were taking pictures with their phones, but this smaller group was well within the barricades, joking and gabbing with two "security guards," also actors. Among the umpteen extras, I noticed Bettina Gerber, who lived in—and had no intention of leaving—the Taliesin house that Thad Manning wanted to buy.

Thad, trailed by three or four functionaries, stepped briskly in our direction. "Are we ready?" he asked, meaning: Has Darnell finished putting Miranda together?

With a flourish, Darnell removed Miranda's smock. "Behold the bitch princess. Fabulous or what?"

Everyone applauded.

"Lovely," said Thad. "Now, then. Let's move to the set for a read-through."

The "set," in this instance, was simply the park bench, a short walk away, which was now surrounded by the tech crew and various assistants.

Although *Home Sweet Humford* was to be a "film" (never a "movie" among the Hollywood crowd), there would be no film involved in the production process, which had been overtaken by high-definition video. The days of massive cameras and film canisters and dollies were gone, with cinematographers relying instead on digital equipment, computerization, and even drones.

Thad led the cast—consisting of Yevgeny, Miranda, Seth with his mother, and Mister Puss with me—as we moved to the park bench. On the far side of the bench, in the background, the extras got into position as autograph hounds and security guards. A hush fell over the entire commons. A few birds gabbed in the tress, rattling the branches. An airplane buzzed faintly where the sky met the horizon.

While discussing the script, Thad addressed the actors by their character names—Miranda was now Suzanne, Seth was Thane, Mister Puss was Oolong. Concluding his comments, he said, "All right. Let's just read the lines. No action. Yevgeny, please begin."

Yevgeny asked Suzanne, "How you teach him to do that?"

"Good," said Thad. "If you'd care to thicken the Russian accent, be my guest."

"*Da konechno*," said Yevgeny. And he laid it on thick.

"That's it," said Thad. "And Suzanne is confused by the question, so she asks her son…"

Miranda as Suzanne: "What were you up to, young man?"

Seth jumped in as Thane, low and surly: "Nothin, hot mama."

Thad gave the kid a steely look. "As *scripted*, please. And bring the register up a notch—you're *twelve*, remember."

Thane rolled his eyes, then delivered the line as directed: "Nothin, Mom!"

"Good," said Thad. "Keep it moving…"

Yevgeny laughed. "No, the cat. How did you teach him to walk on a leash? I have not seen such a thing."

Suzanne: "He just sorta took to it. He's a clever little guy."

Thad asked me, "Brody? Could you hold the cat in position between Yevgeny and Suzanne?"

"Sure." I did as directed.

Yevgeny leaned close to pet Mister Puss. "Hello, kit-cat."

"Fine," said Thad. "Brody, do you think Oolong could possibly meow on cue? I mean, if not, no problem—we'll dub it in later."

"He's a clever little guy," I reminded Thad. "Let's give it a try."

Yevgeny: "Hello, kit-cat."

*Meow.*

After a stunned silence, everyone applauded.

"Very nice," said Thad, impressed. Then he frowned. "Uh, maybe it's just me, but to my ear, it sounded as if Oolong was actually saying the word 'meow,' rather than just, you know, naturally meowing—like a cat. Can we try that again, please?"

I hoisted Mister Puss and turned him to me, nose to nose. "Can you handle that?" Purring, he nuzzled his snout between my shoulder and my ear.

*What's the motivation for my line?*

Reluctantly, I told Thad, "I hate to come across like a stage mom, but I'm wondering if maybe you could explain why the cat decides to meow just then."

"Because," said Thad, whirling a hand while collecting his thoughts and summoning commendable patience, "because Yevgeny just said 'hello' to the cat, and the cat can't very well say 'hello' in return, so he just ... meows. Right?"

"Right, got it." Turning to Mister Puss, I asked with a hint of menace, "Right?"

*Meow.*

"Perfect," said Thad. "That's great."

*Quack.*

"No!" said Thad. "Christ! Cut!"

"We weren't rolling," said Zeiss Shotwell over a loudspeaker that echoed through the park.

"I'm *aware* of that, Zeiss," Thad shouted, clenching his fists to the heavens. Then he spun toward angelic little Seth Douglas. Crouching to face the kid squarely, Thad said with fierce intensity, "You can act like a *professional*—or you can go and act someplace *else*. Understand?"

Jane Douglas tried to intervene. "It *won't* happen again, Thad. Trust me."

"It sure as hell *better* not."

Seth whined, "I didn't say *nothin*."

Yevgeny seemed to enjoy watching the squabble. With a twitch of his brows, he leaned near and whispered to me, "I have not seen Thad angry before. Nice, yes?"

Yowza, I thought. Spank me, hot mama.

When things calmed down, the shoot went much more smoothly, but even then, it was tediously slow, and I gained a new appreciation for the collective effort involved in filming such a seemingly simple scene.

They did several more read-throughs. Then they ran the lines without the script, over and over. Miranda took the leash from me, and the cast rehearsed the action of the scene. The extras were coached and cued, adding their hubbub to the opening and closing shots. And at last they began filming.

Until then, Thad had stood in the midst of the cast, directing the rehearsal, tweaking the delivery of each line, refining every move. But now, for the actual performance before the cameras, Thad moved away and situated himself behind a bank of flat-screen video monitors, where he could check the framing of each camera. When all was ready, he called for quiet, cued the fill-in lighting, cued the video, cued the audio—a clapper board assured everything was in sync—and then he called for action.

I had stepped back as well, and as the scene began, I watched over Thad's shoulder, as did many others.

The scene was shot multiple times, with Thad calling "cut" between takes, each time refining a camera angle, or fiddling with lighting, or adjusting actors within the frame, or simply correcting a flubbed line. After an hour or so, this was followed by a long sequence of establishing shots, reaction shots, and finally, close-ups.

"My God," said Thad, turning to me with a drop-dead smile, "the camera just *loves* Mister Puss. He might've found a new calling."

"Uh-oh," said Darnell, who was standing nearby, at the ready if needed to fix a shiny nose or an errant wisp of hair. From the corner of his mouth, he told me, "I warned the bitch princess: never share a scene with kids or animals."

On the monitors, the actors bobbed and stretched, awaiting their cues while Thad stood quietly, looking over the script with one assistant; with another, he checked a list. Then he huddled in conversation with the man in black, Zeiss Shotwell, director of photography. They studied the monitors, replaying various takes, nodding as they spoke.

Thad's voice came over the loudspeaker. "Looking great, people. But Zeiss thinks that some of these shots might look even better in the afternoon light—and I agree." He concluded, "Break for lunch."

Our friend Nancy Sanderson, the restaurateur who had helped with the dinner party at our loft, had been hired to cater snacks and lunch for the cast and crew. Her van, with crisp black-on-white lettering, FIRST AVENUE BISTRO, was parked on the commons, inside the barricade, in a shady area with picnic tables adjacent to a few tech vehicles, outside the sight lines of the filming. Parked immediately beyond the barricade were a couple of Dumont County sheriff's vehicles, assigned to deputies who were hired for security, and even a paramedics' van—probably a contractual requirement of the guilds and unions working on the production.

Nancy was busy behind a long buffet table, setting things out for the noon rush. Pitching in to help her was Nia Butler, a husky woman of color with a short-cropped Afro. As the city's code-compliance officer, she always wore olive twill pants with an Eisenhower jacket that gave her the look of a motorcycle cop. White shirt, skinny black necktie. Plus, oddly, granny glasses.

I often wondered if Nia's outfit was an actual uniform or if she had simply adopted a paramilitary style of dress to reinforce her authority. I could imagine that she had encountered some skepticism—or outright hostility—among small-town contractors and tradesmen who didn't welcome her visits.

Today, though, Nia was in her glory, since her main reason for being there was not to assist Nancy, but to ensure that everything was up to safety codes. There was plenty that warranted inspection:

Cables crisscrossed the lawn with slapdash abandon. Makeshift power poles sprung up here and there, some of them doubling as supports for awnings, one of which stretched above the catering area. At one end of the buffet table, an oblong galvanized vat was filled with icy water that bobbed with various bottles and cans and coolers, there for the taking.

Not far from the vat, the cables and poles converged in an area overseen by Ellen Locke, the gaffer with the big gun. What was *that* all about? I saw her reach behind some equipment crates and remove a six-pack of Leinenkugel, a regional favorite brewed nearby. Furtively, she stashed it deep in the vat, below the layer of ice. Water splashed over the side, falling to the soggy ground that surrounded the vat.

I frowned. The wet grass, the cables.

Nia Butler, however, stood only a few feet away, unconcerned. If something wasn't up to code, it wouldn't get past her. Nia could be fierce.

But there was another side to this woman, as well. Marson and I had been surprised, that past summer, to watch an unlikely friendship—which had all the overtones of a romance—develop between Nia Butler, thirty-something and single, and Nancy Sanderson, still single in her fifties. Today they worked in tandem behind the buffet table, gabbing amiably while serving the hungry production team, who juggled their plates and phones, catching up on the world after a long morning's shoot.

Moving through the lunch line, I added a few extra shrimp to my plate, no sauce, for Mister Puss, who followed on his leash. When we left the buffet to find a table, I noticed a woman in a huge red hat waving to me from the barricade—it was none other than Glee Savage, intrepid newshound, seeking entry, which would allow a closer perspective for her reporting. When Hollywood came to sleepy little Dumont, that was a front-page story.

"Brody, love, thank you *so* much," she gushed as I escorted her past a deputy. Meandering through the picnic tables, she helped herself to one of Mister Puss's plump shrimp.

I suggested, "Sit with me? *Way* too much food."

"Thanks, doll, but I'm working." And she took off into the crowd, clutching her notepad.

Yevgeny had spotted me, waving me over to a table where he sat with Darnell Passalacqua, Jane Douglas, and her creepy kid, Seth.

Joining them, chatting while eating, I learned that the cast and the senior production crew were all staying at the Manor House, which had been Yevgeny's temporary home for a couple of months. Setting down his glass of iced tea, Yevgeny noted, "Is nice place, yes?"

"Yes," agreed Jane, "the Manor House is *lovely*."

"It's a shithole," Seth muttered. "The Wi-Fi sucks."

If he were my kid, I'd have slapped him.

But his mother said, "Try the chicken salad, honey."

Yevgeny turned to Darnell, sitting next to him, and told him tenderly, "Try the chicken salad." And he winked.

I noticed they were sitting knee to knee, which had a jumbled effect on me. I felt amused: a cliché pairing of ballet star and hairdresser. I felt delighted: good for them. I felt jilted: Yevgeny used to direct his flirtation at *me*. But mostly, I felt relieved: Yevgeny would remain a grade-A fantasy, to be indulged without guilt. (Unless Darnell got hit by a bus. Or whatever.)

My musings were interrupted by Jane saying to Darnell with a warm smile, "Take it slow, sweets."

He grinned back at her. "Yes, bitch princess."

Aha. Though it came as a surprise, I should have expected that all of these outsiders—the cast and crew—were actually insiders of "the industry" and already knew each other. They seemed, in fact, to know each other *very* well.

I watched a nearby table, where cinematographer Zeiss Shotwell and investor Conrad Houghes barked at each other about art versus finances.

At another table, Thad Manning sat quietly conversing with Miranda Lemarr, while Thad's wife, Paige Yeats, kept her distance, making good on her intentions not to intrude upon the starlet's insecurities.

"Hey, Brody."

I turned at the sound of a rich baritone voice, the familiar voice of Thomas Simms, sheriff of Dumont County. Getting up from the table, I greeted him with a handshake that morphed into a quick hug.

Dumont's top lawman had become a close friend since my arrival in town a few years earlier. Always a dapper dresser, Simms wore a dark, well-tailored business suit with an immaculate white shirt and a snappy silk tie—pink and white stripes today. At forty-three, he'd been elected twice as sheriff, rising from the rank of detective. This accomplishment would be a matter of pride anywhere, but it was all the more notable in lily-white Dumont, as Simms was black.

I asked after his wife, Gloria, and their son, Tommy; he asked after Marson. Then I said wryly, "Expecting trouble, Sheriff?"

"Nah. Couple of my guys are working security. Thought I'd drop by for some of the excitement." Looking at the cat at my feet, he laughed. "The way I hear it, a star is born."

"Thad seemed really pleased." I lifted Mister Puss so Simms could pet him, coaxing a purr.

Simms asked me, "Mary's on the road again?"

"I'll say—now she's off to Mexico for a month."

Simms whistled. "Nice and warm there."

Jim Phelps, a local veterinarian, stepped over to us. A mellow old guy, nearing retirement, he wore a corduroy sport coat with suede elbow patches and, as usual, had a pipe in his mouth, though it was rarely lit. He was the quintessential country doctor, and Mister Puss was one of his patients.

"Well, *Jim*," I said, "how nice to see you." Mister Puss stopped purring, wary.

Jim chortled. "Hello there, Brody. Sheriff. Mister Puss." He explained, "Craziest thing—these movie people. Since they're working with an animal today, they're paying me to take the day off and spend it out here in the sunshine, just in case I'm needed. Crazy, huh? But anyway"—he tweaked the cat's cheek—"*thank* you, Mister Puss. I'm at your service." And he strolled away, chomping his pipe.

"Wow," I said to the cat, "you're really getting the star treatment."

With an air of entitlement, Mister Puss yawned.

Someone with a walkie-talkie approached me. "Brody Norris?"

"Yes?"

"Your mother wants to see you."

Through a laugh, I asked, "*What?*"

"Your mother"—he pointed—"she wants to see you."

Oh. My. God.

Inez Norris stood some twenty yards away, out on the street, outside the barricade, waving at me with a broad smile. I hadn't seen her in three years, but even at a distance, I could see she hadn't changed much—she was a healthy woman in her sixties who had long been committed to yoga and meditation and drumming circles and dance—a hippie of sorts, older and wiser. She wore leotards with an East Indian tunic and a billowing mohair stole to ward off the chill of a late-October afternoon.

"*Mom?*" I called, dashing toward her with Mister Puss at my heels.

"Surprise," she said as we embraced over the fencing.

I nodded to a guard, who admitted her. I asked her, "When...?"

"A few hours ago." Glancing down, she said, "And this must be Mister Puss."

I picked him up and introduced them; both seemed charmed.

Inez slung an arm through mine, gabbing about her flight as we walked along the perimeter of the park. I kept an eye out for Glee Savage; this was *not* the moment for a chance encounter after their forty-year estrangement. I noticed that the onlookers in the street had now been joined by a bunch of schoolkids— young ones, who must have been dismissed early from class after a Halloween party. There were zombies and cowgirls; ninjas and superheroes; devils and mice; and a horrid little nun, four feet tall, with gouged and bleeding eye sockets.

Mumbling, I asked, "And where ...?"

"The Manor House, of course—good recommendation."

At a loss for words, I asked, "How's the Wi-Fi?"

Mother Nature had cooperated, producing a spectacular afternoon for the reshoot. The angle of the sun intensified the golden glow of turning leaves. The deep sapphire of the sky was broken only by a few jolly, puffy clouds, which framed the neoclassical lines of the limestone library as if painted there on a backdrop.

Everyone sensed that the quality of daylight had been worth the wait, and excitement was palpable as the crew hustled to adjust fill-in lighting. The scene was already well rehearsed, so Thad called for "places"—we'd soon be rolling. He told Zeiss Shotwell, "Two cameras ought to do it. This morning's reaction shots were dead-on."

Zeiss agreed, positioning two cameramen for wide and medium shots. The third camera was left unmanned, well out of the frame, producing an askew, static image on one of the monitors.

I walked Mister Puss to Miranda and handed her the leash. Then I joined Thad and Zeiss and many others behind the monitors. Inez, my mother, stood next to me; I did a quick scan of the surroundings and found Glee nowhere in sight. The extras were in position behind the park bench. The crowd of hushed onlookers was somewhere behind us on the street, near the catering area and tech vehicles.

Thad called for quiet. And lights. And cameras. And then— action.

The scene ran smoothly, with all of the actors on their marks and on their cues.

"Cut. Great," said Thad. After some minor adjustments of the framing, he said, "Let's run it again. Action."

As the scene played out, Thad nudged Zeiss, telling him, "That cat is amazing—he's stealing the scene."

Through his headset, Zeiss said to one of the cameramen, "Close-up on cat."

They ran that portion of the scene again, with one of the monitors displaying a full-frame image of Mister Puss's face; his eyes and ears followed the action, alert as a cheetah tracking its prey.

"Jesus, *yes*, that's perfect," Thad said quietly.

The fill-in lighting flickered.

With a loud hiss—then *bang*—the lights went out. The monitors went black.

Someone shouted, "Ellen!"

We all turned toward the tech area to see Wesley Sugita, assistant to chief electrician Ellen Locke, as he ran toward her. She had collapsed next to the icy vat of drinks. She lay motionless in the soggy grass next to her assault rifle. One hand still held a frosty Leinenkugel. Peeping from the front of Ellen's red huaraches, her charred toes steamed.

Everyone froze, speechless, trying to comprehend what had happened. Then, among the crowd watching from behind the barricade, the little nun with the gouged eyes let out a deathly shriek, which raised a chorus of cries and whining from the scores of other children.

Inside the barricade, everyone—cast, crew, security—began rushing toward Ellen, but Wes raised both hands, yelling, "No! Wait!"

We halted as he scrambled to disconnect the main power source from the temporary rigging. When the danger had passed, he slumped, waving us forward.

First at Ellen's side were Sheriff Simms, his deputies, and the two medics who tried to resuscitate her—but no one seemed surprised when the effort proved futile.

Miranda Lemarr had brought Mister Puss to me, and I carried him with one arm while stepping over to Sheriff Simms, who was finishing a phone call: "We need you right away, Heather. Thanks."

I knew Heather Vance. She was the county medical examiner.

"Uh, Sheriff?" said Nia Butler, the code-enforcement officer, standing at the far end of the galvanized vat.

As Simms walked in her direction, she used a stick to pull the socket end of a heavy orange extension cord out of the water. Its other end disappeared in the rigging under one of the makeshift awnings.

PART TWO

# NOVEMBER

CHAPTER

5

At our loft the next morning, the first of November, Marson and I awoke before dawn—something of a habit lately, enforced by Mister Puss. Our houseguest had not been shy about sharing our bed each night, where he would end up nesting on one of our pillows. Early that Friday, my slumber had been troubled by a nonstop video loop of Ellen Locke's charred and steaming toes, but I was roused from the dream when I heard the cat purring. His nose touched my ear.

*Up'n at'm.*

Downstairs in the kitchen, Marson fed His Majesty while I checked outside for the paper. As expected, Glee Savage's intended gossip feature had not made it to page one, where a weightier story appeared above the fold.

**Mishap? Or murder?**

*Hollywood tech worker electrocuted while filming Dumont movie*

Compiled from *Register* staff reports

•

NOVEMBER 1, DUMONT, WI — Yesterday's filming of a test scene for *Home Sweet Humford*, directed by Dumont native Thad Manning, ended in tragedy when Ellen Locke, chief electrician on the production crew, reached for a bottle in a tub of water that contained the dangling end of a live extension cord. Locke, 43, was pronounced dead at the scene by attending paramedics.

The plug of the extension cord was later found to be missing its third prong, creating an electrical hazard. The circuit was not grounded until traveling through the victim, who was standing in wet grass.

Dumont County sheriff Thomas Simms happened to be on location with a security detail provided by his department. "I didn't see it happen," he told the *Register*. "Like everyone else on the commons, I was watching the actors during the filming, which was interrupted when the power shorted. It sort of exploded."

Does Simms suspect foul play?

"I'm suspicious," he said. "For that cord to end up in the water by accident, it would take a real numbskull. But everyone on the film crew is a highly trained professional, at the top of their game." With a nod, he repeated, "I'm suspicious."

Dr. Heather Vance, county coroner and medical examiner, was called to the scene and issued a preliminary statement that the victim's cause of death was electrocution. She added, "Because of the suspicious circumstances, however, we'll conduct a postmortem to determine if other factors might be involved."

When asked for comment, Thad Manning said, "We're heartbroken. We're bereft. In our world, a production company is family. In losing Ellen, we've lost one of our own. We're grieving."

Will the film project survive this tragedy?

"Absolutely," Manning answered. "Ellen would be the first to agree: the show must go on. And *Home Sweet Humford* is a film that must be made."

An investigation into the circumstances of Ellen Locke's

death is already underway. Sheriff Simms and his deputies conducted initial interviews with many at the scene of the death late yesterday. He reported, "As far as we know, no one actually witnessed what happened. Tomorrow I'll do some follow-up interviews and try to get more background before these people go home."

Most of the production company resides in and around Los Angeles, where the victim also lived.

Simms explained, "I don't have the authority to order anyone to stay in town—not unless I start arresting people—and at this stage of the game, it's far too early to consider that."

Does the sheriff face an impossible challenge?

"I hope not," said Simms. "But if we're going to get a handle on this, we'll need to move quickly. I intend to wrap it up fast."

When Marson finished reading the story, he set the newspaper in front of me on the counter, then paced a few steps. "It seems our friendly local sheriff may need some extra help. Poor Thomas—a possible murder on his hands, and all the suspects are about to vanish." Marson grinned.

More than once, I had pitched in and assisted Thomas with some amateur sleuthing—an unlikely role for a mild-mannered architect. But hey, whatever works. Not this time, though.

"Nope," I told Marson, "I have bigger fish to fry."

Mister Puss hopped up to the counter and sat facing me, purring, with wide, hungry eyes.

I gave the cat a weary look. "Don't be so *literal*. There are no fish." He looked peeved.

Marson asked, "If not fish, what *do* you need to fry?"

"My *mother*. Inez is in town."

Marson crossed his arms. "You should be thrilled."

I said, "If you knew her like I know her..."

He reminded me, "I grew up with her. I was married to her sister for thirty years."

"Oh. *That*."

He stepped up behind me and put his hands on my shoulders. "What's eating you, kiddo?"

I shrugged, but I knew. "The bad blood with Glee. That feud is older than I am. If they run into each other, they'll be at each other's throat, and with good reason. Inez really ... *betrayed* Glee."

"Perhaps," said Marson, "but she also happens to be the mother of the man I love. I'd like to see her."

I hemmed. "Maybe."

Marson was not the sort to lay down the law. However: "I insist you invite her over for drinks tonight. We can do some catching up."

"Maybe."

"And then, we *are* taking her out to dinner."

As I sulked at the counter, Mister Puss nudged his snout to my ear, purring.

*Buckle up.*

Although Friday was a regular workday, I had promised Inez I would come over to the Manor House for a visit that morning— and now I was under orders to make plans with her for the evening as well. I took Mister Puss.

The palatial Georgian-style mansion on Prairie Street—red brick, white trim, black shutters, third-floor dormers—had been built more than a hundred years earlier by a now forgotten industrialist during the heyday of Dumont's expansion, which had been driven by timber, paper, and printing. With the passing of time, however, the era of private homes fit for nobility had dimmed, then disappeared, leaving the biggest of these houses in search of new purpose as well as new owners.

Such was the case some twenty years ago when the Georgian

mansion—which had grown more than a tad weedy and long overdue for tuck-pointing and new plumbing—found its salvation in an eager young couple from Chicago who, indulging an impulse to become innkeepers, raided their trust funds, snapped up the building for a song, and brought it back to life as the Manor House. The couple, no longer young, still took pride in running one of the most lavish bed-and-breakfasts in all of central Wisconsin.

The stretch of street in front of the mansion, which occupied an entire block, was normally quiet, but that Friday morning it was crammed with cars parked in both directions; others slowly passed by while their drivers gawked. Nearest the house were several vehicles from the sheriff's department. I recognized the unmarked tan sedan driven by Simms. And there was no missing the television truck from Green Bay, with its satellite dish cranked high above the trees.

Mister Puss, on his leash, walked sprucely at my heels as we mounted the limestone stairs of the front terrace and stepped through the main door, which had been propped open to accommodate the traffic.

There was no check-in desk, as the owners had wanted to preserve the feel of an actual home. A service bell sat on a ledge near the central stairway, but I didn't need to tap it that morning, as a woman with a clipboard stood ready to take questions and give directions. I heard voices and activity from several large rooms along the main hall.

Stepping up to the woman, I said, "Inez Norris is expecting me. I'm her son."

"I saw Mrs. Norris in the breakfast room." She pointed.

"Actually," I said, "she's *Miss* Norris, but she goes by Ms."

"I'll remember that." The woman was staring at Mister Puss.

I told her, "He's a service animal. Emotional support."

"Of course," she said skeptically while turning to walk away.

The breakfast room was at the back of the house, painted a cheery yellow, which gave it the feel of a sunroom, with large windows peering out to the vast rear lawn and its formal, symmetrical landscaping, looking rather French.

The small dining tables numbered a dozen or so, but only three were occupied, so I spotted Inez at once, nibbling toast while absorbed in the morning paper. At another table, Yevgeny Krymov sat with Darnell Passalacqua, both of them scruffy and unshaven. Absorbed in each other, they didn't notice me enter.

I stepped over to Inez's table and leaned to kiss her cheek. "Morning, Mom."

"Morning, sweetie," she said with a smile, removing her glasses. "Coffee?"

"Sure." I sat.

Extra cups were set at the table. Inez filled one from her carafe.

"Well," I said with a soft laugh, "you've had quite the homecoming. More excitement than you bargained for?"

"That's one way of putting it." She broke off a tip of her buttered toast and dangled it for Mister Puss, who skittered to her side. Purring, he ate it.

I swallowed some coffee and put down the cup. "I'm sorry if I was less than welcoming yesterday. You sorta took me by surprise. And then, well…"

"*Zap,*" said Inez.

I borrowed her line: "That's one way of putting it."

She tapped the front page of the morning paper. "Any leads?"

"No idea." But she was well aware that I had previously dabbled in local crime solving.

Inez riffled through the *Register* and folded it open to Glee Savage's puff piece, buried between the horoscopes and Dear Abby. "So," said Inez, clucking her tongue, "*she* was there."

I nodded.

"Too bad we didn't bump into each other. Or maybe it's just as well—she'd probably claw my eyes out."

I admitted, "That's one of the reasons I was on edge. But it's a new day, right? Let's celebrate your return. Marson and I want to have you over for drinks tonight, six o'clock. Then dinner somewhere. Are you free?"

She reminded me, "I came to see *you*, dear. I'll be there on the dot."

"Mr. Passalacqua?" said a deep voice from behind me. I knew without looking that Sheriff Simms had entered the room.

I stood to greet him and introduced him to my mother. Simultaneously, Darnell and Yevgeny got up from their table—where they had been gazing dreamily through the window—and joined us, surprised to see me.

Simms explained, "I'm conducting follow-up interviews this morning, and I wonder if you have a few minutes to talk, Mr. Passalacqua."

"*Please*, Sheriff. We're all friends here—it's Darnell." He offered his limp hand.

Simms shook it. "Thanks, Darnell. Got a few minutes?"

"Mm-*hmm*," said Darnell, sizing up Simms.

"And Mr. Krymov," said the sheriff, "I was hoping to talk with you later, but maybe you could join us now, since you seem to be, uh ... together."

Yevgeny and Darnell looked at each other with bedroom eyes. Yevgeny told Simms, "I am at your service, Sheriff."

Then (I had a hunch it was coming), Simms turned to me. "How about it, Brody? Care to sit in?"

I hesitated. "Well, you see, Thomas. I was just—*we* were just— Mom and I—we need some time to catch up."

Inez tossed her hands. "Go, sweetie. We'll have time for that tonight. And believe it or not, I have plans for this morning."

Dubiously, I asked, "Like what?"

"Just plans." Sounding evasive, she added, "Thought I'd visit some old haunts."

Mister Puss was already up and on his feet—at my heel, ready to go.

I gave Inez a parting peck before telling Simms, "Lead the way."

"Library," he said.

Out in the main hall, Simms directed Yevgeny and Darnell into the library, on the right. To the left, in the main parlor, Thad Manning and Paige Yeats sat with the TV crew, recording an interview under the glare of lights on tripods. Simms paused in the hallway to tell me, "I talked to Thad last night and asked if he could supply a copy of yesterday's unedited footage—all of it."

I nodded. "Great idea."

"Thad thought so, too. But he wondered if the other investors might have concerns about security—digital piracy—so he asked me for a 'friendly' subpoena, to cover any liability on his part."

I grinned. "I assume you've made good on that request."

"The subpoena for documentary evidence is now in Thad's pocket. He promised to deliver the video by Monday."

When we stepped into the library, Simms closed the double doors behind us, and Mister Puss sauntered over to the fireplace, plopping on the carpet in front of the hearth. Although the day was not frigid—not for November in Wisconsin—the house felt cold. With its stone floors and leaded windows and high ceilings, it was the sort of interior that begged a cozy morning fire in the confines of the library, which smelled of dust and leather and charred maple. The ticking of a tall pendulum clock underscored the gravity of our purpose—dredging up the truth about Ellen Locke's death.

Yevgeny and Darnell sat waiting at a long wooden table that

displayed a variety of newspapers and magazines. Simms took a chair at the end of the table; I sat down near him. Because Yevgeny was already well known in Dumont, Simms didn't collect extensive background. Darnell, however, needed to fill us in.

Darnell Passalacqua, thirty-one, was born in Puerto Rico and came out at an early age, suffering the typical harassments of a flamboyant sissy in a machismo culture. He fled to Florida for college, where he completed a degree in biochemistry. "Needless to say," he lisped, "this is no longer my thing." After graduation, he moved to San Francisco, where his focus shifted to the beauty industry. From there, it was a short hop to LA and the film industry, "where they say I'm the best in the business."

Yevgeny, of course, had no insights into the emotional dynamics of the production company, but Darnell had been in the thick of it, and he was quick to float a theory regarding what happened to Ellen Locke: "That bitch princess was just *asking* for it."

Simms said, "She had enemies?"

"Many. Don't we all? But the way she *dressed*, sweet Jesús! And those silly guns."

I asked, "What was *that* all about? The guns."

"Batshit loco. She be like Annie Oakley. Shooting squirrels for breakfast—*pow*. Then she eat them raw."

I assumed he was joking. Or at least exaggerating.

Simms said, "She was … strange, yes. But if someone killed her, why?"

Darnell wagged a finger, then tapped it on Simms's notepad as if to say, Take this down. He said, "Thrill kill."

Simms and I glanced at each other.

Darnell added, "Like Hitchcock. Remember the movie *Rope*? Someone thinks up the perfect crime—just for kicks, no motive. Perfect crime needs perfect victim."

Later, Simms asked Darnell for his contact information, in case he was needed for follow-up questions. He added, "I assume you'll be leaving Dumont soon."

Darnell turned to Yevgeny, more than twenty years his senior, and they shared a look of adolescent infatuation.

"Maybe not," Darnell said to Simms. "I think to stay around a few days."

Next to visit the library were sixteen-year-old Seth Douglas, who still made my skin crawl, and stage mom Jane Douglas. Unlike Darnell, they did not intend to linger in Dumont and, in fact, were waiting for a limo to drive them to their plane out of Green Bay.

"Then we'll try to make this quick," said Simms, "but I need to gather the facts regarding everyone's experience with the victim, Ellen Locke."

"Hot mama," said Seth with a low, demonic laugh. He sat playing some sort of game on his phone, which made a racket of pinball sounds and cartoonish explosions. He never looked up from it.

Jane said, "Don't be rude, honey." She tried taking the phone away from him.

He yanked it back, punching at the screen.

I noticed his hair. For the filming, Darnell's magic touch had given the kid an angelic mop top. Today it looked disheveled and greasy.

Simms asked Jane, "How well did you know the victim?"

"Well enough, I suppose. Ellen and I were coworkers, but not what you'd call friends—never socialized. Truth is, her fascination with guns was a real turnoff. I kept my distance."

I said, "There's a grim irony to her death, isn't there? It had nothing to do with guns. She was a gaffer, an electrician—and look at how she died."

Jane groaned. "It was horrible. I can't unsee what happened to her toes."

"*Smokin*-hot mama." Seth laughed.

"For God's sake," said Jane. "Show some respect for the dead."

Seth remained transfixed by his noisy game.

Simms asked him, "Winning any?"

"Can't," said the kid with a grunt. "Wi-Fi sucks."

Miranda Lemarr was next in the lineup of visitors to the library. She, too, was eager to depart for Los Angeles, and Simms said his questions would be brief. When we had settled around the table, Miranda gave Simms her contact information in California, saying she didn't think she could offer much help, but she was willing to try.

I found her every bit as pretty and put-together as the day before at the filming. Paige Yeats had described Miranda as "insecure," but I thought she might simply be shy and perhaps naive—odd traits for someone whose career was making such a rapid rise in an industry known to be highly competitive, at times cutthroat.

What's more, Miranda seemed nervous, which was understandable—she was being questioned in the context of a possible murder. But I wondered if there might have been something else underlying her fidgety manner. She pulled at her fingers, turning them white. She had trouble maintaining eye contact as her glance darted about the room. She bit her lips, requiring a touch-up of lipstick, applied with a shaky hand. Was she "on" something? Or maybe in withdrawal?

Simms must have shared my curiosity. He said, "I believe you just turned twenty-nine, Miss Lemarr?"

"Correct, Sheriff," she answered with a smile and a quick nodding motion that made her hair jiggle, conjuring the image of an antsy Pomeranian.

"And my gosh," said Simms, "your career is really on a roll now.

My wife and I thought you were fantastic last year in *Dreaming Hereafter*."

"That's so sweet of you. Thank you, Sheriff."

His handsome smile turned pensive. "But earlier, I think there were some … problems, right?"

"There were." She stopped shaking, looking calmer. "I was in and out of Betty Ford," she said, referring to the posh, discreet rehab clinic for the rich and famous. She added, "Twice, actually."

Simms smiled again. "Glad you were able to put it behind you. And now, a starring role in Thad Manning's project—it's a big deal, right?"

"Maybe. Hope so. I mean, sure. *Home Sweet Humford* will be a *very* big deal—if it gets finished."

I had tried to keep quiet, but I needed to ask, "Why wouldn't it?"

"It doesn't take much to spook investors. Films get ditched for lots of dumb reasons. But a death—maybe a murder—on the first day of test shots? Not good."

Zeiss Shotwell, director of photography, and investor Conrad Houghes were not buddies, but they knew each other well enough to share a rental car down to Milwaukee, where they would catch their flights home, and they were itching to get on the road, so they doubled up for the interview in the library. Simms and I sat across from them at the long table.

They made an odd pairing. Shotwell, forty or so, with his British airs and erudite manner, wore his usual black slacks and turtleneck—the cerebral *artiste*. Houghes, at least ten years older, was dressed for his role as the LA money guy, crass and sockless, looking nowhere near as hip as he hoped.

In spite of Simms's persistent questions—about the victim, Ellen Locke—Shotwell and Houghes kept gabbing bitchily with each other about the starlet, Miranda Lemarr.

With a loud whistle, Simms gestured a time-out. "What am I

missing here? You've had a death, a *suspicious* death, on your own production crew. Don't you want to get to the bottom of that? I do. That's why I'm here. But *you* two, with your playground pissing match over Miranda Lemarr—if I were just a casual observer, I'd say you were both acting like lovers scorned."

That got their attention. Shotwell said, "That would be a bit of an overstatement, Sheriff. You're not far off, however. You see, I have indeed known the pleasures of Miranda's boudoir. But that was some time ago—no hard feelings, all very up-and-up, don't you know."

With a rude laugh, Houghes declared, "There's a new man in town. And you're *lookin* at'm."

Gag me, I thought.

Simms set aside his notes. "But what about Ellen Locke?"

Shotwell said, "Sorry to sound unsympathetic, old chum, but frankly, I'm glad she's gone. Ellen was a wretched mess." He sniffed.

"And besides," said Houghes, "she's so *easily* replaced. Gaffer gone? Just bring in the best boy. He's waiting in the wings. To be more precise, I just saw Wes Sugita waiting out there in the hall."

Wesley Sugita was next on the list. But after Shotwell and Houghes left the library, Simms and I needed a break before calling him in. As it was nearly noon, the room had warmed up. Even before the fire petered out, Mister Puss had roused himself from the hearth and moved over to the clock, which stood tall between two windows on the outside wall. The cat positioned himself on a square of the cool stone floor, where he could keep an eye on the lazy swinging of the pendulum. On the clock's face, a grinning brass moon kept an eye on the glacial creeping of the heavens.

Standing to stretch a knot between his shoulders, Simms said to me, "Wesley Sugita—best boy, assistant to the gaffer, the chief electrician, Ellen Locke. If Ellen is 'out,' then Wes is 'in.' Is it that simple?"

"Not sure. Maybe *he* can explain it."

Simms said, "And there's something else I want to hear about."

"Me too." I could guess what Simms was thinking: When things went wrong the prior afternoon, when the lights flickered and the monitors went black, when the power surged like a crack of lightning, Wes Sugita was the one who raised the alarm, rushed to Ellen, and kept everyone at bay while he knowledgeably and efficiently restored safety. He knew exactly what to do.

Simms went to the door and spoke into the hall: "We're ready, Mr. Sugita."

When Sugita entered, Simms closed the door behind him, and the three of us sat at the table. He had a serene look about him, as if yesterday's events hadn't shaken him at all. Simms told him, "I'll try to keep this brief. I assume you're leaving for California today."

"I am," he said with a respectful nod, "but I'll make myself available for your investigation whenever needed. If you want me to return, I'll be happy to do so."

We hadn't heard *that* yet today.

He filled in the details of his background: Wesley Sugita was fifty-five years old, born in San Francisco about ten years after his Japanese parents arrived there "after the war." (I noticed that he spoke with no trace of an accent, although his speech was conspicuously polite.) He'd been involved in the film industry for some thirty years and felt that the younger, less experienced Ellen Locke had bypassed him in the pecking order "by sleeping around."

Did he resent her?

"Yes, of course. But we can't always blame disappointment on the success of others."

How did he feel about her zealous affection for guns?

"Many of us thought she had a screw loose."

While there was no hesitation to his answers, his tone struck me as less than candid. He had that Asian veneer of reserve—an inscrutable quality about his manner and features that made it difficult to judge his thoughts or his possible motives.

Simms said, "Forgive me for asking an indelicate question, Mr. Sugita. You mentioned that Ellen 'slept around.' During the course of your professional relationship with her, were you ever intimate?"

"Uh, no." For the first time, he cracked a smile—just a trace, but it was a smile. "You see," he said, "I'm gay."

That angle hadn't occurred to me. I told him, "I am, too, Mr. Sugita."

"I assumed so, Mr. Norris."

Simms laughed.

I said, "Very astute of you, Mr. Sugita. Please, call me Brody."

He nodded. "And please, call me Wes."

G*rrring.*

At six that evening, Mister Puss shot across the living room of the loft to wait at the front door as I followed to answer the bell. When I swung the door open, Inez stepped in from a deep twilight that had fallen over First Avenue.

"Hi, Mom," I said, giving her a kiss.

"Hi, sweetie." She handed me a bottle of champagne. "Thanks for asking me over." Looking about, she proclaimed, "The place is sensational—but of course it *would* be, with you two."

Joining us at the door, Marson leaned in to kiss cheeks with Inez. Then he backed off a step to take a good look at her. Flopping a hand to his chest, he said, "I simply can't *believe* the transformation."

"Beg pardon?" said Inez.

Marson explained, "Last time I saw you, you were my sister-in-law. And now—*poof*—you're my mother-in-law."

"Thanks, sonny," she said in a crotchety voice. She was only three years older than Marson. With a stinging smirk, she asked, "Hear much from Prucilla?"

Inez was referring to her sister, who had been married to Marson for thirty-odd years.

"No," Marson mumbled, "not much," which was an understatement. Marson and Prucilla had barely spoken since he'd left her— for me.

Marson cleared his throat. "Inez," he said, "I've always been concerned about how you might've reacted when I ended things with Prucilla. It was ... complicated."

Inez blurted, "Christ, Marson, what *took* you so long?"

We all had a good laugh—at Prucilla's expense.

Then we had a drink.

And an hour later, we pulled into the parking lot at Moonstruck, a classic Wisconsin supper club on the outskirts of town— the sort of white-linen place where the bar was dressy and the booths were deeply tufted, where meals always began with a relish tray and ended with hand-muddled ice cream drinks, usually involving brandy.

Ginger, the hostess, stepped out from behind her podium to greet us at the door like old friends—everyone was Ginger's oldest, most special friend. She greeted all arrivals with a hug and a "Welcome *home*," and she meant it. When I introduced Inez as my mother, Ginger went gaga. "My God," she said, clutching a stack of menus, "I think I'm going to cry, this is so special." While parading us past the bar, she said, "First round's on me, Johnny."

And we found ourselves at the corner booth overlooking the whole room, the same prime table where, nearly three years earlier, on New Year's Eve, only a day after arriving for my new job in Dumont, I sat with Marson and his wife, whom I hadn't seen since my adolescence, when I had come to town with my mother for a family wedding, leaving a few days later with an impossible puppy crush on my aunt Prucilla's husband. Then, at that New Year's celebration of fresh beginnings, beneath the drifting Mylar streamers and bobbing balloons, beneath the sparkle of glitter and candlelight, beneath the table, hidden by the darkness of draped linen, my knee touched Marson's, at first inadvertently. Then again, deliberately, when … *everything* changed.

And now we were back at that same table, but Marson and I were married, sitting with my mother. And her sister, Prucilla, was gone, but still in town, pampered and peeved as always—now gloatingly, operatically wounded—finding a new zest for life by luxuriating in her victimhood and telling anyone who was still willing to listen: she'd been dumped for her gay nephew.

Inez raised a glass. "To Prucilla."

That entire evening, the mystery surrounding Ellen Locke's death never once crossed my mind.

After the meal, while leaving the restaurant, we paused in the lobby for parting smooches with Ginger, thanking her for the round of drinks. She said to my mother, "After so many years away, I hope you'll enjoy your return to Dumont. Are you staying long?"

Inez sighed. "Afraid not. I need to leave Sunday." It was now Friday night.

"*What?*" I said. "Mom, you just got here."

"It was a spur-of-the-moment thing, sweetie. I wanted to see you. But I'll plan another trip once you're settled in the new house. Can't wait to see that—so proud of you." She gave me a hug.

I felt torn—and guilty. I'd been less than welcoming when she arrived by surprise on Thursday; then Marson had to insist that I set up tonight's dinner with her. And we'd had a wonderful evening. I'd always loved her, but I'd forgotten how much I *liked* her. When I was growing up, Inez was my best friend. Iconoclast, freethinker, firebrand, she raised me in a world of friends where

I was allowed—encouraged—to expand my vision and grow into myself. Tonight, I finally realized how much I'd missed her.

And too soon, she was preparing to leave.

As if reading my mind, she said with a wink, "I'll be back."

Stepping out the door and into the frosty darkness, I shrugged into the Loro Piana topcoat I'd bought three years ago, the week before leaving balmy California. At the time, the coat seemed like a ridiculous extravagance—more a ritual of change than a justified necessity. Little had I known, departing the land of fruits and nuts and palms, how perfectly practical cashmere would prove to be on nights such as this, when autumn winds whispered from the north, a mere hint of the winter that would follow.

CHAPTER

6

Dropping everything, I decided to make the most of what little time was left of my mother's visit. Since she had expressed such curiosity about the new house—I had been phoning her and emailing her about it for nearly two years—I offered to take her out to the construction site on Saturday morning and show her the work in progress.

When I picked her up at the Manor House around ten-thirty, she glanced about the car with an exaggerated look of disappointment.

"What's wrong?" I asked.

She said, "Where's Mister Puss? I was sure you'd bring him."

"Thought about it. But Marson wanted some company at the loft today. He decided, since you're leaving tomorrow, you might enjoy a simple home-cooked supper tonight. Nothing fancy—he's doing his *boeuf bourguignon.*

"Hah!" she said. "Nothing fancy."

I assured her, "Not for Marson."

While driving out to the edge of town, we gabbed and gossiped. I brought her up to speed on all things Dumont, and she filled me in with the latest news from Idyllwild, which had become her permanent home in recent years, up in the mountains that bordered Palm Springs.

The autumn brilliance of October had already succumbed to the dreary brownout of November—like clockwork, the trees that led us out of town had lost their blaze of gold and crimson, dropping dead leaves to the muddied earth from wet black branches. Arriving at the clearing in the ravine, we got out of the car and made our way up the driveway toward the house.

I'd warned Inez not to wear good shoes, and she had wisely opted for the battered pair of sneakers she used for her daily run. (Although my mother had a keen sense of personal style, she was no fashion hound.) Taking my own advice, I'd worn the tan work boots that I stored in the trunk for visits to building sites. They coordinated nicely with my brown corduroys and camel-hair jacket—adding a touch of butch.

The hubbub of construction had ceased for the weekend, but I saw Clem Carter's truck and assumed he was in the house, checking the results of last week's work, making notes for Monday morning.

It was quiet. It was damp—looking as if it might rain. It was sad, I thought.

But Inez could not have been more thrilled. Seeing the house for the first time, even though it was not yet finished, she squeezed my arm and said, "You're right. It's perfect. The perfect house."

When I took her inside and introduced her to Clem, she greeted him warmly and said she remembered his father from forty-some years ago. "Nice man—he ran that hardware store. What was it called?"

Clem Carter grinned, as if it should be obvious. "Carter Hardware."

"Of course." Inez laughed. "I'll bet he's proud of you—look what you've *done* here."

Clem nodded and smiled. "He woulda been. Passed away a few years back."

"Ah."

And Clem resumed his inspection, saying, "Won't be long, Brody. You can start packing."

His words landed with a jolt. Although I could see that completion of the project was at least a month away, and there was therefore no urgency to box up the past three years of my life, it was certainly time to start *thinking* about it. As I strolled Inez through a leisurely tour of the house, my mind was back at the loft: Where, exactly, would our current furniture be placed? What could be used, and what would need to be replaced? What about art?

Inez and I ended our tour on the outdoor balcony that extended from the main room and cantilevered over a stream, which rumbled as it fell some twenty feet over an Ice Age fissure. The water pooled at the bottom before meandering into the distance through grassy knolls of virgin prairie.

Inez breathed deeply, taking it in. Nothing needed to be said.

But when she did speak, she offered, "Let me take you to lunch."

"Sure. But where?" We were truly in the sticks, so I assumed she was ready to return to town.

"A little place I remember. Not far from here."

I was skeptical. She had left Dumont ages ago. I knew of no restaurants anywhere near the new house. Was she ... 'confused'?

In the car, I drove from our isolated property to the intersection of the quiet rural road that led back to town. "Go right," she directed, which would take us north, farther from town.

Making the turn, I asked, "Are you sure?"

"It's a few miles ahead, across the county line."

I felt as though we were heading into uncharted territory. As we passed a sign, LEAVING DUMONT COUNTY, the road narrowed. The vista before us looked like a no-man's-land. Field after field was littered with the twiggy beige debris of harvest.

"There's nothing out *here*," I scoffed.

"Careful. The road doglegs up ahead."

She was right. I slowed the car to take a sharp left and then, a quarter mile later, a sharp turn to the north again.

"I *knew* it," she said with a laugh. "Up there: Polly's Palace."

I slowed the car as we approached the only building in sight, which bore no resemblance to a palace. More accurately, the old roadhouse looked like something out of *Green Acres*, with unpainted siding, weathered gray. The front porch had cracked wooden steps, and the whole structure seemed ready to collapse. I pulled into the gravel parking lot at the side of the building and stopped. The only other vehicles were two massive Harleys. And in every direction, as far as the eye could see, there was absolutely nothing else.

I turned to my mother. "You have *got* to be kidding."

With a wistful, happy sigh, she said, "The summer before college, some of us kids came up here to drink now and then—it was legal at eighteen. Polly, the owner, was a big ol' lesbian, mouth like a sailor, treated us great. Always said, 'If you're off to Madison, better learn to drink,' and she'd buy us a round or two. She can't *possibly* still be here. Let's find out."

"But, *Mom*—"

"Don't be so square." Inez was already out of the car.

I followed, making sure to lock the car behind me.

Inside, my eyes took a moment to adjust; aside from a small pane of glass in the front door, there were no windows. When the interior details emerged from the darkness, I was nothing short of stunned.

Polly, I learned, had been an auctioneer, and over the years she had culled from her work an exuberant mishmash of decorative oddities with which to class up her quirky saloon.

Nothing matched. Tables, chairs, dishes, hanging Tiffany lamps—all different. A full-size suit of armor stood guard over one end of the bar, the length of which was inlaid with pennies. Shelving and sideboards were cluttered with top hats and sewing machines, cowbells and rifles, a silver tea service and a huge brass samovar. Above the salad bar, housed in a long copper bathtub, hung a gilt-framed photo, a faded blowup of a jolly woman (presumably Polly) standing near the bar with her arm wrapped around Liberace, who, from time to time, would escape by limousine up to the Palace when his tours took him through hometown Milwaukee. He wore sequins and one of the silk hats. Polly mugged with a feather boa.

"And believe it or not," Inez told me, "the food is flat-out fabulous." But half a century, I told myself, could take its toll on any kitchen.

Seated at the bar, I was about to learn otherwise. The woman who took care of us was Polly's daughter. Also named Polly, she went by Junior. When Inez asked her if they still served "that incredible shrimp cocktail," Junior gave a thumbs-up and disappeared while Inez and I nursed a couple of craft beers—not really my thing, but hey, I was wearing work boots.

The only other customers, who must have been the Harley riders, were a man and a woman sitting at a nearby table. He was white; she was black. They slouched in their captain's chairs, talking low while feasting on gigantic strip steaks and a bottle of Dom Pérignon—*very* strange for both the setting and the hour. A ritual of some kind? An anniversary? An afternoon tryst? And while I couldn't get a clear look at the man's face, there was something about his manner and his trendy laid-back attire that made me think of Conrad Houghes.

I assumed it was not Houghes—I had seen the brash film investor rushing to meet a plane the day before with Zeiss Shotwell—but the sight of this guy yanked me out of the odd reality of having a beer with my mother, and it crowded my thoughts with the puzzle of Ellen Locke's death, a possible murder, which hadn't crossed my mind since last night. Houghes had bragged about bedding Miranda Lemarr: "There's a new man in town." I pondered the web of intrigue, lust, and jealousy that seemed to ensnare the production company whose gaffer had been a gun nut—until she was electrocuted.

"My God," said Inez, "just *look* at this."

Snapping back to the present, I saw Junior return to the bar, delivering two enormous shell-shaped bowls, each piled with cracked ice and a mound of the biggest shrimp I'd ever seen, still in their bright pink shells. A side tray bore lemon wedges, a heavy crystal goblet of chunky maroon cocktail sauce, and a bowl for scraps.

Inez nearly swooned. "It's exactly what I remember. And this *sauce*—" She swiped a finger in it and licked.

Junior nodded. "Polly's recipe."

I had never been served chilled shrimp in their shells, but the effort of peeling them proved more than worth it. The flavor was astounding, easily the best I'd ever tasted. I picked the most succulent specimen from the mound before me and set it aside, asking Junior, "Could you possibly wrap that? It's for a little friend."

"You bet."

I told her, "We're building a new house nearby. My husband and I—we'll be back."

"I'll look forward to that," said Junior.

Turning to Inez, I asked, "Now, *why* didn't I know about this place?"

Junior said, "Because you didn't ask your mama."

The time spent with my mother that weekend seemed hoggishly focused on food. After lunch, she asked me to take her back to the Manor House, where she wanted to pack for the next morning's return to California, then rest, before coming over to the loft for Marson's *boeuf bourguignon*, his simple supper. "Peasant food," he called it.

*Grrring.*

Mister Puss shot to the door. (The shrimp I'd brought him from

Polly's Palace didn't last two minutes from the time I arrived back at the loft that afternoon. His sniffer locked on the to-go box before I had a chance to hide it in the fridge.) Marson now followed the cat and opened the front door, admitting Inez.

What an unlikely family we made—at least by conventional standards—but family we were, including Mister Puss, the extended visitor who now seemed so naturally at home with us. And despite my doubts, Marson delivered on his plans for a simple supper. No pretense, that Saturday night. No fussing with crystal or silver or flowers. It was "just us." All we needed was each other. Plus, the *boeuf bourguignon* was to die for.

And before I knew it, Sunday morning, I was driving Inez to the airport in Green Bay, kissing her goodbye at the curb, and heading back to Dumont, missing her already. Mister Puss was in the car, secured by his leash and harness, curled in the passenger seat, which had been warmed and vacated by my mother.

During the hour's drive, my thoughts shifted from Inez to the late Ellen Locke. Reviewing the known facts of her death (a purely intellectual exercise, as I had no intention of getting further involved), I decided that her case was simply a mystery and would, in all likelihood, remain forever unsolved. Pity, I thought. On a more positive note, I hadn't heard a peep from Sheriff Simms since Friday, so I congratulated myself for having avoided yet another excursion into the grunt work of crime solving.

I should have been more wary, however, about tempting fate. As if on cue, my phone rang. The readout confirmed my inkling. I answered the call: "Good morning, Thomas."

Mister Puss looked up from his snooze.

Simms asked if I could sit in on a meeting the next morning with the medical examiner, Heather Vance. There would also be a meeting that afternoon with Thad Manning, who was delivering the test footage.

Needing to focus less on the road and more on the phone, I pulled the car into the empty parking lot of a rural dance bar, which looked depressingly seedy in the Sunday sunshine. I reminded Simms, "I'm an architect. I'm flattered that you value my instincts, Thomas, but you're the pro. I don't want to get in your way. I'd probably just bungle things up."

"Don't sell yourself short, Brody. You've been a huge help before. And when it comes to bungling things up, I should never have told the *Register*, 'I intend to wrap it up fast.' What was I *thinking*?"

I assured him, "You were thinking you were up to the task—which you are."

Mister Puss stood and moved over to my lap.

Simms said, "How 'bout it, Brody?"

I hesitated. "Sure." Petting Mister Puss as he stretched to my shoulder, I asked Simms, "Are cats allowed?"

He laughed. "Whatever works." And we rang off.

With the cat purring in my ear, I stared vacantly through the windshield and told myself aloud, "Well, you're a sidekick again."

*Saddle up, buckaroo.*

Heather Vance was not only the county coroner and medical examiner, but over the course of two prior investigations of mysterious death, she had become a close friend. In one instance, we posed as a couple and were said to "look good together."

At thirty-two, Dr. Vance didn't fit the image of someone whose calling was so grim. Heather was young and blond, even perky, and I always saw her, on or off the job, wearing outfits that were stylish and colorful—no mannish gray pantsuits, no scrubs and clogs, no biohazard gloves. What's more, she drove a zippy red roadster.

She worked in a bleak building near the back of the county

complex, behind the courthouse and the sheriff's headquarters. Her own office was bright and cheery—no skeletons, no jars of formaldehyde, no grisly display of autopsy photos.

When I entered her office with Mister Puss on Monday morning, Simms had already arrived and was standing next to Heather, looking through a file folder. They turned and smiled, rushing over to crouch and greet the cat. I reminded them, "Hello?"

"Hey, Brody," said Simms as he stood, clapping an arm over my shoulders.

Heather gave me a hug. Waving us toward her desk, she said, "Let's get started."

Simms and I sat in two chairs facing the desk as she settled in behind it. I unclipped Mister Puss's leash, and he hopped up to the sunny windowsill behind Heather, where he sat and sniffed the potted plants.

Simms told me, "Heather has some initial results."

"I do," she said. "This isn't complicated, at least from my perspective. The victim, Ellen Locke, a forty-three-year-old Caucasian, died Thursday afternoon while working on the technical crew of a film production. The cause of death was electrocution by a live extension cord submerged in water, grounded through the victim's body; she was standing with bare toes in wet sod. The mechanism of death was cardiac arrest, which was virtually instantaneous. Blood tests revealed trace amounts of alcohol and recreational drugs in the victim's body, but that's not considered a factor in her death."

Heather paused before concluding, "As I said, this isn't complicated from my perspective. Cause of death: electrocution. Mechanism: cardiac arrest. However, where this *does* get complicated—manner of death—that's up to you guys."

I couldn't help noticing that she had used the plural. I was one of the guys. I was on the team.

Simms looked up from the notes he was writing. "Manner of death. Four options. First: natural causes."

"Nope," Heather and I said in unison. She elaborated: "The victim was healthy. She didn't die of disease or old age. She was electrocuted. That is *not* nature's course."

Simms said, "Second option: suicide."

Heather suppressed a chuckle.

I said, "That would be *way* bizarre. If she intended to kill herself—and there's no reason to think she did—she could easily have used a gun, since she was so into them. Plus, it was obvious *why* she stuck her hand in the vat of ice water—not to kill herself, but to retrieve a bottle of beer she'd stashed there. I saw her do it."

"Yeah," said Simms, "a number of people witnessed that. We can safely rule out suicide. So that gets us down to the last two options: Accident? Or homicide?"

Heather and I looked at each other. We both shrugged.

Simms said, "If the manner of death was a tragic accident, our work is done. On the other hand, if it was homicide—murder—our work has just begun."

Again I noticed the plural: "our" work.

Heather asked him, "Have a theory?"

He nodded. "My forensics team made an exhaustive investigation of the death scene. They examined the entire physical setup of the electrical and the rigging. They talked to everyone involved in setting it up as well as everyone who was working in the vicinity of the vat, including the catering crew. And you know what?"

Mister Puss jumped down from the window and came over to hop into my lap, looking up to watch Simms as he spoke.

Simms told us, "Hidden in the rigging under the awning— with its grounding prong removed—that extension cord had no discernible purpose, other than its availability to be dropped into the vat when needed. Needed for what? Bottom line: We've got a murder on our hands."

Again the plural.

That afternoon, I needed to return to the county complex to meet Simms at his office, where Thad Manning had agreed to hand over a duplicate of the test footage that was shot the prior Thursday.

Because the sheriff's headquarters was located downtown, only a few blocks from the Miles & Norris architecture offices, I decided to walk to the meeting. The weather was pleasant enough—for November in Wisconsin—and I thought Mister Puss would enjoy the exercise, so off we went, fetching plenty of stares. Though I was thoroughly accustomed to the cat's impressive leash manners (I had taught him well), there were others who found the spectacle of us parading down First Avenue to be worth a lingering gape.

Inside headquarters, however, no one batted an eye as we traversed the long terrazzo-floored hallway toward Simms's office—we had done this many times. When we arrived, the deputy barely looked up at us as she jerked her head toward a door, saying, "He's expecting you."

Entering the office and not finding Simms there, I knew from experience that he would be waiting beyond a second door, which opened into an adjacent conference room where we had previously sussed out the details of untimely death.

"Hey, Brody," said Simms with a smile as we entered. "You too, puss-cat."

The room had a high ceiling and a big window with venetian blinds that were tilted to admit sunlight but no view; there was nothing to see beyond the glass other than a blank brick wall of the jail. Opposite the window was a wall of dusty wooden bookcases containing cockeyed binders of forgotten forms and reports. It was an oddly pleasant space, in an old-timey kind of way, looking nothing like the sterile, fluorescent interrogation rooms that are such a cliché of every cable cop show.

Simms took a chair at the head of the conference table and asked me to sit down. Mister Puss hopped into the chair next to mine and curled up for a nap with the tip of his tail touching his nose.

I said, "I'm glad to help, Thomas, but what exactly would you like me to *do*?"

With a calming gesture of both hands, he said, "For now, just listen—and think. We can both benefit from a measure of 'passive absorption' before deciding on a more active strategy. I've seen you do this before. Just stay in touch with your intuitions."

I removed a notepad from my pocket. "Easy enough, but what if—"

The door opened as Thad Manning was shown into the room. The deputy—she was normally the picture of stone-faced efficiency—wore a wide-eyed grin, as if she couldn't *believe* she was in the company of the Hollywood heartthrob himself. With an awkward bob of her head, she backed out of the room and closed the door.

Simms and I rose to welcome Thad. Mister Puss deigned to open an eye as Thad approached the table and joined us.

"There you go, Sheriff," he said, handing over an external hard drive, which was about the size of a small paperback. "That's a digital copy of everything we shot on Thursday—three cameras, *many* takes, plus close-ups and reaction shots. The scene lasts only a minute, but it involves a couple hours' worth of raw, theatrical-grade video."

Simms turned the gizmo in his hand, eyeing it curiously. "How do I watch this?"

"You'll need to connect it to a computer."

Simms nodded. "Someone in the department can figure it out."

"Sheriff?" said Thad. His face wrinkled with concern.

Smiling, Simms reminded him, "My name's Thomas."

Thad returned the smile. "Thanks, Thomas. I was just wondering: You've probably talked to … *everybody* by now. Any idea what happened to Ellen Locke?"

"We know she was electrocuted."

"Yeah. But I mean, any idea *why*?"

Simms glanced at me before saying to Thad, "If you're asking if she was murdered, I'm now working on the assumption that, yes, she was. But I still need a motive."

Thad lifted a palm to his brow. "Christ."

Simms asked, "How well did you know her? What'd you think of her?"

Thad was forthright. "I didn't much *like* her—with her survivalist crap and her guns. Abrasive, too. But she was good at her job, and she was available, so we hired her."

I said, "This is a difficult question, Thad. Does Ellen's death, if it proves to be murder, in any way jeopardize production of your film?"

He sat back, looked at the ceiling, and exhaled heavily. "I hope not. But realistically, who knows? If it's not already obvious, trust me: the film industry is one weird, crazy business. It's built on dreams and risk and luck. It depends on inspiration and money. At its best, it's art. Too often, it's creative backstabbing and wars of ego."

A spicy stew, I thought. A recipe for trouble.

"But those of us who are in it," said Thad, "we love it."

Simms said, "You mentioned money, risk, and luck. And on your first day of filming—murder. Will that spook your investors?"

"Maybe. Not necessarily. But one of them is itching to paint this as an omen."

I guessed: "Conrad Houghes."

Thad nodded. He told Simms, "Connie's been dead set against location shooting in Dumont—wants to do it cheaper, closer to home. He'll try to *use* Ellen's death to force that decision. Got a text from him yesterday. Says we need to sit down and hash this out again. Tomorrow."

I asked, "In Dumont? Didn't he return to California on Friday?"

"I thought so," said Thad, "but he might be back already."

Conrad Houghes's actual whereabouts on that Monday afternoon—California or Wisconsin—intrigued me. On Friday, he was rushing off to Milwaukee to catch a flight home. On Saturday, I saw someone who reminded me of him at Polly's Palace, not far from the Dumont County line. And now, he was trying to set up a face-to-face with Thad Manning for the next day.

Thad and his wife, Paige Yeats, were still staying at the Manor House, where Houghes also had stayed during the run-up to shooting the prior week's test scene. Thad was under the impression that Houghes was back in Dumont, but Thad had not seen him; they had communicated only by text.

In the conference room at sheriff's headquarters, I pondered this chronology while Simms continued to question Thad about various members of his cast and production crew. Interrupting, I said, "I have an idea."

They both turned to me with expressions of interest.

Mister Puss yawned, stood up in his chair, and looked at me, blinking groggily.

I asked Thad, "Have you set up your meeting with Houghes yet?"

"Tomorrow morning at eleven, then maybe lunch—depends how it goes."

"Where?" I asked.

"Probably the Manor House, but we haven't nailed that down. I wasn't sure of my schedule."

"Perfect. Tell him you have an earlier meeting with me, at the loft—maybe you're thinking of building a house."

"Maybe I'll need to," Thad said wryly. "Bettina Gerber has no intention of leaving my uncle Mark's house."

I laughed. "We can talk about that later, if necessary. Meanwhile, the point of this is simply for Houghes to meet you at the loft. You can discuss your business there. I'd like to be around."

Sheriff Simms nodded. He told Thad, "Brody agreed to help with some of the background of this case—off-the-record, so to speak. The investigation has just begun, and people are likely to be more candid in *his* presence than they would be in mine. So, if you're willing…"

"Say no more, Thomas." Thad took out his phone and texted the meeting arrangements to Conrad Houghes.

I reached over to Mister Puss and twiddled beneath his chin. His juicy purr rumbled in the quiet of the room.

Marson never failed to amaze me. Twenty-four years my senior, he was not only a highly experienced designer, but also a man of precision and discipline, a "perfectionist" who wore that badge with pride. Yes, he was set in his ways, but they were good ways—reasoned and sturdy and informed.

What amazed me, however, was not his boundless self-confidence, but that he managed to project it without ego or airs. He was not a stuffed shirt. He was no pompous tyrant.

Quite the contrary. He was a *gentle* man, refined and caring. He loved me, certainly, but he also believed in me, never failing to nurture and encourage.

Which is to say: Marson did not merely tolerate my occasional forays into amateur sleuthing. Rather, he supported me without question. Granted, he might occasionally stoop to some good-natured ribbing, calling me "Sherlock," but he never let me doubt that my problem-solving skills as a designer could be effectively applied, when needed, to a puzzle of suspicious death.

So on Monday night, when I told him that I had contrived to have Thad Manning meet with Conrad Houghes at our loft the next morning, he simply asked, "Do you want the place to yourself? Or should I be here, too?"

Interesting question. I had assumed I would be alone with Thad and his investor, since Marson had work to do at the office (for that matter, so did I). But if Marson was also at the loft, Houghes would be less likely to wonder why I was hanging around.

I told Marson, "Know what? You're invited—I could use a beard."

"Sure thing, Sherlock." And he picked up the phone to leave a message at the office for Gertie, letting her know we'd be at home the next morning.

Tuesday, around a quarter to eleven, I followed Mister Puss to the front door and admitted Thad Manning, who was looking dreamy in a bulky baby-blue cable-knit sweater—it was a chilly morning.

I gave him a hug (I mean, come on, that sweater, he was asking for it), then walked him over to the dining table, where Marson fussed with set-dressing the supposed aftermath of a busy design conference—pens and notepads, laptop and sketchbook, coffee mugs and doughnut scraps, plus, most prominently, a scattering of unfurled floor plans and blueprints, their corners anchored by an assortment of whatnot—stapler, pepper mill, a pair of bookends, and on and on. I had to give Marson credit. For someone with such an ordered mind, he'd created a bang-up mess.

Marson offered, "Can we get you something, Thad? Coffee?"

"The doughnuts look great—what's left of them."

I assured him, "We've got whole ones in the kitchen. Hold on." And I ducked away to fetch him one, choosing a plump cherry-glazed specimen, which I brought back to him on a saucer.

"Yum." He eyed it lustfully before biting into it. Bright pink and crumbly, it looked luscious against his powdery blue sweater.

While he ate and perused the plans on the table, the three of us gabbed. Then he set aside the saucer with half of the doughnut. "These drawings. Wow!"

Marson said, "They were handy. That's the house we're building. It's Brody's work. Nice, huh?"

"Nice?" Thad turned to me. "It's beyond … well, I'm speechless."

I assured him, "We can't *wait* to have you over."

*Grrring.*

Mister Puss, as usual, beat me to the door. Marson remained with Thad at the dining table as I welcomed Conrad Houghes and brought him inside. He glanced about, telling me, "Great digs—not very 'Dumont,' if you know what I mean."

I knew exactly what he meant. Our home had an urban vibe. I told him, "As far as we know, this was the first residential loft conversion in town."

"So you *live* here."

"Right. Our offices are just a few blocks away."

Thad called from across the main room, "Hey, Connie."

I brought Houghes over to the table and introduced Marson as my husband and business partner. They greeted each other, shaking hands.

Marson said, "I'll have this cleared in a jiff—our meeting ran a little long." And he set about removing the mess he'd so carefully staged.

I invited Houghes and Thad to be seated at the table, offering, "Coffee?"

They looked at each other and shrugged. "Sure."

"I'll start a fresh pot," I said, stepping to the kitchen.

Excusing himself, Marson said vaguely, "I need to get a few things organized upstairs." He carried an armload of clutter up the spiral stairway and disappeared on the mezzanine.

Which left Thad alone with Houghes at the table while I puttered with the coffee. Because of the open plan of the loft space, I could keep an eye on them, not twelve feet away. I could also hear every word they said.

"Welcome back," Thad said to Houghes, sounding more amused than sincere. "I didn't expect to see you so soon. I thought you were flying back to LA on Friday. Did you go?"

An evasive reply: "You'd be surprised."

"Are you still at the Manor House? Haven't seen you around."

"Nope," said Houghes. "Too rich for my blood."

Thad laughed. "Spare me, Connie. You're *made* of money. It's who you are."

"In good times, maybe."

Sounding less glib, Thad said, "Well, you can't win 'em all. Ups and downs. Roll of the dice."

"I'm *aware* of the clichés, thank you very much."

"You don't sound happy, Connie."

"I'm *not*. As you probably know, I've had a bad investment or two lately. No secrets in Tinseltown."

"The way I hear it," said Thad, "you've had a whole *run* of bad investments. But your luck has changed, Connie. With *Home Sweet Humford*, you're banking on a winner. I'm invested in this as much as you are. More, in fact, because my reputation's on the line—my future *career* depends on this picture. And now I have more confidence than ever. Now we have the test scene. The footage is gorgeous. It's totally validating."

"*Validating?*" said Houghes, attempting but failing to lower his voice. "Are you fucking nuts? Ellen Locke *died* working on that scene. They're saying it might've been murder. In my book, that's some seriously bad juju."

Thad insisted, "Juju won't make or break this picture. Whatever happened to Ellen—yes, that's awful, and we need to get to the bottom of it. Fortunately, the local sheriff is determined to resolve it. Meanwhile, the picture's on solid ground. All systems go."

"You are tempting *fate*," said Houghes. "Cut your losses—get out of Dumont—do it now. Move the location shots to New Mexico."

With an exasperated laugh, Thad countered, "You are *so* transparent. You don't give a damn about Ellen. You don't give a damn about juju. All you give a damn about is saving a few bucks."

"So crucify me."

The coffeemaker beeped. I asked, "Black? Cream or sugar?"

They both mumbled that black was fine, so I filled two cups and took them to the table. As I set them down, Thad said, "Why don't you join us, Brody?"

"I'd hate to intrude." Though of course I was itching to sit in.

"Not at all." Thad reminded me, "It's your house."

So I popped back into the kitchen to pour myself a cup of coffee, then returned to the table and sat. Mister Puss had been perched on the back of a loveseat in the living room, with a watchful eye trained on our guests. He now hopped down to the floor, pranced over to us, and jumped into my lap. His head peeped over the edge of the table, like a periscope spying on the visitors.

Houghes said, "Brody, you're friends with Thad, right?"

Thad assured him, "You bet we are."

Gosh, I thought.

Houghes continued, "So, Brody—talk some sense into your friend. Tell him that Dumont may be a lovely little town and all, but the lovely little town of Humford belongs in New Mexico."

"I, uh ... I'd never advise an artist on creative matters."

Thad winked at me.

Gosh, again. I hid my grin behind a slurp of coffee.

Houghes tried another tack: "If you saw that a friend was about to step in front of a bus, wouldn't you say something?"

The way Houghes slouched in his chair, he really did remind me of the guy I noticed at Polly's Palace on Saturday. I wondered about the black woman and the two Harleys in the parking lot.

Responding to the hypothetical about the bus, I said to Houghes, "Miranda Lemarr. You're friends with her—intimate friends, from what you told Sheriff Simms and me on Friday— you kinda bragged about being the 'new man in town.' So I assume you wouldn't let Miranda step in front of a bus. But she's also an artist, an actress. Would you advise her on creative matters?"

Houghes eyed me warily. "What does she have to do with any of this?"

"She's in the film. She's the star. The film's success will be her success. Would you second-guess her creative judgment?"

He hesitated. "Miranda is a beautiful woman. She's truly gifted in many ways. But her judgment? Let's just say she could use some help in that department."

Thad turned to me. Speaking quietly, he said, "Miranda has a history of serious drug issues. We hope that's behind her."

I nodded. "When Sheriff Simms and I interviewed her last Friday, she was frank about that." I could have added, but didn't, that her past substance abuse was widely known, or at least rumored.

Houghes told me, "I'd like to think that I helped Miranda through some of that."

I was bold enough to ask, "You love her?"

He seemed surprised by his own answer: "Yeah. I guess I do."

I wondered: What about the black woman, the Harleys? Had I in fact seen Houghes on Saturday?

He added, "Truth is, Miranda and I sorta helped each other. When I first got to know her—not just as friends, but 'involved'— I couldn't believe my own luck. I mean, she's young and hot. Me, not so much. So even though I knew there were problems, I was more than willing to ignore that. And I ... well, I paid a price."

Thad and I exchanged a quizzical look. I asked Houghes, "Care to elaborate on that?"

He nudged his coffee aside and slouched in his chair again, staring at the ceiling. "Do you have any idea what it means to a guy like me to 'own' the affections of a stunning woman like Miranda? Do you know what that feels like?"

I did not. Not directly. But with a bit of psychological transference, I could easily switch up the scenario and replace Miranda with a hot guy—fantasized or real—so, sure, I could understand how Houghes felt about Miranda. He was talking about blind passion.

He continued, "The better I got to know Miranda, I realized she was pretty messed up. The drugs, I mean—prescription or street stuff, didn't matter to her, she'd try anything, then come back for more. It was a part of her life, a part of who she was. And because I needed to be a part of who *she* was, I allowed her to become, as they say, a bad influence. Now, I'm the first to admit that I was never a choirboy, but she took me *way* over the deep end. And yes, that had something to do with my run of bad investments. I needed to clean myself up, and I begged her to make some changes, too."

Thad said, "Good for you, Connie. Miranda heard you."

"She did. Took a couple of stints at Betty Ford, but she managed to pull herself through it. She wouldn't like to hear me say so, but I'm proud of her."

I asked, "Why wouldn't she want to hear *that*?"

"Because she'd probably find it patronizing, like something a father might say. I don't want to go *there*—even though I'm old enough. I'm her lover, and I plan to keep it that way."

"Okay, then," Thad said brightly, lifting his coffee cup to Houghes as if toasting him. "All's well that ends well."

"Not … exactly," said Houghes.

Thad turned to look at me. Mister Puss looked up at me.

I asked Houghes, "There's more to the story?"

"Uh, yes," he said with a tone of understatement. "Before Miranda got her act together, she wasn't just *doing* drugs; she was pushing them. I mean, not like a street pusher, not even for profit. But she had her suppliers, and in turn, she supplied a few friends—just acquaintances, peeps in the industry."

Thad exhaled a quiet sigh. "Yeah, I'd heard that. But it ended, right?"

"Right. Miranda stopped supplying when she stopped using. Once she got her head together, her career really took off. Her whole persona changed, and so did her roles. Before, she was doing edgy stuff—artsy flicks that verged on porn—but after she got straightened out, honest to God, her natural beauty just seemed to blossom. And you know how she has that innocence, that vulnerability? I still can't quite believe the transformation. She got … *wholesome*. It comes through loud and clear in the sort of roles her fans are loving. Who'da thought? Miranda Lemarr is now the girl next door." Houghes paused before adding, "That's when the trouble began."

I said, "Let me guess: the source of that trouble was one of Miranda's peeps."

"Bingo."

"Who?" said Thad.

Houghes turned to me, eyeing me cautiously. "You were there with the sheriff last week, when he was doing interviews. You're not *working* for him, are you?"

"Me?" I gave Houghes a get-real look. "I'm a mild-mannered gay architect." Which was true enough, as far as it went.

"I guess it's bound to get out eventually—like I said, no secrets in Tinseltown." Houghes leaned on his elbows, facing Thad and me across the table. Lowering his voice, he explained, "The troublemaker was Ellen Locke."

Thad slumped in his chair and held a hand to his forehead.

Mister Puss moved up to the tabletop, where he sat watching Houghes, switching his tail.

I asked Houghes, "Ellen? Really? Do tell." I had a hunch he was about to deliver a breakthrough.

He said, "Ellen Locke was playing an extortion game, threatening to go very public about Miranda's past—and the fact that Miranda had been dealing heavy drugs to her. There was meth involved. Ellen wanted money, and we're talking significant cash, to forget everything she knew. She even threatened *me*. I laughed at her, the hateful bitch. I mean, hell, people *already* think I'm a shit, so what's to lose? Miranda, though? Whole different story. Old rumors don't mean much in Hollywood. But new allegations that America's sweetheart is a meth addict and pill pusher? *Whoa*—so much for those blockbuster new roles as a goody-two-shoes."

Marson appeared at the top of the stairs. "Getting sorta quiet down there. You boys playing nice?"

"Just wrapping things up," I told him. And in fact, I had gleaned more from our conversation than I'd hoped.

Marson spiraled down the stairs and stepped into the kitchen. "Then it won't bother you if I'm rattling around?"

We assured him we were finished and got up from the table.

Thad told me, "Thanks for putting up with us. Sorry for the inconvenience."

"Not at all." And I walked them to the door.

Houghes asked Thad, "Lunch somewhere?"

"Not today." Thad shook his head. "Not hungry."

As they stepped out to the street, Houghes gave Thad a parting reminder: "It's not too late. I want you to really think about New Mexico. It is *way* more friendly to the bottom line, and I can't afford to lose my shirt on this. I can't even *risk* it. So get out of Dumont."

"Thanks for the advice," said Thad, sounding testy. "I'll give that some serious consideration—*not*."

Houghes persisted. "And while you're at it—"

"And while *you're* at it," Thad interrupted, "maybe you can tell me where you were this past weekend."

With a coy smile, Houghes replied, "None of your business."

Then he turned and walked away.

Within three minutes after they left, I got Mister Puss into his leash and harness, then drove us over to the sheriff's headquarters.

When we arrived at the deputy's desk outside Simms's office, she told me, "He's not here. But you might find him out in the break area. It's—"

"Got it," I said. "Thanks." And I walked Mister Puss out the front of the building.

We turned at a driveway that led toward a garage and maintenance area in back. A clearing among some scraggly trees contained a few metal picnic tables intended for staffers on break. Cigarette butts littered the matted, patchy grass. Although it was a pleasant day and a decent setting for whiling away the noon hour, the smokers had opted to dine elsewhere, perhaps at any of the old corner joints that served booze. At one of the picnic tables, Thomas Simms sat alone, picking at a brown-bag lunch arranged neatly in front of him.

He broke into a smile as he spotted me. "Hey, Brody," he said, rising.

"Don't get up. Sorry to interrupt your lunch." I sat on the bench opposite him. "Looks good," I said.

"Gloria's meat loaf is flat-out the best I've ever had—better than Mom's ever was—so I always bring a sandwich to work the next day. Want half?"

"Wouldn't think of it. Enjoy."

Mister Puss had worked his way under the table and reached his paws up to Simms's knee.

"Hey there, puss-cat." Simms asked me, "Okay to share some 'people food'?"

I rolled my eyes. "Ever heard the expression 'cast-iron stomach'?"

Simms laughed, feeding the cat a generous hunk of meat loaf. "Pickle?" he said to me, extending a spear.

"Sure." I chomped off the end of it.

Wiping his fingers on a napkin, Simms asked, "Social call? What's up?"

"Not a social call, Thomas, but it's always a pleasure. I just came from the loft—where Conrad Houghes had his meeting with Thad Manning. They asked me to join them."

"Terrific. Learn anything?"

"*Did* I. At first, it was just Houghes whining about the expense of doing location shooting in Dumont. But then he opened up about his relationship with Miranda Lemarr. And that's when it got … interesting."

"Needless to say," said Simms, "I'm … interested."

So I told him the whole story: Miranda's drug issues. How she supplied her peeps, including Ellen Locke. How Houghes helped Miranda get clean. Most significantly, how Ellen tried to blackmail Miranda.

"Well, now"—Simms balled up the waxed paper that had wrapped his sandwich—"it seems we now have a solid, workable motive for what happened to Ellen Locke."

Mister Puss, having exhausted Simms's generosity with the meat loaf, returned to my side of the table and hopped up onto the bench.

"By my count," I said, "we have *two* workable motives. First, of course, Miranda wanted to protect her career, so she had plenty of reason to silence Ellen Locke and get her out of the way. But a second possibility is Conrad Houghes. He despised Ellen—called her a 'hateful bitch.' He wanted not only to protect Miranda but also to preserve his relationship with her. By his own description, his devotion to the hot young starlet borders on fetishism." As if resting my case, I took another bite of the pickle.

"Hmm," said Simms. "Both Houghes and Miranda had plenty of *motive* to kill Ellen Locke. But I'm wondering: Did either of them have the means and the opportunity?"

Contemplating this, I said, "By 'means,' we're asking if they had sufficient knowledge of electrical matters and consequences. And 'opportunity' is simply the chance to rig it up, unseen."

"Exactly. When it comes to electrical knowledge, the principles are pretty basic—it's not like you'd need a degree in electrical engineering." He laughed.

But I could think of two people with such a degree, the owners of the Taliesin house on Prairie Street, Harlan and Bettina Gerber, one of whom was at the murder scene.

Mister Puss had begun to purr. He walked his front paws up my arm, reaching my shoulder.

"As for opportunity," Simms continued, "no one admits to *witnessing* anyone rig up the extension cord over the vat. The video could be of help. So far, we've only taken a quick look; it needs a lot more study. But I think we're finally on track."

Mister Puss stretched his snout to my ear. He had been at the murder scene. Had he witnessed something? His purr grew louder.

*Done with that pickle?*

Simms smiled at me. "Nice work, Brody." With a satisfied nod, he declared, "Progress."

# 8

But then things came to a standstill.

By Friday morning, three days later, life had returned to normal in Dumont. Marson and I had resumed regular hours at the office, venturing out to check progress at a handful of building sites. I'd talked to Sheriff Simms about the murder once or twice, but there were no developments on that front to capture the public's attention, so the tragedy of the prior week began to recede from the headlines, from the word on the street, from the conversations of ordinary people going about their ordinary business. I began to wonder if the case of Ellen Locke's electrocution was destined to be forgotten and filed away, unsolved.

Then, a week and a day after the murder, while the morning coffee was brewing, I retrieved the *Dumont Daily Register* from outside the loft and found a front-page reminder of the puzzling death, from our favorite local gossip columnist.

**Inside Dumont**

*Miranda Lemarr returning soon for
advance promotion of film project*

By Glee Savage

•

NOVEMBER 8, DUMONT, WI — Miranda Lemarr, Hollywood's sweetheart, was in Dumont last week to appear in the filming of a test scene for *Home Sweet Humford*. The broadly autobiographical memoir, written and directed by Thad Manning, was inspired by his youth in Dumont, a setting he has reimagined as Humford, a generic "Hometown, USA."

The film will not enter full production until spring, but it's never too early for buzz, so Miss Lemarr will be returning to Dumont—possibly next week, according to sources—where she will pose for publicity stills at various locations, yet to be announced.

When this reporter reached Miss Lemarr by phone in California and asked her to confirm the return visit, she said effusively, "It's true! And I can't wait. I wish I could've grown up there. Dumont is just ever so adorable."

But how did she react to the death of crew member Ellen Locke during last week's filming?

Miss Lemarr grew pensive while answering. "Ellen was a dear friend, loved by all who knew her. Her death was a terrible shock—no pun intended. We miss her every day."

Is any sort of memorial planned?

"That's a good question. No one's said a word about it, at least not to me."

Here at home, we reached out to Sheriff Thomas Simms, asking if he could report any developments with the investigation of Locke's death.

Responding to the *Register* by email, Simms wrote, "This case has posed some significant challenges. The victim, as well as most of her coworkers and many potential witnesses, was not a resident of Dumont County. I don't have the jurisdiction to compel cooperation from California law enforcement or from persons of interest there."

Simms continued, "Here in Dumont, we are treating Miss Locke's death as a possible homicide, and our ongoing efforts have produced a number of promising leads. At this time, however, I have nothing further to report."

Meanwhile, gentle reader, if someday soon you happen to be visiting the local library—or dropping your kids at school, or raking the lawn, or simply waiting at a stoplight—and you think you caught a glimpse of Hollywood royalty, you'll probably be right.

So be on the lookout for Miranda Lemarr. She's coming to town. And you read it here first.

Marson handed me a slice of buttered toast smeared with a thick layer of apricot jam. "Must be slim news on the police beat if it's a footnote to Glee's celebrity gossip."

"Afraid so," I said, setting the paper aside on the kitchen island. Mister Puss jumped up to the countertop and watched me as I ate a corner of the toast. I dragged a finger through the jam, then painted the cat's nose with it. He stretched his barbed tongue to lick it clean. He purred for more.

I swiped the toast again and let him lick my finger.

Marson poured our coffee. "Have you talked to your mother?" It was five days since Inez had flown home.

"Sorry, forgot to tell you—she sends her love. She called yesterday afternoon, at the office. Gabbed a few minutes, but I was busy. She asked how the house was coming along." With a laugh, I added, "She wondered if we'd set the date for the housewarming."

Marson winced. "Seriously?"

"She asked," I assured him. "But I doubt if she thought we were that far along. I think she just wanted to let me know she's eager to come back."

"Nice." Marson set down his coffee. "Know what, kiddo?"

"Nope. What?"

"It hardly seems possible, but after all this time—we started planning the project two years ago—we need to be ready to move *next month*."

That woke me up. My eyes bugged. Mister Puss tilted his head, giving me a curious stare. I told Marson, "And we haven't even *thought* about packing."

"Oh, I've thought about it..."

I knew what he meant. Packing and moving would be a tedious and disruptive ordeal, certainly. But that wasn't our underlying concern. That wasn't the reason we'd been ignoring the need to begin the process. Our procrastination had nothing to do with laziness—and everything to do with sentiment. Although we had never intended for the loft to be our permanent home, it was the only home we had known together. Our time there, not yet three years, had been filled with love and countless happy moments. Leaving would be hard.

On a more upbeat note, we had made plans to meet Yevgeny Krymov and Darnell Passalacqua for dinner that evening at Moonstruck.

The parking lot was predictably crowded that Friday night, forcing Marson to find a space well removed from the restaurant's door. Bracing ourselves against the cold, we hustled across the asphalt side by side. Marson said, "Now, tell me about Darnell again." They had not yet met.

I explained, "He's the film crew's hair-and-makeup guy. Thirty-one, Puerto Rican, a real fireball. He met Yevgeny at the Manor House, where they're both staying. Then they got to know each other at the filming last week. Seems they clicked—to put it mildly. Darnell's work in Dumont is done for now, but he stuck around for Yevgeny."

As we approached the entrance, a car backed out of a space near the door, and just as it pulled out to the street, another car pulled into the lot, claiming the prime spot. It beeped its horn and flashed its lights, so we waited.

The car's doors opened, and out popped Darnell and Yevgeny.

Darnell, who had been driving, banged his door shut and hollered into the night, "Yoohoo-oo! Wait up, bitch princesses—it's cocktail time!"

As we strolled over to greet them, Marson laughed, leaning to ask me, "Fireball? You weren't kidding, were you?"

Yevgeny must have heard Marson. As they hugged, Yevgeny told my husband, "He keeps me young."

Marson assured him, "I know *that* feeling." Although Marson and I were a few years older than Yevgeny and Darnell, each couple's age difference was twenty-some years.

After introducing Marson and Darnell, we all piled through the restaurant door and into the small lobby. Ginger stepped out from behind her podium for a round of hugs and kisses and greetings of "welcome home." When she came to Darnell, she asked anyone, "And *who* is this ravishing creature?"

With a throaty growl, Darnell said to her, "I am destined to become your new best friend, doll." (He must have judged it a tad early in their relationship to give her the "bitch princess" treatment.)

And with a flourish of menus, Ginger paraded us through the dining room, pausing as usual at the bar to tell Johnny to send us a round on the house, then leading us straight to the corner booth that overlooked the entire room, which was filled to capacity.

While that booth was considered Moonstruck's most desirable, it could feel cramped, since the horseshoe-shaped seating at the round table necessarily left the front open for access. Meaning, it was a cozy fit for four grown men, seated knee to knee. Good thing we were all friends. I ended up between Marson and Yevgeny.

Darnell kept the conversation going at a manic clip. Although there were times when I wished he would give it a rest, Yevgeny lapped up Darnell's antics like a kid with a crush. And I couldn't help noticing that Darnell now referred to Yevgeny as Zhenya, the diminutive form of his Russian name, which the ballet dancer had previously invited me alone to use when addressing him. Hearing this, I first felt a tinge of disappointment in the ebb of his fickle affections—as if I'd been dumped. But upon reflection, I was relieved to dismiss that fantasy, sharing a wave of the obvious joy Yevgeny had found in connecting with someone who didn't need to hide his gaga devotion. Very gracious of me, I thought.

Plus, I had the consolation of Yevgeny's knee under the table, which wasn't shy about resting against mine. Neither was Marson's, on my other side.

Through drinks and appetizers and well into dinner, the conversation remained frothy, with Darnell leading the charge. When the table had been cleared, however, just as coffee was being poured, Marson changed the topic to murder.

"I've been wondering," he said. "The three of you were right there last week—right *there* when that woman was electrocuted. All three of you were involved in the movie. So was she. It must have been horrible, like losing a member of the family."

"I was just looking after the cat," I reminded him.

"I was just doing a guest cameo," said Yevgeny. "Never met the woman."

With an exaggerated lisp, Darnell said, "I could not *stand* Ellen Locke. Her loss is no loss. She is not missed."

Not expecting such candor, Marson asked, "Really?"

"Darnell has shed no tears." He flailed one hand dramatically. "Darnell weeps not."

His words, I figured, were meant to amuse. I asked, "So … why don't you tell us how you *really* feel?"

He blew me a kiss.

"*Lyubovnik,*" said Yevgeny, "don't waste those kisses."

Darnell twitched his brows at me. "I love when he talks dirty Russian."

Yevgeny laughed. "I called you my lover boy."

Darnell planted a wet one on Yevgeny's lips—which quieted things down.

Marson cleared his throat. "Anyway," he said to Darnell, "since you're the only one here who actually knew Ellen Locke, and since Brody has more than a passing interest in figuring out what happened, I'm just curious: What's your best guess?"

I had already heard Darnell's theory and found it no less bizarre when he repeated it to Marson.

"Thrill kill," he said matter-of-factly.

Marson shot me a puzzled look.

Darnell elaborated: "Nobody liked Ellen, at least nobody *I* know. She was the perfect target as a random victim. The person who killed her could have no motive at all—just the thrill of pulling it off and then getting away with it."

Marson looked horrified. "Why would *anyone* do such a thing?"

"Just for kicks." Darnell shrugged. "And think about it—the way she died—the bang, the smoke. Pure theater." He leaned over the table with a look of pop-eyed enthusiasm, reminding us, "A week later, and everyone's *still* talking about it."

Marson and Yevgeny weighed the pros and cons of this hypothesis with Darnell.

I didn't say a word, though. Darnell had now pushed his thrill-kill theory twice, with that evening's explication marked by an intensity that seemed almost gleeful. What was driving that? Was it merely the product of his splashy personality—plus a couple of drinks?

Or: Was he daring us to believe that he himself might be the killer? Was that part of the thrill?

My musing was interrupted when Darnell said, "She's coming back for a photo shoot. I think they're jumping the gun—but for me it's a job."

I asked, "Miranda Lemarr? I saw the piece in the paper."

Darnell sing-songed, "That's ri-ight. The bitch princess her-self—but I love her. I make her beautiful."

I stage-whispered, "According to the paper, it's very hush-hush."

"Top secret." Nodding gravely, Darnell mimed zipping his lip. Then he blurted a squeal of laughter and leaned close over the table, confiding, "Early Tuesday morning, that nice little restaurant downtown. First Avenue Bistro."

"How 'bout that," said Marson. "Nancy Sanderson's place."

Darnell became pensive. "It gives me something to do."

Yevgeny smiled. "Bored with me already?"

"Oh, *no*. Never, Zhenya. But if I stay, I need to work. Maybe I could open a salon—something classy, for women *and* men."

I told him, "Dumont could use a place like that."

"And if you stay," said Yevgeny, "we'll need to find a house. That is, if you want to stay with me."

Darnell was struck temporarily—and uncharacteristically—speechless.

Out of the blue, Marson asked, "Do you gentlemen have plans for Thanksgiving yet? I know, it's three weeks off, but it never hurts to nail down the holidays."

I chimed in, "Great idea. Chances are, that'll be our last bash at the loft."

Yevgeny turned to Darnell. "Should be fun. You'll still be here?"

There might have been some groping under the table as Darnell replied coyly, "It's one more reason to stay."

Yevgeny turned to Marson and me. "Count us in. Thank you, my friends."

As the evening grew late, the room had grown noisier. The full house lingered, splurging on supper-club drinks for dessert—pink squirrels, brandy Alexanders, grasshoppers. The menfolk indulged in hearty laughs while the women competed for decibel dominance. The ladies were winning.

We tussled over the check—Marson won the honors—then we slid out of the round booth, squeaking across the burgundy leatherette. Crossing the crowded room, we waved goodbye to Johnny, who smiled and said something from the other side of the bar, but we couldn't hear a word of it.

After sidling our way out to the lobby, we said our good-nights to Ginger and thanked her for the royal treatment—the prime booth, the comped drinks. She was everyone's best friend, at least for a couple of hours at Moonstruck.

"We're open every night," she reminded us over the din while delivering a round of smooches. "Don't be strangers, now."

When she made her way to Darnell, he told her, "Good night, bitch princess."

Ginger had made the grade.

Outside—more hugs and kisses in the cold night as we left Yevgeny and Darnell at their car before hustling off toward the back of the parking lot.

When Marson and I climbed into his Range Rover and thumped the doors closed and sat there in silence—with the exception of the ringing in our ears—Marson turned to ask me, "What was *that* all about?"

"Which part?" I asked with a laugh.

"Thrill kill."

With my jollies nipped short, I replied, "Good question."

## 9

Four days later, I was up before daylight and out of the house with Mister Puss; Marson was still in bed. It was the Tuesday morning of Miranda Lemarr's publicity shoot in Dumont, which would include photo sessions at scattered locations around the city, with an early start at First Avenue Bistro.

Although Darnell Passalacqua had spilled the beans on Friday night regarding the secret logistics of Miranda's visit, I was informed of the same details on Saturday by Thad Manning, director of the film project, asking if I could bring Mister Puss to appear in some of the stills with Miranda.

That Tuesday morning, it had rained overnight—at least it wasn't snow, yet—so I picked up the cat to carry him from the loft to the car. He purred in my arms as I switched off the kitchen lights, preparing to step out into the chilly dawn. I asked, "Ready for your close-up, Mister Puss?"

*It's Oolong, dah-ling.*

The restaurant was only a few blocks away, on the same street as our loft. Cruising past it, I noticed that the blinds at the windows had been drawn, and there was a sign on the door, reading CLOSED FOR PRIVATE EVENT. Thad had told me to park in the small lot off the alley behind the building.

Although I intended to be early, I seemed to be the last to arrive, squeezing into the sole remaining parking space. Conspicuous among the cars already there was Glee Savage's vintage Gremlin hatchback, custom-painted a metallic shade of fuchsia and adorned with retro whitewalls and baby moon hubcaps. The vehicle, which she had bought new some forty years earlier, reflected a sense of style and pizazz that was uniquely hers. Needless to say, there was nothing else like it in town.

Far less conspicuous was the generic-looking tan sedan that I recognized as Sheriff Simms's unmarked cruiser. I had clued him to Miranda's schedule, and he agreed that he should drop by.

Entering the Bistro through the rear door, I set Mister Puss on the floor. Having never been to the restaurant, he explored what he could within the radius of his leash, sniffing at the swirl of aromas that emanated from the kitchen and filled the dining room. As expected, Nancy Sanderson had gone out of her way to please the crew that had invaded the Bistro that morning. Several tables were lined up near the kitchen, arranged as a buffet for coffee and juices and pastries and bacon and delicate little breakfast sandwiches.

The photographer (I had wondered if it might be Zeiss Shotwell, but it was someone else) and his three assistants stood in a cluster near the buffet, gorging themselves while Miranda was made beautiful by Darnell. His makeup supplies were displayed in a huge open tackle box that sat on one of the dining tables next to Miranda's chair. She sipped coffee through a straw while Darnell wielded a shrieking hair dryer.

Thad Manning was there, discussing angles and lighting with the set dresser. Glee Savage sat alone by one of the windows, taking notes on her steno pad. I was surprised to see Nia Butler, the city's code-enforcement honcho, who was giving Nancy a hand with the food; I wondered if they had spent the night together.

Sheriff Simms stepped over to me, looking handsome as ever, dressed to the nines at the crack of dawn. I noticed the glint of a leather shoulder holster beneath the lapel of his jacket, which reminded me that he wasn't there out of curiosity—he was working. "Morning, Brody," he said, clapping a hand on my shoulder.

Then he hunched down to pet the cat. "And good morning to you, Mister Puss."

"Please," I told the sheriff, "he's getting into character—it's Oolong."

Simms roared with laughter. Snatching a piece of bacon from the buffet, he broke it in half, then shared it with the cat. "I beg your pardon, Mister Oolong."

When Darnell switched off the hair dryer and turned his attention to Miranda's makeup, the noise level in the room dropped, allowing breezier conversation. I went over to the window table where Glee was writing notes. She closed her pad as I leaned to give her a kiss, avoiding the wide brim of her hat; she always wore a hat "on the job," and today's was a shocking orange—more accurately, tangerine—lending some bright autumnal flair to the gray morning.

"Brody, love," she said, "keep me company." In the spirit of things, she greeted the cat as "the mighty Oolong." He purred.

When I sat, the cat hopped into my lap. I said to Glee, "You're at it early today."

"Part of the job, sweets. I'll follow this caravan all day, if they'll let me."

I smirked. "I'd like to see them try to stop you."

She winked at me. Then we huddled over the table, exchanging gossip, hers regarding details of *Home Sweet Humford*, mine regarding the murder, although I didn't say a word that hadn't been reported already. When it became apparent that neither one of us had anything newsy to spill, Glee wondered aloud, "Suppose I could sneak in a little interview with Miranda before this gets started?"

I glanced over at the starlet. She sat there with a glazed look as Darnell motor-mouthed while working on her. I told Glee, "She'd probably welcome it."

And Glee was on her feet, fishing the phone out of her purse for a few photos of her own, moving toward Miranda Lemarr and pulling up a chair. Miranda came to life, smiling as she gabbed with the reporter.

"Hi, Brody." It was Nancy Sanderson stepping over to the table. She then sat in the chair Glee had vacated. With a soft laugh, she said, "I'm sure my regular breakfast crowd is wondering what's up."

I had known Nancy for nearly three years, having met her shortly after my arrival in Dumont. Marson and I frequented First Avenue Bistro, so she knew us as loyal customers, and we turned to her whenever we needed assistance with our entertaining at home. We shared an interest in inventive cuisine, tastefully presented. She was a true foodie and a good friend.

But that friendship always seemed to be held at arm's length. Nancy had a perpetual air of reserve about her—not that she was cold and certainly not haughty, but she seemed to draw a strict line between friendship and privacy. I knew that she was a lesbian, but now in her fifties, she had never allowed herself to commit to someone else. In a word, she seemed repressed.

So I didn't expect her to ask me, "Isn't she *gorgeous?*"

I must have looked bewildered.

Nearly gushing, Nancy explained, "Miranda Lemarr! At the film shoot in the park, I nearly swooned when she went through the catering line—she was *so* nice, *so* genuine. She took time to tell Nia and me that everything was 'delish.' Can you believe it? Delish! Nia just froze. I thought she was going to faint—in fact, I had to hold on to her. We giggled all night about it, in spite of... 'what happened' that afternoon."

So. I'd just learned not only that Nancy had a perfectly healthy libido, but also that she and Nia Butler, the butch black code-enforcement cop, were in fact spending their nights together. It seemed that Nancy was making considerable headway in overcoming her commitment issues. I smiled. Good for her.

"*Anyway,*" she continued, leaning near, "do you think I'd be out of line if I asked Miranda for a selfie with Nia and me? I'd *love* to get a framed blowup, then hang it here in the dining room— maybe near the door, where everyone could see it."

"Nancy," I said, "let's go ask. If she's agreeable, I'll be happy to shoot it for you."

She flumped a hand to her bosom and followed me and Mister Puss, waving a hand for Nia Butler to join us.

Miranda Lemarr seemed flattered by the request, asking Darnell if she was "good to go" for a selfie. Darnell powdered her nose and removed her smock with a flourish befitting a matador, then finger-wagged for Nancy and Nia to come hither so he could pretty them up. They tittered as he primped. Thad Manning stepped in to pose the three ladies, and Nancy handed me her phone, saying, "A gazillion thanks, Brody."

But Miranda said, "Frank? Why don't *you* take care of this?"

The photographer stepped over, asking me, "May I?"

"Yes, *sir*," I said, handing over the phone.

And he went to work, directing and snapping what seemed like a hundred shots before saying, "Nice. Really nice," as he returned the phone to Nancy.

Nancy thanked him, then thanked me again, adding, "I almost forgot—what a pleasure it was, meeting your mother."

Stupidly, I asked, "Inez?"

"Well, *yes*"—Nancy laughed—"during her visit."

With a swell of anxiety, I glanced about for Glee Savage, who, as far as I knew, was clueless that her old nemesis had been in Dumont lately. But Glee was out of earshot, back at the window table, typing on a tablet.

Confused, I asked Nancy, "Did Inez introduce herself at the filming in the park?"

"No, I saw her meet up with you that day, but I didn't know who she was. Then, the next day, Friday, she came in here—alone, for lunch."

I recalled that when I visited Inez at the Manor House that Friday morning, she mentioned having plans for the day. Sounding evasive, she explained, "Just plans. Thought I'd visit some old haunts."

And now I knew that those plans had brought her to First Avenue Bistro, which was *not* one of her old haunts—it didn't exist until many years after Inez left Dumont. And while she was at the restaurant, she became acquainted with Nancy. What was that all about? Or had Inez simply gotten hungry and asked someone to recommend a good place for lunch?

Nancy excused herself, needing to look after things in the kitchen. I watched her cross the dining room, meeting Nia just outside the kitchen, where they lingered to ogle Miranda Lemarr while swiping through the pictures on Nancy's phone. They giggled and gabbed like schoolgirls—totally out of character for both of them.

As I settled in a chair near Miranda, Darnell replaced her smock and continued his transformation of the starlet, preparing her not for selfies, but for publicity photos that would be seen by millions. While rifling through his enormous tackle box for sponges, puffs, tubes, and powders, he chattered nonstop about Yevgeny, saying, "This might be it—true love, *fabulous* sex, my sweet Zhenya. Makes me think I could settle down here—and be so, so happy." With that exaggerated lisp, he added, "Seriously, blissfully satisfied."

Miranda rolled her eyes. "We've heard this before, Darnell. What about that stevedore from Long Beach?"

Darnell let out an appalled shriek. "That *tramp*? Ignacio was a brute—he had his moments—but no style, no elegance, and certainly no stamina. Ignacio is *dead* to me."

Sheriff Simms joined us, pulling up a chair.

Mister Puss hopped up to my lap as I said to Miranda, "Someone's been looking forward to working with you again." The cat placed a paw on Miranda's knee, purring.

"Awww, hi there, Oolong darlin." She twiddled his chin.

One of the photographer's assistants came over to check something with Darnell, speaking in whispers that burst into full-throated laughter.

Simms said, "Miss Lemarr, I know how busy you are today, but after the shoot, while they're putting things back in order here, maybe you and I could find somewhere to talk—somewhere more private?"

"Anything to help, Sheriff," she said, wide-eyed. "But I'm not sure where. This is pretty chaotic."

It was. The hubbub was not only noisy, but there were far too many eyes and ears in the room to allow a confidential discussion of murder and its possible motives. I suggested to Simms, "There's that little park across the street."

"Bingo," he said. "And maybe you can join us, Brody." I knew that was coming. He said to Miranda, "If things work out afterward, let's try to get together."

She said, "Sure, Sheriff," and he stepped away to answer his phone.

Which left me with Miranda and the cat, plus Darnell and the photographer's assistant, named Alexis. Darnell said to her, "Have you heard? I seem to be in love."

She assured him, "I've heard, all right. You fell for a dancer."

"A *dancer*?" he scolded. "Yevgeny is a *star*."

"Hope it works," said Alexis, sounding sincere. She was younger than Darnell, maybe mid-twenties, not long out of college. Perky and earnest, more cute than pretty, she seemed content to share in the glamour of Hollywood from behind the scenes.

Darnell asked her, "Have you talked to Jane?"

"Yeah, just a few days ago. She's fine. Sends her love."

I asked, "Jane Douglas?" I hadn't seen the stage mom of horrid little Seth Douglas since the day after the murder, when they were waiting for a limo to drive them to their plane out of Green Bay.

"Right," said Alexis. "You know her?"

"Just from the day of the test shoot."

"Ah. I wasn't around for that."

"Count yourself lucky," I said with a halfhearted laugh. Then I asked Darnell, "You're close, you and Jane?"

"Like *this*," said Darnell, raising two crossed fingers. "We go way back, to my first job in LA. A few days after we met, she called me her BFF. Darnell is more with-it today. Back then, I wondered if she was being dirty."

"But she wasn't," I thought aloud. "The two of you are best friends forever."

Darnell shrugged. "Who knows? Best friends—sure. Forever—that's a *long* time."

I admired his pragmatic logic, but I was more intrigued by the apparent depth of his relationship with Jane Douglas. I'd assumed they were just film-industry chums.

Turning to Miranda, I said, "I'm sorta surprised Jane and Seth aren't here today—to have the kid in the publicity shots with you."

She made a puke face, accompanied by a gagging sound. "I'd like to wring that little monster's neck. If he was really *my* kid, I'd slap the shit out of him." She flipped her hands, smiling. "But he's not—I'm just his movie mom. And I'm more than happy to spend the day with my sweet, sweet Oolong."

Mister Puss hopped over to her lap and stretched to give her a chin bump.

"Awww," said everyone who was watching.

Pondering Seth's creepy behavior, I said, "That kid's a handful, all right. Jane seems fully aware of his problems, but powerless to correct them. It's almost as if she's ... *afraid* of Seth."

"He scares the crap out of *me*," said Darnell.

"Me, too," Miranda and Alexis chimed in unison.

"Me, three," said Thad Manning, who picked up the gist of our confab while walking past with a clipboard. "But Seth is box-office magic."

As Thad stepped away, I said to the others, "If Jane can't control Seth, what about the kid's father? Where is he?"

Miranda said, "Not a clue. This is my first encounter with the Douglas family, or what's left of it. If that little devil even *has* a father, he's sure not around." With an exasperated sigh, she added, "Probably ran for the hills—and I can't say I blame him."

Darnell and Alexis were looking at each other, as if weighing shared knowledge.

I said, "Darnell?"

He began tidying up the makeup table, returning things to his tackle box. "My BFF Jane, she had some rough times." His vocal delivery had lost its usual joshing mania as he continued, "Her husband died a few years ago. His name was Nate. It was ugly."

Darnell then stepped behind Miranda's chair and kissed the top of her head. Removing her smock, he said, "All set, my beautiful bitch princess. You're on."

After two hours of preparation, the photo shoot itself lasted only thirty minutes, but it was lively, and all the bystanders seemed to have fun watching the professionals at work. Boppy music played from a boom box as Frank cajoled smiles and mugging from Miranda in her role as Suzanne. Many of the setups included Mister Puss as Oolong, drawing comments from those around me that he was stealing every shot. "That cat just *loves* the lens," declared Frank—more than once.

Darnell confided to me, "Now and then, I groom animals for a shoot. But your little boy? Doesn't need a thing—he's a natural."

I felt an unexpected swell of pride in the little guy. I told Darnell, "Now, if I could just get him to focus on better grades."

Darnell let out a hoot, which drew a shush from Frank: "We're *working* here."

And when the work was done, Miranda and Mister Puss received a round of applause. The starlet hadn't been able to eat while in makeup, so she now grabbed a big gooey cinnamon roll—plus a slice of bacon for Mister Puss, telling him, "You've earned it, darlin."

Sheriff Simms stepped over to ask her, "Is this a good time?"

"Let me just tell Thad where I'm going."

And a couple of minutes later, after she polished off the cinnamon roll, wrapped her hair in a chiffon scarf, buttoned up a trench coat, and donned a huge pair of dark glasses, we slipped out the front door—Miranda, Simms, Mister Puss, and I. By then, well past nine o'clock, the clouds had given way to brilliant sunshine, which had warmed the morning and burned off the overnight drizzle. With downtown office workers now planted behind their desks, traffic on First Avenue was so sparse that we could cross the street without even looking both ways.

Several years earlier, after a fire in an abandoned head shop had left a charred plot of land amid a row of storefronts, the city had installed a "pocket park" to fill the gap. Despite the tainted circumstances of its inception, the little park felt as if it had always been there, nestled between the brick walls of adjacent buildings. Quaint lampposts. A patch of green, a neat square of boxwood hedges, a few lacy honey locusts that had dropped their tiny yellow leaves. A sputtering fountain to mask the street noise. A pigeon or three. A pair of benches.

Simms sat down with Miranda. I settled on the other bench, at a right angle to theirs, holding Mister Puss's leash. He stayed on the ground, crouching, where he could keep a close eye on the dorky pigeons, too dumb to notice him.

Simms said, "Thanks for making time for me, Miss Lemarr."

"I hope you'll call me Miranda, Sheriff."

"That would be a pleasure. And I'm Thomas."

Their easygoing friendliness was in marked contrast to her interview at the Manor House on the morning after the murder, when Miranda acted shy and fidgety, causing me to wonder if she was on drugs. Though I was pleased to see that she was now in much better spirits, I had to wonder: What had changed?

Simms said, "I'll get right to the point, Miranda. It's been nearly two weeks since Ellen Locke was killed. Back in California, you've had some time to decompress and think about everything that happened that day. Do you recall seeing anything that now strikes you as suspicious?"

She mulled the question briefly. "Nothing at all, Thomas."

"How well did you know Ellen?"

"Not very."

Simms eyed her askance. "But she was trying to blackmail you. Right?"

Miranda wasn't expecting that. She began pulling at her fingers, as she had done at the previous interview. Bowing her head, she mumbled, "Yes. She wanted money—or she'd tell about some stuff I'm not too proud of."

Simms asked her gently, "Why didn't you mention this before?"

"Because I'm ashamed of it." She raised her head to look at him. "But I didn't kill Ellen. I would never hurt *anyone*."

I was inclined to believe her. So, apparently, was Simms.

He said, "What can you tell me about Conrad Houghes?"

With a soft smile, Miranda said, "I suppose you already know we have a 'thing' going on. We're not *living* together, but we've talked about it. Who knows?"

Simms studied her with a quizzical look.

"What?" she asked.

"Sorry. None of my business, but that guy, well … he doesn't quite strike me as your type."

She laughed, nodded. "Too old for me? A little rough around the edges? I know. But who's to say? When it works, it works. I guess I just needed something totally different." She paused before adding, "Different from Zeiss."

"Zeiss Shotwell," I said. "You used to be a couple, before Houghes."

"Yeah. It was nice, for a while. Zeiss, you know, he's all *British* and sophisticated, the artsy-fartsy director of photography. Really had me charmed. Bottom line, though—total prick. It's all about *him*. Nothing would surprise me about that guy, not anymore. He's capable of *anything*. As far as I'm concerned, he was perfect for Ellen. A match made in heaven."

Simms and I exchanged a bug-eyed glance.

I said to Miranda, "You mean, Zeiss Shotwell and Ellen Locke, they were …?"

"Well, *yeah*. He moved in with her. Not common knowledge, but I'm sure of it."

A voice called, "*Miranda?*"

I turned to see Thad Manning standing in the open doorway of the restaurant. He called, "Ready to move on."

Miranda stood. "Gotta go."

Simms stood. "Let me see you back." And he escorted her toward the street.

As they were leaving, she turned and twiddled her fingers. "Bye, Oolong."

While I sat pondering this enticing new detail, I patted my knee, summoning Mister Puss. He hopped up to the bench, purring. Then he stretched his paws to my chest and reached his snout to my shoulder.

*The plot thickens.*

# 10

Zeiss Shotwell had said nothing to Simms and me about his relationship with Ellen Locke. In fact, when we interviewed him
at the Manor House, he said, "Sorry to sound unsympathetic, old
chum, but frankly, I'm glad she's gone. Ellen was a wretched mess."

Had Zeiss told us a brazen lie? Or was Miranda Lemarr mistaken that Zeiss had been not only involved with, but living with,
the victim? Or—an even more intriguing possibility—did Zeiss
actually feel contempt for the victim while ingratiating himself
into her heart and into her home?

When Zeiss made the "wretched mess" comment at the Manor
House, Conrad Houghes was sitting right next to him, and their
conversation centered not on Ellen's death, but on Miranda's
boudoir. Didn't Houghes *know* that Zeiss had been living with
Ellen? Or was it more logical to assume that Miranda was mistaken about that? Or was she lying about it?

Considering them as a foursome—Ellen Locke, Zeiss Shotwell, Conrad Houghes, Miranda Lemarr—I could make no sense
of their conflicting stories, but I knew they were interconnected
by a web of passion, drugs, and blackmail.

On Wednesday, the day after the publicity shoot at First Avenue
Bistro, my morning got off to a more typical start at the loft, since
I didn't need to deliver Mister Puss for his photo call at dawn.
Instead, Marson and I arose at the civilized hour of seven and

then had to lure the cat out of bed with our breakfast clatter in the kitchen.

The cat was soon gobbling whatever Marson had set out in two little Art Deco bowls (Mister Puss was surely the only cat in town who routinely enjoyed his meals from Puiforcat "pet dishes") while I sat at the kitchen island, nursing my first few sips of steaming black coffee. Marson stepped outside the front door to retrieve the *Dumont Daily Register*, then returned, nudging the door shut behind him.

"Wow!" he said, looking at the front page while walking to the kitchen.

Uh-oh. I wondered: Washington meltdown? Pandemic coming? Martial law?

"Looky here," he said, flopping the paper in front of me on the countertop.

I agreed: "Wow!"

Under a banner headline, STARS SHINE BRIGHT IN DUMONT, a huge photo was displayed across the width of the page, showing Miranda Lemarr and Mister Puss during yesterday's shoot at the Bistro. Glee Savage had captured on her phone a playful moment with Miranda having a nose-to-nose "conversation" with the cat. Frank, the publicity photographer, could be seen directing the action as a blurred silhouette in the foreground, with the recognizable interior of the Bistro in the background. But the focus—the sparkle and life—of the image was the interaction of the beautiful starlet with the exotic Abyssinian. Mister Puss, mugging as Oolong, was closer to the camera than his human costar, with his head bigger than life on the printed page.

Running directly beneath the photo was Glee's story, peppered with gushing clichés, including "the magic of Hollywood," "tinsel and glamour," and last but not least, "a star is born"—referring to Mister Puss.

The cat in question had finished his breakfast and jumped up to the countertop. Planting himself next to my coffee mug, he glanced down at the paper and then, looking up at me, yawned.

"Gosh," said Marson, "Mary will be *thrilled*. We need to save her a copy."

His words came as a jolt of reality. We had both become so accustomed to a morning ritual that included coffee, the paper, and Mister Puss, it was difficult to imagine that his days with us were limited.

An hour or so later, after I was put together for the day, I was about to leave for the office when my phone rang.

"Hey there, Brody." It was Sheriff Simms. "Sorry to call so early."

"Not at all. What's up?"

"I've been reviewing all this video from the murder scene."

I noticed that in Simms's parlance, the test shoot for the film and its location, the city commons, were now collectively "the murder scene."

He continued, "It's tedious. Most of the footage is useless and repetitious."

"Destined for the cutting-room floor," I mused.

"But my main problem," he explained, "is the equipment. Sure, we have a tech guy at headquarters, and he connected the external drive to my computer. Showed me how to play it. It works. But, I mean, we have *office* computers here. They're not made for this— too slow, small screen, so-so video. Some of these test scenes, I'd like to get a better *look* at them."

I understood his dilemma. Professional filmmaking involves state-of-the-art video, requiring specialized hardware and software for proper viewing or editing. Sleepy little Dumont had no television stations, and as far as I knew, there were no commercial video-production services in town. Then it clicked.

I told Simms, "Questman Center."

"Really?"

The performing-arts complex, designed by Marson and principally funded by Mary Questman, was devoted to live performances in three theaters. But their back-of-house facilities included a video studio and editing suite, used primarily for interviews, archival recordings, and promotional work.

"It's just what you need," I said.

Simms laughed. "You've got connections over there, right?"

"Let me see if I can arrange something."

Questman Center's newly installed executive director, Paige Yeats, happened to be the wife of Thad Manning, whose film project had been visited by a murder that needed solving.

"When would you like to come over, Brody?" said Paige when I phoned.

After lunch, around one-thirty, Mister Puss and I sat in my car, waiting for Sheriff Simms to meet us in Questman Center's parking lot.

Two weeks into November, the cold nights could still warm up to pleasant afternoons. The trees had lost their leaves, so the black branches spread out in bold relief against a cloudless blue sky. The low slant of late-autumn sunshine created deep, jagged shadows in the rocky crags of a glacier-carved ravine that had once backdropped a city park. Now, though, this geological quirk served as a spectacular setting for Dumont's growing cultural campus, dominated by the dramatic forms of Questman Center and its component theaters. Nearby, workers busied themselves with construction of the new county museum, designed by Marson. My own project, the main library, was still a vacant patch of land beyond the museum.

Spotting the sheriff's tan sedan pull into the parking lot, I got out of my car and walked Mister Puss on his leash toward the plaza in front of the theater complex. Simms was soon out of his car and moving briskly to meet me.

I called to him, "Hi there, Thomas."

"Hey, Brody." Stepping up to me, he shook hands. "Thanks for setting this up." He crouched to pet the cat. His other hand held the hard drive containing the video.

When he stood again, I asked, "Yesterday, Miranda Lemarr—do you think she was on the level when she told us Zeiss Shotwell was involved with Ellen Locke?"

"Good question. If they *were* involved—and Shotwell went out of his way to imply they were *not*—we'd have good reason to find him suspicious. But I dunno…"

I nodded. "It doesn't add up, does it? Let's say Shotwell *was* the killer. That would mean: he was the one who rigged the extension cord and, later, at the right moment, let it drop into the vat of icy water. But Ellen was killed *during* the filming, while Shotwell was busy—he was standing a few feet away from me the whole time. If Shotwell dropped the cord in the water, it was at least twenty minutes before Ellen was electrocuted."

Simms scrunched his face. "He'd be taking a huge chance—*anyone* might've stuck their hand in the vat before Ellen got around to it. And that makes no sense at all."

"Unless…," I said, "unless his intended victim wasn't Ellen, but somebody else."

Simms's shoulders drooped. "Oh, Lordy."

I shared his dismay. If Ellen's death was merely the result of poor timing, the puzzle had become exponentially more complex. I told Simms, "Let's take a look at that video."

We passed through the front doors and into the expansive main lobby. On a Wednesday afternoon, there were no performances, so we were alone. A light shone from the doorway of an office behind the ticket counter, but otherwise the vast space was nearly dark, with only the dim glow of a few security lights defining the perimeter. As I led Simms toward the far side of the building, traversing what must have been half an acre of teak parquet flooring, it popped beneath our feet and echoed softly in the hushed, empty space.

Finding the hallway that led back to the offices, I took Simms into the reception room outside the executive director's suite, where a perky young male secretary—TIMOTHY, according to the nameplate on his desk—glanced up from his keyboard, then stood. "*Gentle*-men, good afternoon," he said, sizing us up, looking very interested. He might have had better luck with me, but he was staring at the straight black sheriff. Then he noticed the cat on the leash. "Oh! A furbaby—how *adorable*."

I said, "Miss Yeats is expecting us. The name is Oolong."

Flummoxed, Timothy scrolled his computer. "Let me, uh ... take a look."

I heard Paige Yeats laughing—her voice was unmistakable. Then she appeared in a doorway. "It's all right, Timothy. Come on in, guys."

As we entered her office, I casually turned from the doorway to see Timothy's gaze following us. When I winked at him, he winked right back.

"Well," said Paige, "it's week two on the new job, and I'm still trying to get this place organized. Sorry for the mess."

It wasn't that bad—a few open boxes tucked behind the desk, a stack of framed pictures waiting to be hung, various mementos and certificates already tacked to the wall above a credenza. The office itself was roomy and comfortable, with good contemporary furnishings, a space meant not only for work, but also for receiving and entertaining important guest artists, replete with a sofa, upholstered chairs, and even a small bar, fully stocked. A huge plate-glass window, floor to ceiling, flooded the room with natural light and revealed a jaw-dropping view of the ravine behind the building.

"If you're slow settling in," I told Paige, "that must mean you're already busy on the job. From what I hear, that alone would be a big improvement over Basil Hutchins. Welcome to Dumont. The Center needs you."

"*Thank* you," she said with a coo. "Please, guys, have a seat."

Mister Puss was first to land on the sofa; I joined him. Simms sat next to us. Paige took one of the chairs.

With a thoughtful scowl, she said to me, "Odd that you should mention Basil Hutchins. As of this morning, no one's heard a word from him. We've been trying to get in touch, but still can't track him down."

"Last I heard, he was on his way to the Canary Islands, and there were severe storms in the Atlantic off the coast of Africa." I added, "But that's been weeks."

"Ouch," said Simms. "That does *not* sound good."

Paige said, "I never met him, but we're concerned about him, of course. More to the point, though, his files and record-keeping were a mess—what we can find of them. I could use some guidance, but I'm beginning to think I'll just start from scratch."

"Sometimes, Paige," said Simms, "that's the best way. A clean slate. I'd bet money you can untangle it."

"Sweet of you, Thomas. And I'd bet money *you* can untangle the sordid details of Ellen Locke's death."

"That's why we're here." He leaned forward on his knees, as if to close the distance between Paige and him, asking, "To the best of your knowledge, was Ellen in any way 'involved' with Zeiss Shotwell?"

Paige looked as if she might laugh. "No," she said, "why do you ask?"

"Someone seems to think they were living together."

"It's news to me. Truth is, I never hung out with *either* of them, but I find it hard to imagine those two 'together.'" She added finger quotes.

Entering the conversation, I asked, "Why's that?"

"Well, Zeiss is a bit of a flake, and he certainly has no short-age of ego, but he's also intelligent, creative, and one of the most erudite and articulate people I've ever known. Ellen, on the other hand, was … not."

"How well did you know her?"

"Not well at all."

Simms asked, "What did you think of her?"

"Couldn't *stand* her." Paige stopped, took a deep breath, and exhaled. "Sorry. Not kind to speak ill of the dead, let alone the murdered."

Simms said, "I'm sure it's an emotional time for all concerned."

"It is." Paige nodded. "On top of which, I'm going through lots of changes right now. All good, but also stressful: New job. New town. Pregnant."

I said, "If this is too personal, just say so. But I'm wondering: You're a film star in your own right, but now you're essentially giv-ing that up for Thad—supporting *his* dream to switch from acting to directing, moving to *his* hometown, and staying here to start a family with him. You don't strike me as a second fiddle, so that's a *lot* of love."

She grinned. "I guess you're right. But starting a family, that's something both of us want, and I want to be around to raise and nurture our child, leaving little time for Hollywood. Truth is, I've sorta lost interest in acting, and that's why *this* job is so important to me—a fresh challenge, a new way to prove my worth."

Simms said, "You have nothing to prove, Paige."

"Don't be so sure," she said with a low laugh. "When you're the daughter of Glenn Yeats, you enter the world with a heap of advantages. I've never had illusions about that, and it's always made me wonder if my life has any semblance of 'reality.' I've never struggled. Anything I've accomplished has been—let's face it—handed to me. To be honest, I suspect that my acting career had some 'help' behind the scenes. But Questman Center? Entirely different. I landed this position fair and square. I'm thrilled."

Sitting there, listening to this, I knew otherwise. Mary Quest-man had been blunt with me when explaining her plan to install Paige as executive director: Paige's father was a multibillionaire with a known taste for philanthropy and a soft spot for the arts.

I told Paige, "And the board is thrilled to have you at the helm."

"Full steam ahead," she said with a broad smile. Then she frowned. "Things would be perfect—if we could just get out of the Manor House. I mean, nice place, but it's like living in a hotel. And a few months down the road—baby makes three."

I asked, "No progress with the house on Prairie Street?"

"Zilch. The Gerbers haven't budged. Thad sent them a higher offer, and they haven't even responded. Bettina was an extra in the test scene, and I tried to make nice with her, but she wouldn't talk to me."

With no subtlety whatever, I reminded her, "If you decide you need an architect..."

"Rest assured, Brody, you'd be the first person we'd turn to. But Thad is showing no signs of giving up on this. Anyway"—she stood—"you're not here to stew over house hunting. Let me check to see if they're ready for you in the studio."

When she stepped over to her desk to make a phone call, Simms and I and Mister Puss got up from the sofa. Simms checked his phone for messages. I moseyed over to the credenza to snoop at the collection of mementos Paige had displayed on top of the cab-inet and on the wall.

As expected, there were a number of awards and statuettes re-lated to her acting. There were citations from various charities, as well as photos of Paige and Thad posing at galas with other Hollywood glitterati. What surprised me, however, were the other items, all with a common theme: gun control.

There were membership certificates from organizations that

sought to "fix or repeal" the Second Amendment. Photos showed Paige behind the podium at various rallies, with banners supporting stricter registration laws and opposing assault weapons. She had been awarded a plaque with an engraved depiction of firearms in a trash can.

"Okay, Laurencio," she said on the phone, "I'll bring them down."

I had caught Simms's eye and beckoned him to the credenza. He was studying the mementos when Paige stepped over to ask, "Ready, guys?"

"Sure," said Simms, "but I'm curious: How long have you been so stoked about gun control? I didn't realize you were into it, but it seems you're quite an activist."

She beamed. "Ever since college—in that sense, I haven't grown up. When you believe in a higher cause, you stick with it. It's worth fighting for." Then she said, "Oops. Sorry, Thomas. We're probably not on the same page. I mean, you're a cop."

"Think about it." Simms tucked his thumbs in his belt, spreading his suit jacket to reveal his shoulder holster, which was not a decorative accessory. "I have no problem with the notion of keeping guns out of the wrong hands."

Nor did I myself have any problem with Paige's "higher cause." However, it brought to mind a logical question that I wanted to suppress, but could not. Trying to keep things breezy, I asked Paige, "Did you and Ellen ever lock horns over this?"

Paige rolled her eyes. "That's putting it mildly. She and I often ended up working on the same set, and I admit it, I can't hold my tongue when I know I'm right. California's not an open-carry state, but she always managed to make her fetish known. So we had a few shouting matches; a couple were doozies. No more, though. And as far as I'm concerned, the world's a better place with one less gun nut."

Simms and I glanced at each other.

Noting this, Paige told us, "But it's unkind to speak ill of the dead." Her tone made it clear she felt only contempt for Ellen Locke.

Paige took us down to the lower level of the Center, a labyrinth of tech areas and rehearsal spaces, where the scene shop had direct access to install complete sets on the stages of all three theaters. The concrete floors, cement-block walls, and harsh fluorescent lighting stood in stark contrast to the teak-and-velvet refinement of the public areas above.

The video studio and editing suite were at the end of a long corridor, well removed from the bustle and noise of the shop areas. Paige led us in and introduced us to Laurencio, the A/V director. After instructing him to be at our service, she left.

Laurencio was young, mid-twenties, like the twinky Timothy up in the executive offices. He was also uncommonly cute, but in a straight, Latin, nerdy-glasses kind of way—which I found achingly attractive, perhaps because he was so clearly off-limits. (Not that I would seriously consider straying from Marson's affections, but hey, a guy can kick the tires now and then.)

He took the external hard drive from Simms and asked us to get comfortable in the dimly lit editing room, where we sat in big swivel chairs at a long table, facing a seven-foot display. Mister Puss hopped up to my lap as Simms took a few pages of notes from the inside pocket of his jacket and unfolded them on the table.

"Holy *crap*," said Simms with a laugh as a still image of a crowd on the commons appeared on the oversized screen—sharp and brilliant and richly detailed.

Laurencio, who had been fussing at the main control panel, stepped over to us and handed Simms a remote, explaining, "Each take from each camera is on a separate file, which you'll find listed on the menu, here." He tapped a button, bringing up the directory. "The basic 'play' functions are just like your home TV. You'll find the audio isn't nearly as good as the video—it's just the sound picked up by each camera, which is later replaced with audio from dedicated files."

"No complaints," Simms assured him, trying out the control. "This is fantastic."

"Great. If you need me, I'll be working on another project, right over here."

I told him, "Thanks so much."

He eyed me for a lingering moment before saying, "You're *very* welcome, Mr. Norris."

Huh? Was he kicking the tires? Did my trusty gaydar need a tune-up?

As Laurencio stepped away, Simms shot me a grin.

Although the video was dazzling, the novelty soon wore off. Simms had told me his earlier viewing was "tedious." And in fact, most of the footage was useless and repetitious. Mister Puss fell asleep in my lap.

Simms ran through each file, frequently fast-forwarding, occasionally making notes, then turning to ask me, "Nothin, right?"

Each time, I responded with a nod, each more weary than the last.

We were most interested in two blocks of footage: everything shot just prior to the afternoon takes, when someone might have been most likely to rig the lethal extension cord—and everything shot just before and after the electrocution. Unfortunately, the video following the electrocution was very brief, as the shorted main circuit killed the juice.

We took a second look at the end of the morning's shooting, before the break for lunch. The wide-angle camera showed the group of extras playing autograph hounds in the background. The only face I recognized was that of Bettina Gerber, who'd been recruited by Thad Manning in hopes of softening her resistance to selling him the Taliesin house he wanted. On-screen, there was nothing at all remarkable about her—she was a face in the crowd.

After that scene, when the lunch break was called, one of the cameras was left askew, recording longer than the others, focused in the distance on an area that included the catering table and the adjacent icy vat. In the course of two minutes, before the camera was shut off, Simms and I saw moving through the lunch line everyone we had considered as having a conceivable motive for wanting to kill Ellen Locke: Miranda Lemarr, Conrad Houghes, Zeiss Shotwell, Darnell Passalacqua, and the victim's assistant, Wes Sugita.

Some of the others moving through the line were not under active consideration, but they intrigued me: Bettina Gerber, meeting up with her husband, Harlan, who had previously said he would not be present at the shoot. The uber-creepy Seth Douglas with his mom, Jane. And Paige Yeats, who had stayed in the background that entire day, not wanting to steal the spotlight from the film's insecure starlet, Miranda.

None of them did anything that looked suspicious.

Most of them reached into the vat, including the cateress, Nancy Sanderson, and her love interest, Nia Butler—harming no one.

As for the victim, Ellen Locke, she appeared in none of this.

I said to Simms, "I wonder if we can get a closer look at the rigging above the vat."

Simms swiveled his chair toward the control board. "Hey, Laurencio?"

The A/V director turned to us. "Yes, Sheriff?"

"Can we zoom?"

"Sure." Laurencio came over to us and demonstrated how to do it. "You'll lose definition, of course, but you've got a lot to work with."

I watched him return to his console, wondering if he'd glance back. Which he did.

Simms enlarged the image on the screen, pulling back when it started to pixelate, giving us a good look at the rigging and the awning over the vat.

"Interesting," I said.

"Yeah," said Simms. "Not even a *trace* of orange up there."

The extension cord that electrocuted Ellen Locke was a bright utility-orange. "So," I said, "if the cord was already up there, it was completely hidden. And if it *wasn't* already in place, someone was waiting for the right moment."

"Meaning," said Simms, "there was forethought and intent."

"Meaning," I added, "it was no accident."

Simms nodded. "It was murder, all right."

When we zoomed out to the full image again, Simms said, "Let's have another look at the last footage of the day."

For the afternoon shoot, with the glorious natural light, Thad Manning and the photography director, Zeiss Shotwell, had decided to use only two cameras; the third was left unmanned but recording. It gave us an angle similar to the footage that had captured the lunch line, so we watched that video file intently:

The onlookers from the street are standing two or three deep, milling and gabbing while following the action of the scene being shot in the park. Many are children in Halloween costumes. Most of the adults are holding phones, some above their heads, taking photos and videos of the day when Hollywood came to Dumont. Ellen Locke, in her bizarre getup with an assault rifle slung over one shoulder, moves into the frame, reaches deep into the galvanized vat, and freezes for a few seconds before spasmodically dropping to the ground with steam rising from her toes in the wet grass. The crowd begins to notice. The video begins to jerk and flicker as Wesley Sugita rushes into the frame from the opposite direction. Just as the horrid little nun with the gouged and bleeding eye sockets opens her mouth to scream, the screen goes black.

Simms and I sat there, breathless. I asked him, "What do you think?"

"Two things," he said. "First, when you add everything up, Wes Sugita is still our most obvious suspect. He checks all the boxes: motive, means, and opportunity. So I need to question him again—not easy when he's two thousand miles away."

I understood Simms's logic, but I wasn't convinced he was on the right track.

He continued, "Second—and I feel like a dunce for not thinking of this earlier—did you notice all those people taking pictures? I need to make an immediate appeal for the public to send us whatever they have."

"Now, *that*," I said, "that's a great idea." I didn't mention that I thought it was a better idea than going after Wes Sugita.

Simms wrote a note to himself, then said, "As long as we're here, let's take one more look at the final scene."

"Sure, Thomas, my time is your time." But I really did need to get back to my office.

Thomas pulled up the file containing the close-up of Mister Puss, which was recorded immediately prior to Ellen Locke's death.

With a soft laugh, I said, "Thad was right—Mister Puss really did steal that scene."

At the mention of his name, the cat roused himself from my lap, hopped up to the tabletop, and stretched. Then he noticed his huge mug on the video screen and began to purr.

"What a ham," I told Simms.

Simms rolled the take again, displaying a full-frame image of Mister Puss's face; his eyes and ears followed the action, alert as a cheetah tracking its prey. The other actors in the scene were barely visible, but when things went wrong at the galvanized vat, their training had taught them not to break character, not to turn and look. Mister Puss, however, simply reacted by instinct and seemed to be watching some disruption.

On the tabletop in front of us, Mister Puss purred louder, transfixed by the picture on the screen.

Simms backed up the video and froze it on the frame where the cat's eyes turned away from the scene. Then Simms zoomed closer on the cat, till his eyes filled the frame. Each golden eye contained a convex reflection of the entire surroundings, the whole crowd assembled in and around the park, a vast landscape meeting the sky in an arc at the horizon—but it was impossible, of course, to discern any detail.

Simms looked at the screen, looked at the cat on the table, then looked at me. "If only the little guy could tell us what he saw."

We both laughed. Everyone knew that Mary Questman thought her cat could talk.

Simms got up and moved over to the control board, returning the remote to Laurencio, who chatted with the sheriff while keeping an eye on me.

I leaned toward Mister Puss, who stepped near me on the table. His purr rumbled as he slid his snout across my cheek, rising to my ear.

"I'm listening," I told him. "Spill it."

*Hot mama.*

Crossing my arms, I gave him a look.

*What a creep.*

Seth Douglas had been there in the scene with Mister Puss, mere inches out of the frame. And I had already witnessed, more than once, how the obnoxious kid was the very embodiment of creepiness. He made my skin crawl. But at the moment, I was consumed by another idea that made me far more uneasy.

What if Paige Yeats was at the bottom of this? It seemed unthinkable.

# 11

Paige Yeats had a "higher cause." She said it was "worth fighting for." She also said, "The world's a better place with one less gun nut."

She had strongly held beliefs. Fine. But if she had used those beliefs to justify zapping Ellen Locke to the hereafter with charred toes, there would be consequences—not only for Paige and for hubby Thad Manning but, more broadly, for Dumont and for Questman Center for the Performing Arts, which would be cast adrift, minus its newly acquired lifeline to the staggering assets of Paige's father, Glenn Yeats.

Ten days had passed since Sheriff Simms and I spent an afternoon reviewing the video files, and Mary Questman was now expected home in about a week. What would *she* think if—after leaving Dumont for a long and restful holiday, after leaving her beloved Mister Puss entrusted to the care of Marson and me, after leaving her namesake Questman Center in the capable hands of promising new leadership—what would Mary Questman think if she came back to a perfect shitstorm?

That Saturday morning, Glee Savage ran a little update.

**Inside Dumont**

*Trouble brewing for local film project*
*as cast fears return to Dumont*

By Glee Savage

•

NOVEMBER 23, DUMONT, WI — Everything got off to a beautiful start three weeks ago when Hollywood heartthrob and Dumont native Thad Manning began shooting test scenes here for *Home Sweet Humford*, his first film project as director.

That day ended in tragedy, however, when the film crew's chief electrician, Ellen Locke, was electrocuted by a live extension cord in a vat of icy drinks. From the outset, circumstances of Locke's demise were deemed suspicious, and now, according to Dumont County sheriff Thomas Simms, his investigation is treating the death as a homicide.

The performing arts are riddled with superstitions and taboos ("break a leg," "the Scottish play," etc.), so it's little wonder that *Humford*'s production team is feeling spooked by the murder of a crew member on the first day of filming.

"I've never thought much about omens," said investor Conrad Houghes by phone from California. "But come on —this does *not* bode well for the project."

Zeiss Shotwell, director of photography, echoed those sentiments, telling the *Register*, "The show must go on—stiff lip and all that—but I don't know anyone on the cast or crew who's itching to resume filming in Dumont."

And that reluctance has now spread from the production team to the guilds and unions representing them. A spokesperson for the acting guild told us, "Our first concern will always rest with the safety of our members. We're considering revoking our approval of this project if the circumstances of Ellen Locke's death are not quickly resolved, with the assurance there is no ongoing danger."

Thad Manning, whose interest in the project is not only financial, but deeply personal, told us, "The unsolved murder is threatening the future of this film, at least in Dumont. Sure, we could move the on-location shooting somewhere else, or scrap it altogether, but I'm determined not to do that. Without Dumont, there can be no *Home Sweet Humford*. I hope not to disappoint the community."

Sheriff Simms told the *Register*, "My department is doing everything within its power to solve this crime and to enable Mr. Manning to continue filming here. However, the investigation has been seriously hampered by lack of access to persons of interest."

Last week, Simms issued a public appeal for photos and videos that were made by onlookers during the October 31 filming.

Simms now reports, "We've been flooded with submissions, and we thank the people of Dumont for responding. To date, though, we have discovered no new evidence that sheds light on Ellen Locke's death."

The investigation might have come to a standstill, but activity at our loft that Saturday morning was anything but leisurely. We had gotten word from Clem Carter, our builder, that we could expect to move into our "perfect house" by mid-December—within a month—so Marson and I had entered a phase he described as "pre-packing." Nothing was boxed up yet, but the boxes themselves had appeared, and we were making lists, which grew longer by the day.

Like most cats, Mister Puss had a fixation with boxes—nesting in them, curling into impossibly cramped spaces—so he welcomed their appearance with playful abandon, but he also seemed wary of this disruption of the natural order. What, exactly, was going on?

Marson was fine with all this. An obsessive planner and a stickler for detail, he threw himself into the task at hand—while I found it dizzying. Needing any excuse to come up for air, I was cheered when my phone rang. It was my mother calling.

After the usual greetings, Inez said to me, "You sound stressed, sweetie."

I laughed. "I was about to say the same thing to *you*. What's up?"

She paused. "You'll never guess who just sent me a letter."

"You're probably right." I stabbed at it: "Brad Pitt? Michelle Obama?"

"Glee Savage."

That stopped me cold. "Oh? What'd she ... want?"

"I was afraid to open the envelope. She's had forty years to stew at me—and with good reason. After so long, I thought the silence would last beyond the grave. And I was comfortable with that. I mean, no news is good news, right?"

"*Mom*," I said, "what did she want?"

"She heard that I was recently in Dumont. She wonders if I'm planning a return visit. She wants to talk."

"Interesting. What was her tone?"

"Vague," said Inez. "Do you think it's a trap?"

"Don't be nuts. What's a life-shattering betrayal between friends?"

"Jesus..."

"She reached out to you, Mom. I think you should respond."

The line seemed to go dead.

"Still there?" I asked.

"Yes. God, I dread this. Do you happen to have her email address?"

"Sure." I gave Inez the address and wished her luck. We rang off.

From inside one of the brown corrugated boxes, Mister Puss peered out at me, with only his ears and eyes visible above one of the flaps.

Marson walked past the dining table, scratching something on his clipboard. "Was that Inez?"

As I began to explain why she called, my phone rang again. This time, it was Sheriff Simms.

"Hey, Brody. Sorry to bother you at home."

"No bother at all. Any progress?"

"A little. Late yesterday, Wesley Sugita called me. I'd already talked to him a couple of times last week, questioning him about his quick response at the murder scene. He must've thought I was accusing him of being *too* efficient, as if he'd planned it all—and in fact, that's a possibility I haven't ruled out. So he was nervous. And he called me last night to say that he was flying back to Dumont—wants to help the investigation and, presumably, clear himself."

I recalled, "He promised full cooperation when we interviewed him at the Manor House. He offered to return if needed. I was impressed—it was the attitude of a concerned citizen."

"But it could also point to guilt," said Simms. "He seemed a little too eager to please. He's arriving this afternoon."

Because Wes had told us he was gay, and because I had established a measure of trust with him, Simms asked if I could sit in when they met later that day. Naturally, I agreed. Simms also wondered if the three of us could meet on "friendlier ground" than his office at headquarters. I offered the use of the conference room at our Miles & Norris architecture offices. On a Saturday, no one else would be there.

Simms was waiting at the curb in his tan sedan when I arrived to open up, shortly before four o'clock. He had dressed as nattily as he would for any workday—smartly tailored dark suit, boldly striped silk tie—and I wondered if he and Gloria had plans for a nice dinner out later on. Or, more likely, did he mean to impress upon Wes Sugita that this meeting was serious business?

I had brought Mister Puss along (Marson was happy not to have him underfoot while getting things organized at the loft), and Simms greeted both of us warmly as I unlocked the street door and stepped inside. Unclipping the cat's leash, I realized that my logic for bringing him had nothing to do with keeping him out of Marson's way. Rather, I meant to impress upon Wes Sugita that this meeting was *not* such serious business—just a productive chat among friends.

Good grief, I thought. Was I playing "good cop" to Simms's "bad cop"?

Waiting in the outer office for Wes to arrive, I asked Simms, "How are Gloria and little Tommy? Haven't seen them in a while."

Simms beamed. "Thanks for asking—they're great. Tommy's still loving school, third grade now—has a sleepover tonight with some Scout friends. Which means, Gloria and I are looking forward to some nice, quiet alone-time at home this evening." He winked at me, confirming that the suit was not for a night out, but for Wes.

And moments later, Wes pulled up at the curb in a bland blue compact that had the stripped and sanitized look of a rental car. Parking behind Simms's unmarked cruiser, he peered through the side window to check the address of the building, then got out of the car.

I opened the office door, telling him, "You found it. Welcome back, Wes."

"Thanks, Brody." He hustled across the sidewalk and through the door, wearing a puffy yellow ski parka, rubbing his hands as though they were freezing. It wasn't all *that* cold for a gray afternoon in late November, but it was a far cry from California weather.

Simms greeted him matter-of-factly, as if Wes had popped over from next door.

I asked Wes, "Would you like some hot coffee? Easy to make some." When he declined, I said, "Then let's get comfortable in the conference room."

He and Simms followed as I led them back through the offices. Mister Puss brought up the rear.

Closing the door behind us, I invited them to sit at the oblong table that occupied much of the room where Marson and I normally met with design clients; today, though, the topic was murder. Simms set a folder on the table and spread out a few files. I'd brought a small notebook. Wes was empty-handed.

Simms said, "Tell us why you're here, Mr. Sugita," which I found abrupt.

But Wes was unfazed by Simms's tone—or he was too polite to show it. He said, "Thank you for making time for me, Sheriff. I flew here today because I hope to shed some light on what happened to Ellen Locke."

"Do you *know* what happened?" said Simms. "Do you know who did it?"

Wes shook his head gently. "No. I wish I had simple answers for you, but I don't. Ellen didn't have many friends—I wasn't alone in disliking her—but I did work with her, so I probably knew her better than most. If there are insights you'd like me to share, just ask."

Simms looked at me with a subtle nod, prodding me to pick up the conversation.

Just then, Mister Puss hopped up from the floor to sit in Wes's lap, purring.

"Sorry," I said, "let me take him."

"But I like cats," Wes assured me with a broad smile, a rare display of emotion. "Good, good kitty," he said, petting Mister Puss. "Beautiful Oolong."

The purring intensified.

"Wes," I said, "you told us before that you 'resented' Ellen. She was younger and less experienced than you, but as gaffer, she became your boss."

"Correct. However, I couldn't blame my disappointment on the success of someone else. Such thinking is not only unwise, but irrational."

Simms said, "That's a commendable attitude. I doubt if I could've been so philosophical about it."

I wasn't sure how to interpret Simms's words. Was he paying Wes a compliment? Or was he trying to pin him with a motive for murder?

Wes shrugged. "Philosophical restraint sometimes has its re-wards—karma, many call it. You see, Sheriff, although I played no role in Ellen's death, her untimely passing has already advanced my career. Thad Manning has asked me to take over for her in *Home Sweet Humford*—if the project moves forward."

"Karma," Simms repeated, making note of it.

I said to Wes, "Last time we talked, you were forthright about being gay, which I didn't see coming. If you'll pardon a personal question, may I ask when you first came out?"

"I 'found myself' during college, and once I understood it, I accepted it. You're younger than I am, Brody, so you may not get this: I was never closeted, but I've always been discreet. An Asian thing, maybe."

Truly curious, I asked, "Is there someone special in your life?"

"There has been, a couple of times, but I'm single now and no longer looking. What's the expression? I'm 'wed to my work.' And I love my job. It's magic."

Simms was searching for something on his phone. "Can you take a look at this, Mr. Sugita? It's a short video clip that was captured by one of the cameras at the time Ellen Locke was elec-trocuted." Simms held the phone so Wes could see it, then played the video. Mister Puss raised his head from the edge of the table and watched it, too.

I could see it well enough to recognize the action:

Ellen Locke, in her bizarre getup with an assault rifle slung over one shoulder, moves into the frame, reaches deep into the gal-vanized vat, and freezes for a few seconds before spasmodically dropping to the ground with steam rising from her toes in the wet grass. The video begins to jerk and flicker as Wesley Sugita rushes into the frame from the opposite direction before the screen goes black.

Simms asked Wes, "When you ran toward the vat, what did you think had happened?"

"I thought Ellen had probably been killed. Electrocuted."

"But you didn't try to help her?"

"The only way to 'help' her was to shut everything down. I assumed she was already beyond helping, so my first concern was to ensure that others were safe—there were *kids* right there."

I asked, "Wasn't that a huge risk—to yourself?"

"I was the only one who could fix it. It's my job."

Looking a bit chastened, Simms tucked his phone away.

"When we sat down today," I said to Wes, "you told us that you probably knew Ellen better than most others because you worked with her. Did you ever socialize?"

"God, no. Off the job, I saw her as little as possible."

"But were there times when you needed to connect after hours, so to speak?"

"Sure."

I fished: "Were you ever at her home?"

Simms perked up.

Wes said, "Now and then—to drop something off or look over a script."

"What sort of place did she have? House, apartment, condo?"

"Small house. One of those bungalows just off the Ten in Rosemead. Decent neighborhood. God-awful decorating—I mean, you saw how she *dressed*."

Simms was taking notes.

I asked, "She lived alone, right?"

"She *did*," said Wes, "but not lately. Last couple times I was there, so was Zeiss Shotwell. I mean, he was *living* there."

Simms and I gave each other a blank look.

Wes asked, "Zeiss never mentioned that?"

"No," said Simms.

Two sources—Wes Sugita and Miranda Lemarr—had now told us that the murder victim had been living with Zeiss Shotwell, who, three weeks earlier, had supplied Sheriff Simms with contradictory contact information before checking out of the Manor House and leaving Dumont.

Immediately after our meeting with Wes Sugita, Simms ran a check on the Los Angeles address given by Shotwell, finding tax and postal records linking the property to him. Shotwell, therefore, had not exactly *lied* about it, but thanks to his whopping omission, he was no longer a mere person of interest; he'd landed squarely on the suspect list.

Then Simms went home for some alone-time with his wife.

And I took Mister Puss back to the loft, where Marson had put in a full day of pre-packing. We decided on an easy dinner at the nearby First Avenue Bistro, leaving the cat to romp with the cardboard boxes.

Nancy Sanderson saved "our" table for us—an unexpected gesture, considering how late we'd phoned on a Saturday. She greeted us at the door, then led us through the crowded dining room to the corner table, between the fireplace and the front windows, where we could keep an eye on the entire room as well as activity on the street. At that hour, Dumont's main drag was hardly cosmopolitan, but it offered an animated note of connection to the outside world. Off to my side, a glowing fire of oak and birch lent its crackle to the demure hubbub of the well-dressed patrons, whose amiable chatter drifted through the cozy room.

Nancy recited a few specials—the lamb *en croûte* sounded perfect for the weekend before Thanksgiving—turkey and yams could wait. Nancy then left menus and stepped away to get the bottle of Bordeaux we ordered. While she moved between the tables, I glanced back toward the street door. Near it hung a large framed photo, one that had been shot in that same room eleven days earlier, the picture of Miranda Lemarr posing with Nancy and her special friend, Nia Butler. All three women looked radiant in the captured moment.

When dinner was finished and coffee was poured, the earlier seating was long gone, and Nancy came over to the table, asking if we had a few minutes to review our catering needs for Thanksgiving. Good idea, so we asked her to sit with us.

Because we had done this many times, there was little to decide other than the final number of guests, which was still in flux but probably eight. We wouldn't need Nancy or staff for serving or cleanup, and the meal itself was predictably traditional. Marson would take charge of the bird, start to finish.

Marson told Nancy, "I hope you won't be working the whole day. Will you have some time for your own celebration?"

"Sure," she said, closing her notepad. "I have a couple other jobs like yours to deliver, but the restaurant is closed that day, so I'll be clear by midafternoon. And guess what—Nia offered to cook for the two of us."

"Wow," I said with a broad smile, "there's a switcheroo. Did you accept the offer?"

"You *bet* I did."

We all laughed.

I couldn't help thinking that Nancy Sanderson and Nia Butler, the city's code-enforcement officer, were such an unlikely couple, but it was heartwarming to know that they had found each other. "By the way," I said to Nancy, "that photo of you gals with Miranda turned out *great*."

"It really did." Then Nancy's smile faded. "But I'm worried about the movie."

"How so?" asked Marson.

"Well, I just hope Thad Manning is able to *finish* it—here in Dumont. You probably read about the trouble with the production unions. And *now*, Nia tells me, the city is considering pulling the film permits. I mean, look what happened at the test shoot—murder." Nancy slowly shook her head, adding, "An unsolved murder."

Marson and I turned to look at each, perplexed.

And over his shoulder, I could see through the window to the darkness of First Avenue, where a pair of hunched figures passed under a streetlamp, talking. It was Darnell Passalacqua, the hair and makeup artist, with Wesley Sugita, the assistant electrician who had just been promoted to gaffer, replacing the late Ellen Locke.

# 12

Three days later, on the Tuesday morning before Thanksgiving, I was beginning the workday at my office, sorting and trashing the scores of emails that had arrived overnight, when one of them caught my attention, escaping the junk folder.

From: Mary Questman
To: Brody Norris, A.I.A.

Brody, love, although my days in San Miguel will soon draw to a close, I wonder if I could ask a favor of you prior to my return.

Looking through my calendar last night, I found that Mister Puss is now due for a booster shot—distemper, I believe. Had I returned as originally planned, this would all be taken care of by now, but Mexico has been such a delightful getaway, I'm afraid I simply lost track.

If you have time, could you possibly take Mister Puss to see Dr. Phelps? He'll know what needs to be done, and he can charge the services, as usual, to my account. My apologies for the inconvenience, Brody.

Hoping all's well on the home front. Please extend my love and smooches to both Marson and His Majesty. And I meant to ask: Did our little one in fact appear in Thad's movie? So eager to hear all about it!

All my love,
Mary

Mary was clearly overdue for an earful. But I had no inclination to dampen the remainder of her time away, so I responded that I was more than happy to accompany Mister Puss to the vet. I signed off with love, then tapped SEND.

The cat had come to the office with Marson and me, which was now routine. Sunning himself in a shaft of morning light from the east window, he lifted his head to look at me, perhaps wondering why I had grown so quiet. When I patted my knee, he sauntered over and hopped into my lap, purring.

I told him, "Mary wants to hear all about your movie."

He purred louder, reaching his paws to my shoulder.

I said, "She's coming home soon. I know you've missed her."

*Yes. A little.*

Meanwhile, I had learned from Thad Manning that Zeiss Shotwell, the cinematographer, was arriving from California that afternoon to meet with Thad, review the test footage, and brainstorm a path forward, should it become impossible to continue shooting the location scenes in Dumont. They would hold their meeting at Questman Center, where Thad's wife, Paige Yeats, had offered use of the facility's conference room and video equipment.

Thad had invited me to sit in on this meeting and asked me to invite Sheriff Thomas Simms as well. Simms jumped at the chance, and we agreed to meet the others at Questman Center at two o'clock.

Shortly before noon, Simms phoned me. "Hey, Brody. I've got an idea. Does Zeiss Shotwell know for a fact that you're gay?"

I had to think back. "He might assume that I'm gay, but I don't recall saying anything to him about it—never mentioned Marson, for instance." With a laugh, I asked, "Why?"

"He has a reputation as a womanizer, and from what I've heard, he seems to have no qualms about trying to poach attached women."

I said, "That would fit—how about that 'love circus' he had with

Miranda Lemarr, Ellen Locke, and Conrad Houghes?"

"Exactly. So here's my idea: What if you show up with your pretty 'wife' today? It could add an unexpected dimension to a very dry meeting."

"I like it. Have you talked to Heather?"

"Way ahead of you," said Simms. "We'll meet you in the parking lot at two."

We were speaking of Heather Vance, the county medical examiner. She had done "decoy" duty before, posing as my other half. We looked good together—we were both in our thirties, both young professionals approaching middle age, both sharing a certain sense of style that gave us the appearance of a convincing couple.

Naturally, I phoned her at once to ask what she was wearing. (When duty calls, I may occasionally portray a straight man, but hey, you can't leave wardrobe to chance.) Good thing I asked. The tie I'd worn to the office would have been a hideous clash with her outfit, but after a quick switch with Marson, I was good to go.

Shortly before two, outside Questman Center, I was waiting in my car with Mister Puss when I saw Simms pull into the lot. Heather Vance had ridden with him. Moments later, we were standing together on the terrace in front of the entrance.

We agreed that Heather would use her real name, but there would be no mention of her job. Then we made our way toward the lobby doors.

But Heather stopped. Looking at me, she shook her head.

"What?" I asked.

"I have *never* seen a straight man walk a cat on a leash."

I countered, "Have you ever seen a gay man do it?"

"Just you."

Simms laughed.

She had a point. "Okay," I said, handing the leash to Heather. Mister Puss sat, looking up at me, bewildered.

With hands on hips, I peered down at him. "Be nice to Mommy."

Squinting up into the sunlight, he appeared to wink at me.

Once inside, I led the others across the vast lobby to the executive suites, where the swishy receptionist, Timothy, told us, "She's expecting you."

Paige Yeats welcomed us into her office, where Thad Manning had already arrived, accompanied by Zeiss Shotwell, who was dressed in his usual black outfit. On that cold afternoon, he had added a black silk scarf to his black wool turtleneck.

Noting the cat on the leash, held by Heather, he said to me with mild surprise, "I thought Oolong was *yours*."

"He is," I said, "but not when Mommy's around."

Heather and I exchanged a doting glance. Mister Puss rubbed against her ankles, purring. We were the perfect little family.

Zeiss also purred, giving Heather the once-over. "I don't believe we've met."

"Heather Vance," she said, "a.k.a. Mrs. Brody Norris." She extended her hand.

Zeiss clasped her fingers, telling me, "I admire your taste. How long have you been together?"

Heather answered for me, "We go way back. But it seems like … yesterday."

Paige Yeats, who had been clued to this ruse, told Heather playfully, "Watch out for *that* one, Mrs. Norris. He's a bit of a home-wrecker."

"Nonsense," Zeiss assured Heather. Under his breath, he added, "It's just that some homes are more prone to wrecking than others."

"Well, now," said Thad, "since everyone's here, shall we get down to business?"

Paige told him, "Everything's set up in the conference room. Laurencio should be waiting for you."

Aha, I thought—the adorably geeky Laurencio. Whatever would he think when I showed up with my "wife"?

Thad led us out of Paige's office and down a short hall to the conference room, which served primarily as Questman Center's boardroom, sumptuously appointed with wood-paneled walls, deep wool carpeting, a long granite-topped table, and a dozen high-backed executive chairs, upholstered with supple leather the color of wet cement.

At one end of the table, a video display covered most of the wall. The room was outfitted with all manner of A/V equipment, tastefully concealed. Laurencio had arranged several remote controls on the table, and he set about instructing Thad in their use while the rest of us—Zeiss, Simms, Heather, and I—filed in and chose seats.

Noticing me as I entered the room, Laurencio looked up from what he was doing and blushed. "Hi there, Mr. Norris. Nice to see you again." Then his jolly expression collapsed when he realized that Mister Puss was in the care of Heather.

I stepped Laurencio and Heather aside to introduce them, explaining, "It's not what it seems, Laurencio. But there's a reason. Play along with us, okay?" I touched his arm.

He responded with an eager nod.

Then he told Thad, "You're all set, Mr. Manning. If you need anything, I'll be downstairs in the studio. Use the call button."

As Laurencio was leaving the room, I cornered him outside the doorway. "Is there teleconferencing from this room?"

"You bet."

"Can you spy on us from downstairs?"

"I wouldn't quite put it that way, but ... sure."

I asked him, "Switch it on, okay? The sheriff and I will come down after a while to take a look."

"Got it." And Laurencio bounded down the stairs at the end of the hall.

Stepping back into the conference room, I closed the door and joined the others at the table, sitting between Sheriff Simms and

Heather Vance, who held Mister Puss in her lap. Thad Manning sat with Zeiss on the other side of the table. Zeiss had positioned himself directly across from Heather, and he wasn't subtle about establishing eye contact with her.

While Thad recited some preliminary concerns regarding the impact of Ellen Locke's murder on the future of his film, my gaze drifted toward the various baffles in the ceiling and along the walls, where speakers and electronics were kept out of sight. In one of the black crevices, I noticed a red pilot light blink on, and I assumed that we were now being watched by Laurencio downstairs in the editing suite.

Sheriff Simms said to Thad, "My office is well aware of the urgency you feel in wanting the murder resolved. I want that, too—every bit as much as you do. Logistics and jurisdictions have made this case a tough one to get a handle on, but we *are* working on it, and we're making some progress now."

"That's *great*," said Thad, cheered by Simms's words. "What can you—"

"Hold on," said Zeiss. "I flew out here today to review the test shots and discuss artistic contingencies. But all I'm hearing is talk about the investigation. So what are we here for? The film? Or the murder?"

"Both," said Thad, sounding annoyed. "Completion of *Home Sweet Humford* depends on bringing Ellen Locke's killer to justice. If we don't do that, it may be impossible to continue filming here. And without Dumont, there's no *Humford*. It's that simple."

"Why?" said Zeiss. "Look, Thad, I know this town has emotional significance for you, and I agree—it's a lovely setting, reminds me of a charming little village where I used to visit a favorite aunt each summer in Shropshire. I also agree—the test shots were beautiful. I hope we can proceed here. But if not, good God, don't scrap the project. Just find another town."

"Now, don't *you* start," said Thad, disgusted. "Christ, you're sounding like Connie Houghes. In case I haven't been clear, I'll say it again: without Dumont, the project is dead. Period. Full stop—old chap."

Zeiss tossed his hands. "Look. I can shoot a gorgeous film for you. Anywhere. But I can't solve a murder for you."

I said, "But maybe you can help."

Syrupy sweet, Heather told Zeiss, "I'm *sure* you can."

Caught off guard by her wiles, he smiled while primping a lock of hair behind his ear. Eyeing her, he asked softly, "You, uh, think I can help, do you?"

"Oh, *yes*," she purred.

Zeiss purred.

Mister Puss purred.

Zeiss turned to Simms. "How might I be of help, Sheriff?"

Simms said simply, "Tell us about your relationship with the victim."

"Relationship?" said Zeiss. "With Ellen? We rubbed shoulders, as they say, while working on various projects. You see, Sheriff, Hollywood's a smaller town than most people think. Everyone in the industry seems to know each other."

"You mean," asked Simms, "you and Ellen Locke weren't romantically involved?"

Zeiss blanched. He hesitated before saying, "We had *very* little in common."

"Then why would you move in with her?"

"You can't be *serious*." Zeiss's protest was unconvincing.

Simms persisted: "A bungalow in Rosemead, correct?"

"Wherever did you hear such a thing?"

"Two sources," said Simms. "As you've already noted, Hollywood's a small town."

Heather jumped in. With a soothing tone, she said to Zeiss,

"Sometimes, circumstances can 'look bad'—on the surface—but deep down, I'm *sure* you have nothing to hide. I've always admired a man with the courage to step up to his civic duty." She broke into a flirty smile.

I wondered if she was about to blow him a kiss, and I feared she might be overplaying it. But it worked.

Zeiss squared his shoulders. With a sniff of resolve, he told Simms, "It's true. I did stay with Ellen—briefly. From the start, I never thought it would last. We were so different. After all, she was an aficionado of guns, which I find abhorrent." Summing up their relationship, he bragged, "It was just sex—and quite good, in fact."

Simms asked, "Now, *why* didn't you mention this before?"

"You never asked me—not specifically—if I lived with her. And in fact, I was merely *sleeping* with her. I never changed my residence from the LA address."

"So you're no longer 'sleeping' in Rosemead?"

"Of course not. Ellen's place was a dump."

Simms checked his notes. "And when was the last time you slept there?"

Zeiss looked bewildered. "I'm not sure. Before Ellen died, certainly—which was nearly four weeks ago."

"You never went back to pick up your stuff?"

Zeiss asked archly, "Stuff?"

"Your *things*. Clothes and such."

"I never moved *in*, Sheriff. Toothbrush and razor—that's about it."

This, I thought, didn't quite square with what Wesley Sugita had told us about his visits to Ellen Locke's house: "Last couple times I was there, so was Zeiss Shotwell. I mean, he was *living* there." To my ear, that was not a description of a man with a toothbrush.

Thad Manning was experimenting with one of the remote controls. A still from the test scene appeared on the large video display—a postcard-perfect image of Miranda Lemarr and Mister Puss, both looking impossibly beautiful in the golden glow of the afternoon sun, with a backdrop of Dumont's downtown commons that rivaled the best work of an Oscar-worthy set designer.

"Just *look* at that," said Thad Manning. "It's magical. *This* is the reason *Home Sweet Humford* belongs in Dumont."

Heather said, "It's amazing, Zeiss. You're a *very* talented man." She winked at him.

Zeiss winked back.

Sheriff Simms pulled the phone from his pocket and checked its display. "I need to take this," he said, rising. "Excuse me."

This was our agreed-upon cue to clear out of the room and leave Heather alone with Zeiss.

Thad rose from his chair and took one of the remotes from the table. "I need to check on something downstairs with Laurencio."

"Honey," I said to Heather, "maybe I should step outside with Mister Puss. He's acting kinda squirmy."

The cat gave me a quizzical look.

"Good idea," said Heather, handing me the leash.

I walked Mister Puss to the door, then turned back to see Zeiss eyeing Heather like an alley cat sizing up a mouse. With a tone of concern, I asked Heather, "You'll, uh … be all right?"

She tossed her head back and laughed airily. "Don't be *silly*, dear. Take your time."

I stepped out of the conference room and closed the door.

Simms and Thad were waiting for me. We rushed through the hall to the stairs and went down to the tech level, where we followed another hall back to the video studio and, beyond it, the editing suite. Laurencio was waiting for us as we scrambled through the door. "The show's about to begin," he said.

Simms, Thad, and I took seats at the table facing the seven-foot video screen, which displayed a live picture of Heather and Zeiss upstairs in the conference room. Laurencio tweaked the audio, and we could hear their conversation clearly. Mister Puss hopped up to the tabletop and sat, watching the video as intently as the rest of us. Laurencio then moved over from his console to stand behind us, joining the audience.

Upstairs, Zeiss Shotwell wasn't wasting any time. With his elbows on the table, he leaned toward Heather, sitting across from him. "You're a beautiful woman," he said. "It must be … frustrating. Here in Dumont."

Heather sighed. "How did you guess?"

Zeiss grinned. "I can be most perceptive."

She leaned on her elbows, reflecting his pose across the table. Quietly, she asked, "Can you keep a secret?"

He mimed zipping his lip.

"I think"—she choked on her words—"I think my husband might be gay."

Zeiss chortled. "I have to admit, that was my impression. I mean, could he *be* more obvious?"

"Thanks," I said to the screen.

Simms laughed. Laurencio patted my shoulder.

Heather told Zeiss, "So there are times when I have to wonder what it might be like to … to …"

"Yes?" asked Zeiss. "What it might be like to … what?"

"To be with another man—a real man."

Zeiss froze, smiling. His eyes looked ready to pop out of their sockets.

"And that's my secret," said Heather. "You promised to keep it."

"Trust me," he said, "it's strictly *entre nous*. May I confide in you as well?"

Heather nodded.

He said, "I wouldn't want this getting back to the others."

"Strictly *entre nous*," she assured him.

I looked over my shoulder to ask Laurencio, "Can we record this?"

"Already doing it." Laurencio pulled out a chair and sat next to me.

Zeiss said to Heather, "I hope they get this murder business straightened out. Then the film can remain in Dumont, which would mean: I'll be spending plenty of time here. I'd really like to … to *know* you better."

"Likewise, I'm sure," she said, sounding ditzy.

Zeiss rose from his chair and stepped around to Heather. Then he sat on the table mere inches from her, looking down at her. "You'd be available?"

"Mm-hmm." She licked her lips. "And you, Zeiss?"

"That's *my* secret."

"It's safe with me. You *are* unattached, right?"

"I am now," he said. "You see, my involvement with Ellen Locke was … complicated. But it's over." With a laugh, he added, "Obviously."

Heather shared the laugh. Then she frowned. "What do you mean, 'complicated'?"

"We were married."

Upstairs in the conference room, Heather drew a faint gasp.

Downstairs in the editing suite: "Holy shit." "Bingo." "Pay dirt."

Zeiss continued, "We both wanted it secret. We were very different people, but oddly, we met each other's needs. Imagine my surprise when I found out about her insurance. That—plus her other assets—it was quite a windfall."

Sheriff Simms mumbled, "Do tell."

Heather said to Zeiss, "As I recall, Brody mentioned that you filled out an affidavit during a previous interview. You said you were single."

Zeiss reminded her, "By that time, Ellen was already dead."

"Ahhh," said Heather, smiling up at him.

"Which brings us back to your question. And my answer: I am indeed 'unattached.'" Twitching his brows, he reached for Heather's hands and pulled her up from the chair. "Let me get a better look at you."

While listening to this, Simms scratched some notes.

Thad Manning kept his eyes on the screen, shaking his head with dismay.

Laurencio and I turned to each other, sharing a grimace. His knee touched mine.

Zeiss told Heather, "I like what I see."

Heather asked, "Do you also like yams?"

Zeiss rattled his head. "What?" He pulled Heather close to him.

She explained, "It's almost Thanksgiving, and I always fix some candied yams."

"All right…"

She added, "I like mine with pineapple."

Sheriff Simms stood and moved to the door. "Upstairs *now*—before he lands her on the table."

We had agreed that Heather's safeword would be *pineapple*.

And we had just discovered that Zeiss Shotwell had a motive for murder.

## 13

Wednesday, the day before Thanksgiving, felt as if the holiday had already arrived. Marson stayed home from work that day, fussing with preparations for Thursday's big dinner at the loft.

I had phoned the veterinarian's office about the booster shot for Mister Puss, and the receptionist suggested Wednesday at eleven. "Not much on the books that morning—we'll be closing at noon."

So Mister Puss curled up in the passenger seat as I drove him out to the edge of town for his appointment with Jim Phelps. It had been a cold night, with frost, and the day had dawned bright and crisp. By late morning, the frost had vanished, and the bucolic landscape of fields and fence posts whisked past me under a theatrically blue autumn sky. It was still cold; the car's heater lent a soft background whoosh to the sound of the radio, which played something frisky and Baroque—probably Vivaldi.

With no other vehicle in sight, the pleasant setting was conducive to stray thoughts as I drove along the rustic road.

I recalled the moment, the prior afternoon, when geeky Laurencio's knee bumped mine under the table in the editing suite. It had been inadvertent, surely. Or it might have been a test, a subtle signal he sent, intended to gauge my response—and I responded in no way whatever. Except that I did not pull away from him. Except that I instantly fantasized about slipping his glasses off and running ten fingers through his thick dark hair, raven black. Except that I would never act on that impulse. Except that I considered it. Except that it still stuck in my mind.

And I recalled rushing upstairs with Sheriff Simms and Thad Manning, responding to Heather Vance's invocation of "pine-apple," then bursting into the conference room where she and Zeiss Shotwell had engaged in a coy dance of deception, teasing the topics of murder and infidelity.

She was fine. Zeiss had not "landed her on the table," as Sheriff Simms conjectured. In fact, when we interrupted them, Heather had gained the upper hand, landing Zeiss in her own chair and towering over him in her heels, with one of the stilettos poised pointedly at his groin. "Try *that* again," she told him, "and you'll be singing falsetto."

And I recalled wondering if Simms would confront him on the spot with what we had learned—that Zeiss Shotwell had been married to Ellen Locke, whom he claimed to abhor while profiting from her death. But Simms didn't mention that we'd heard Zeiss tell his secret to Heather, strictly *entre nous*.

I had to give Simms credit. My own inclination would have been to pounce on Zeiss, cuff him, and haul him downtown. But that was a cop-show cliché, and I realized that Simms had a more farsighted approach. He'd overheard Zeiss confiding to Heather in the context of planning a tryst, but that wasn't proof of murder; it could easily have been braggadocio. Better to let Zeiss believe, at least temporarily, that he was not under suspicion. Simms's circumspection served to remind me why *he* was the sheriff—and I was but a mild-mannered, if somewhat nosy, architect.

Glancing up ahead now, I saw the folksy wooden sign with bent-twig lettering that announced I was arriving at the practice of James Phelps, DVM, so I slowed the car and entered the gravel parking lot, which was empty. The earlier appointments, if there were any, had ended, and I hoped the kindly doctor's little patients were now on the mend, resting comfortably at home.

A split-rail fence separated the parking area from a patch of wild-looking lawn, with a path down the middle leading to the quaint offices, clad in shake shingles that had weathered long ago to a silvery gray. Though Mister Puss was wearing his leash and harness, I carried him from the car to the door. As I swung it open and stepped inside, a bell on a spring heralded our arrival.

The receptionist looked up from her computer. "Good morning, Mr. Norris. All set for Mister Puss. Have a seat—Dr. Jim will be with you in a minute."

Having been there several times before, I picked my usual chair near the window, next to a pile of magazines, and set Mister Puss on my lap, where he could keep an eye on everything—including an aquarium, which was soothing, and a parrot in a cage, which was annoying, and a lethargic snake in a terrarium, which still creeped me out. But the cat had no interest in these lowlier denizens of the animal kingdom. Instead, he watched TV.

A cable news program played at low volume on an older set—with a picture tube—mounted near the door. A commercial was running, promoting the region's largest flooring and carpeting business, owned by Walter Zakarian, a local fop and widow-walker. For many years, he had appeared in his own commercials wearing a cape and crown, brandishing a scepter, and calling himself the Karastan King. "If you're shopping *anywhere* else," he decreed, "you're paying too much!"

Dumont was a small town, and I knew Walter Zakarian well enough to understand that he was an aging, portly closet case. He had a condo in Puerto Vallarta, which he visited for sex holidays with paid talent, discreetly removed from the Karastan Kingdom by thousands of miles because he thought it was "better for business" to limit his local escapades to the seduction of wealthy older women.

He had tried this with Mary Questman, and she had played along with his game for a while (enjoying, apparently, his carnal ministrations), but when she tired of him, she turned the tables and tossed him out like an empty husk. She moved on.

And now she had literally moved on—traveling again after so many years, leaving Dumont to rediscover a bigger world—while Walter languished with his crown and scepter, fooling no one, itching for his next furtive getaway with a trick in the tropics because it was better for business. I truly felt sorry for him, but my pity would only offend him, so it was never discussed.

Thirty seconds later, a toothy talking head in Green Bay announced an update on a "perplexing matter down in Dumont," then cut away to an interview of Paige Yeats, recorded in her office at Questman Center.

The reporter, Sunny Skyes, who doubled as the station's weather hostess, explained to viewers that the famed Hollywood actress had recently taken over as executive director of the performing-arts center, succeeding Basil Hutchins, who had retired to the Canary Islands. "But six weeks later, his whereabouts are still unknown?"

"That's right, Sunny," said Paige, "and frankly, we're worried. At first, we attributed this to a disruption of communications, caused by a storm. But that situation has long passed, and we still haven't made contact with him—or even his extended family. We've tried, but it's radio silence."

Sunny was asking a follow-up question when Jim Phelps stepped out to the waiting room.

"*Hi* there, Brody. Sorry to keep you. Dawdling on the phone with Mrs. Courtney—says her Pekinese is going deaf, but I think little Pooh-Bah is just sick of hearing *her*." Laughing, he waved for me to follow. "C'mon back."

The parrot shrieked as I walked Mister Puss to the back hall.

Phelps laughed again. "Don't mind her. She just gets lonely out there."

I thought, I'd shriek too, stuck alone with that snake.

Phelps closed the door of the consultation room behind us as I set Mister Puss on the stainless-steel exam table and removed his harness. Then I sat in a molded pink plastic chair while the vet fussed with a syringe and a vial. An adjacent counter was filled with medical instruments, sell-cards for pet medicines, and a baby scale. The hospital-blue walls were decorated with faded Currier and Ives prints and yellowed charts showing the innards of dogs and cats. Bright fluorescent lighting competed with slashes of sunshine from the venetian blinds.

I told Mister Puss, "Not much longer."

He gave me a look, as if annoyed by the cheery small talk.

Phelps chewed the tip of his unlit pipe while talking. "So Mary's down in Mexico?"

I explained, "She tacked it onto her last trip, to Sedona. She's been in San Miguel a full month, but due back soon."

Phelps chuckled. "My preliminary diagnosis is that she's contracted a full-blown case of wanderlust—but it's totally benign."

"She's got the travel bug, all right. And it seems to agree with her. She's always struck me as sprightly for her age, but now she seems *reborn*."

"Good for her," said the doctor.

"But she was concerned that Mister Puss was overdue for his booster. Distemper?"

Phelps shrugged. "It could've waited, but we'll get him taken care of." Then he set down the syringe and perused the cat's charts. "It was the damnedest thing when she first brought him in here— eighteen months ago, out of the blue. I guessed he was about a year old then. Mary said he just landed on her doorstep one morning. Mighty strange. Beautiful cat like that—gotta be a purebred."

Mister Puss struck a regal pose on the exam table.

I stood to pet him, and he began to purr.

"Thataboy, Brody," said Phelps, setting the syringe on the table.

"Twiddle his face and ears."

As I did so, Mister Puss stood, reaching his paws to my shoulder. The purring intensified.

At the same time, Phelps ruffled the cat's shoulders and haunches, telling me, "He won't know what hit him."

*Like hell I won't.*

And Phelps deftly injected the loose skin behind the cat's neck.

The purring stopped. Mister Puss shot me a cross-eyed look of betrayal.

The vet disposed of the syringe, then gave the cat a once-over, checking eyes, ears, teeth, pulse. "Yep," Phelps joked, "he'll live. Oughta be good for another twelve thousand miles."

I got Mister Puss into his harness again while Phelps washed his hands. He asked over his shoulder, "Big plans for Thanksgiving?"

"Marson and I are having some people over to the loft. It's our last shindig there—moving next month."

"Nice," he said.

I asked, "How about you, Jim? Any plans?" I'd heard he was widowed, and I wasn't sure about extended family, so I thought he might be in need of an invitation.

He nodded. "Driving over to Appleton. Kendra always has a mob. Always a good time—*way* too much food."

I was glad to know he wouldn't be alone, although I had no idea who Kendra was. When I placed Mister Puss on the floor and attached his leash, Phelps spritzed the exam table with disinfectant.

He asked, "Any news on that gal who got electrocuted?" He'd apparently heard, or guessed, that I was again doing some side-kicking for Sheriff Simms.

"Actually," I said, "do you have a couple minutes?" I'd previously confabbed with him when puzzling over stymied investigations, and I admired his common sense. Plus, he'd been present during the test shoot as medical backup for the feline member of the cast.

"Sure, Brody," he said, "I've got all the time in the world—at least today I do." Then he led Mister Puss and me out of the exam room, across the hall, and into his office.

Closing the door behind us, he exchanged his lab jacket for the corduroy blazer that hung on a peg. "Make yourself comfortable," he said, and I took a seat on the small sofa. Its tufted brown leather squeaked as I settled in with the cat. Phelps sat across from us in the maple captain's chair at his desk. The room had the persnickety-sweet smell of cherry pipe tobacco.

I was about to say something, but there was a rap at the door. It opened a crack, and the receptionist poked her head in. "I'm leaving, Jim. Have a great Thanksgiving."

"Thanks, Judy. See you Monday."

She said goodbye, closed the door, and retreated down the hall. I heard her exit by a door at the back of the building, where the staff parked.

"So, then," said Phelps, "we were talking about the 'accident.'"

I nodded. "But it wasn't an accident. Sheriff Simms says it was murder."

"Yeah"—Phelps dug at his cold pipe with a tool that resembled a flattened nail—"I read about that. So tell me: Who did it?"

I laughed. "Don't know. Not yet."

"But I'll bet you have a few ideas."

"Too many," I admitted.

"So"—he banged the pipe in a heavy green glass ashtray—"how do you sort them out? The suspects."

I had to think about that. Good question. "A suspect is typically evaluated by weighing his or her motive, means, and opportunity to commit the crime. So let's take those in reverse order:

"Opportunity. We've figured out that the extension cord was dropped into the vat of ice water sometime after the lunch break, so whoever did it was *there*, on the scene, at the time of the murder. But there were well over a hundred people at the scene, working or watching, so that doesn't help us much."

Phelps said, "I was there. You were there. The sheriff was there. The killer was there. But who?"

I continued, "Who had the 'means' of committing the crime? Now, this is interesting. Because Ellen Locke was an electrician, it seems ironic that she was killed by electrocution, doesn't it? Was the killer sending a message, dropping a clue? Maybe. More to the point, who had the 'means'—or the specialized knowledge—to rig things up for fatal mischief? At first, I wondered if the killer might be another electrician, and that's certainly a possibility. But on the other hand, it wouldn't take an electrical engineer to pull this off. Anyone who was there that day should've been able to predict the effect of dropping a live extension cord, without a ground prong, into a tub of water."

Phelps said. "Yeah, any dummy knows that. Me. You. The sheriff. The killer."

"Which brings us," I said, "to the motive. In the end, the solution to a crime always seems to boil down to its motive."

"Logical." Phelps leaned back in his chair, letting his eyes drift to the ceiling. "If you know exactly why it was done, you know who done it. So: Why did someone want this woman dead?"

"We've discovered plenty of motives. And that's the problem."

Phelps grinned. "You don't say."

"Think about it. There must be thousands of reasons for killing someone, but most of those can be lumped into a handful of classic motives for murder."

"Self-defense," suggested Phelps.

"Sure. If someone is trying to kill you, and the only way to save yourself is to kill them instead, that's not 'murder.' But if the self-defense is less noble, less justified—let's say, defending yourself against a secret you don't want revealed, defending yourself against blackmail—that's murder."

Phelps said, "Another biggie: money."

"Of course. Money, greed, avarice. Since time immemorial, people have found wealth worth killing for."

"Hate," said Phelps.

"You bet, Jim. Hate, revenge, resentment. In a sense, pure hate seems like the most raw and unvarnished of motives."

Phelps added, "And let's not forget the passions of the flesh."

"Let's not, indeed. Passion, jealousy, unrequited love. It's the stuff of tragic romance—from Shakespeare to drugstore bodice rippers—and over the ages, *many* have died as victims of an over-active libido."

Running through this litany of mayhem, I had no trouble at all matching each motive we covered to individual suspects I'd considered in the mystery of Ellen Locke's death. But we had not yet covered all the possibilities.

Jim Phelps seemed to be pondering these options as well, fingers to chin. Then, looking up at me, he asked, "Have I missed anything?"

I nodded. "This may sound a little offbeat, but I can think of at least two other reasons to kill. First, what about the prospect of a murder with no motive at all—a perfect crime, a 'thrill kill' for the pure sport of it?" (I could not shake the utter weirdness of Darnell Passalacqua promoting this theory.)

Phelps looked at me with a skeptical arch of his brows.

"And second," I said, "what if Ellen Locke died as the victim of someone who was devoted to some 'higher cause'?" (I could not dismiss the cavalier attitude of Paige Yeats in declaring the world "a better place" with one less gun nut.)

Phelps paused in thought. "I dunno, Brody. Thrill kill? Higher cause? Those are fancy motives—movie motives, so to speak.

Seems to me, more often than not, you've got to really *hate* a person to want to kill'm."

"Makes sense," I said. But I thought Jim's reasoning arose mainly from his own innate goodness—as a person and as a veterinarian. He was the personification of wisdom and contentment, which seemed unfathomably distant from the worlds of Hollywood, glamour, wealth, and murder.

At my side, Mister Puss snoozed and gurgled, sleeping off his vaccine.

CHAPTER

14

$W$hile conversing with Dr. Jim Phelps, I had described our Thanksgiving plans at the loft as a "shindig." I might have been tailoring my vocabulary to my audience—Jim was a country veterinarian, and a folksy one at that. More accurately, I should have described our Thanksgiving plans as an elegant late-afternoon dinner party.

Marson and I had hosted gatherings such as this many times, and it's safe to say we knew how to entertain tastefully, with flair. (I mean, two gay men with design degrees—piece of cake.) But we had never hosted such an event in the afternoon, nor had we ever hosted Thanksgiving.

Since my arrival in Dumont, Mary Questman had always claimed dibs on that holiday, extending invitations we enthusiastically accepted. Her grand old house on Prairie Street, with its traditional charm and silken gentility, was the perfect setting for a celebration focused on food and hearth and home. Not only was Mary a gracious hostess, but she employed a full-time housekeeper, Berta, who knocked herself out for a week in advance, preparing culinary wonders no Pilgrim could match. The house was filled with the mixed aromas of allspice, sage, cinnamon, and cloves. The table and crannies were festooned with pumpkins, gourds, Indian corn, and horns of plenty.

This year, however, Mary was in Mexico. And our downtown loft, more chic than cozy, would require a different approach to celebrating the harvest. There wasn't much leeway with the traditional meal (Marson, with Nancy Sanderson's help, had covered the basics and "all the fixins"), but our decorating for that Thursday's feast had none of the seasonal exuberance that Mary and Berta had lavished on their guests. Marson deigned to put out a gourd or two, but otherwise we relied on the simple elegance of white candles and white flowers.

Plus, we would be moving soon (within three weeks), so our restrained décor had a decidedly nontraditional twist—stacks of packed corrugated boxes were piled in growing pyramids at the corners of the main room, which we reasoned was not altogether out of keeping with the loft's industrial aesthetic. At least, that was our story.

Our guest list evolved until the last minute. We had first invited Yevgeny Krymov, the ballet star, with his new love interest, Darnell Passalacqua, the hair-and-makeup artist. They'd accepted on the spot. Meaning: the party was on.

So we quickly followed up by inviting Thad Manning and Paige Yeats. A month earlier, when I invited them to a get-acquainted dinner at the loft, I assumed the Hollywood power couple was far too busy and would politely decline. But they did indeed accept that invitation, and I was no less surprised when they expressed their eagerness to return and celebrate Thanksgiving with us. Meaning: we were a party of six.

Marson, however, has this symmetry-and-balance thing, which caused distress at the prospects of one woman at the table with five men. So we turned, of course, to Glee Savage, who happily agreed to join us "with bells on." Meaning: we were seven, which may be a lucky number, but it's also an odd number, and in Marson's book, that created an impossible challenge at a rectangular table.

I suggested inviting Sheriff Simms and his wife, Gloria, and their son, Tommy, which would top us off at ten guests. Marson thought it was a splendid idea, but when I phoned Thomas about it, I learned they would be out of town to visit Gloria's family.

Then I thought of Heather Vance, the county medical examiner and my occasional decoy "wife." She was single; she might jump at the invitation. But when I phoned, I learned that she, too, would be out of town—flying off to faraway Buffalo to be with her family. Meaning: our guest list was stuck at seven.

Marson fretted over this until late Wednesday evening, the night before Thanksgiving, when Heather called to inform me that a blizzard in Buffalo had closed the airport there for at least twenty-four hours. Could she *possibly* horn in on our celebration? Marson was overjoyed. Meaning: we were a party of eight.

Five men, three women—not gender parity, but close enough. Plus a cat.

Our guests were expected at four. They would arrive in the waning daylight, dine during twilight, and be stuffed by dark.

Nancy Sanderson had cleared out by early afternoon, and Marson's turkey was still in the oven, so everything was under control in the kitchen. We gave the table a final spiffing before we headed upstairs to dress. Mister Puss followed us up the spiral stairway, then sat on the bed, watching us.

We decided against jackets. It seemed unlikely that Yevgeny, Darnell, or Thad would wear them, and we didn't want them feeling underdressed—God forbid—so we opted for nice slacks and sweaters. Marson stuck with his usual palette of black, grays, and silver, while I went with warmer tones; we both wore white dress shirts under our sweaters to give us a matching element. Details, details.

Checking his hair, Marson said to my reflection in the bathroom mirror, "Starting the holiday season without Mary—doesn't seem quite right, does it?"

"It doesn't," I agreed. "They don't even *have* Thanksgiving in Mexico."

"I'll bet the Americans do. I wonder if they have turkey."

"Dunno. But she'll be back in town soon enough—with plenty of time to get her game on for Christmas."

Marson turned to me with a warm smile. "Remember our first Christmas Eve together—at Mary's?"

"How could I forget?"

It wasn't the black-tie dinner at Mary's that Marson was referring to. It was the noteworthy fact that we were twenty minutes late, which Marson would normally find inexcusable. And we were late because I had just presented him with my plans for the new house, prompting a bout of spontaneous lovemaking.

I now said to him, "Can you believe it? Two years later, and we're about to move *into* that house."

He offered his arms. "And it's still just the beginning."

We kissed like young lovers. Things were getting a bit ... spontaneous again. Over Marson's shoulder, I saw Mister Puss spectating, giving us an odd look from the bed.

*Grrring.*

So much for spontaneity.

Mister Puss shot down the stairs, leaping the last six feet to the floor. Marson and I followed. He asked me, "Care to guess who's first?"

"Easy," I said, checking my watch. "Gotta be Glee—with bells on."

*Grrring.*

I bellowed rudely, "Keep your shirt on!"

We could hear her laughing outside as I swung the door open.

"Happy Thanks-*giving*, boys," she warbled while whooshing in from the cold, looking fabulous in a big hat, big heels, and a big furry shrug with matching muff—everything in shades of maroon and umber. She carried a wicker picnic hamper.

"Welcome, doll," I said, giving her a smooch, "but you didn't need to bring anything."

She assured me, "It's *nothing*—just a sour cherry pie with merlot and rosemary—and a lattice-top crust. Whipped it up this morning."

"How clever," said Marson, kissing her. "No such thing as too many desserts."

She handed him the basket, which he whisked away to the kitchen. Then she turned to ask me from the corner of her mouth, "Is the bar open?"

"Mm-hm." Slipping my arm through hers, I escorted her back to the kitchen island. "What'll it be, doll?"

"Too early for a martini?"

I reminded her, "It'll be dark before you know it."

"Sold."

While I fixed her drink, Mister Puss sauntered over and rubbed along Glee's ankles.

She scooched down to pet him. "How art thou, O mighty Oolong?"

*Meow.*

"Stick with me, small fry, and someone might slip you a gizzard."

*Grrring.*

Mister Puss led the parade to the door as we all went to greet the next arrival. There were two: Yevgeny and Darnell, looking happy and coupled and a bit tousled, as if they'd just arisen from a nap that turned spunky.

Yevgeny carried a bottle in a gift bag, which Marson took to the kitchen.

With both hands, Darnell bore a lavish arrangement of cut flowers and pine sprigs in an oblong ceramic bowl.

I told him, "Fabulous—I have *just* the spot for that." After leading him over to the middle of the room, I helped him place it on the low, square cocktail table, where the flowers were backdropped by the fireplace and its flickering tiers of candles.

Darnell gently grasped my elbow and leaned near, speaking low: "Would I sound too silly to say I'm in love?" With that lisp, he did.

I said, "Not at all, Darnell. I couldn't be happier for you—and for Yevgeny. It seems you've really clicked."

He twitched his brows. "That's one way of putting it."

From the bar, Yevgeny called over to Darnell, "Your usual, my sweets?"

Darnell shot a thumbs-up as I leaned to tell him, "Hang on to that one."

*Grrring.*

It was Heather Vance, who joined the party at the bar, bearing a small wrapped gift—a stout cylinder, maybe four inches long.

Marson stepped over from his kitchen duties to greet her with a hug. "So glad you could join us—you *saved* my table."

"And *you* saved my holiday. Thanks for including me on such short notice." She handed my husband the gift.

He said, "You shouldn't have."

"Trust me, it's *nothing*—didn't have time to come up with much."

He shook it. "Shall I open it?"

"Definitely." Heather shot me a grin.

Marson unwrapped a can of pineapple. With a confused smile, he thanked her.

I laughed, explaining, "Inside joke."

"But useful," he said. "I'll find a nice bowl and set it out with the yams."

Within a few minutes, we were all tippling and gabbing while avoiding two obvious, but stressful, topics—the murder and our impending move from the loft. Marson set out the tray of nibbles Nancy Sanderson had prepared for us, and Mister Puss was soon making the rounds, mooching shrimp.

*Grrring.*

The cat was torn between two impulses. Curiosity never failed to propel him to the door, but this time, the lure of the shrimp won out, and he stuck close to the crowd at the bar while Marson and I went to greet our remaining guests.

Thad Manning and Paige Yeats stepped in from the cold, beaming their perfect Hollywood smiles. We had done this before, but it still felt unreal—having such luminaries of the entertainment world in our modest home, right there in sleepy little Dumont. I hugged them both. So did Marson. They seemed thrilled to be with us, and even though they were two skilled actors, the warmth they exuded was plainly no act. Paige carried a small gift, extending it to Marson. "We hope you'll both like this—we thought it was very 'you.'"

"How considerate. Thank you," said Marson, placing it on the console table near the door. The box, eggshell blue, was wrapped with a white satin ribbon, topped with a bow. Something told me it was *not* a can of pineapple.

Within half an hour, Marson was ready to begin moving things from the kitchen to the table, so he invited everyone to linger with their drinks in the living room while he tended to his duties. As I ushered the others toward the fireplace, I explained, "I'd better give Marson a hand."

But Yevgeny insisted, "Let *me* help, Brody. You stay with your guests." And before I could protest, he had slipped off to the kitchen.

We arranged ourselves on the loveseats around the cocktail table, with Glee and Darnell keeping the conversation lively. Heather huddled with Paige and Thad, who were intrigued by her work as the county coroner. I made sure everyone's glasses were topped up.

Keeping an eye on the kitchen, I wondered if Marson would find Yevgeny more of a hindrance than helpful, but I was surprised to note that the architect and the dancer were a well-choreographed pair, making efficient progress with our meal's finishing touches.

I'd never had reason to guess that Yevgeny knew anything at all about cooking, but there he was, with his sleeves rolled up and a dish towel tucked into his belt, tending to the serving dishes while Marson carved the bird, dangling scraps for the cat. Whenever Yevgeny needed this or that, he didn't ask Marson about it. He just seemed to *know* where to find it—as if he owned the place.

Around the cocktail table, our conversation shifted from the trivia of the day to the aromas from the kitchen, which were now so overwhelming, we spoke of nothing but food, practically bouncing in our seats as we awaited the call to dinner.

"Dinner," announced Marson, accompanied by the tinkle of a silver bell, "is served."

Gathered at the long Parsons table, we all agreed that we had much to be thankful for. As hosts, Marson and I sat at the two ends of the table and expressed our gratitude for the company of our friends.

Along the outer side of the table, facing the kitchen, Glee sat in the middle, separating Darnell and Yevgeny, who was adjacent to me. Glee was grateful for her long tenure at the *Register*, which had allowed her to contribute to Dumont's social and cultural life. Darnell and Yevgeny, of course, were simply thankful for finding each other, and we all joined in wishing them happiness.

Along the other side of the table, which faced out toward the front windows, Thad sat in the middle, between his wife, Paige, and Heather Vance, who was adjacent to me. Heather was grateful not to be snowed in at an airport. Thad and Paige gave thanks for fresh beginnings: life in Dumont, new career callings, and a baby on the way.

Marson circled our gathering and poured wine. Then we all paused for a toast: to friendship, to love, to each other.

While the food was being passed, Mister Puss hopped up to my lap, purring, which I was inclined to interpret as gratitude for the temporary home Marson and I had made for him during Mary's absence—but I suspected his real purpose was to beg for a handout, so I slipped him a sliver of turkey from the platter in front of me, then dropped him to the floor beneath the table, where he could explore his possibilities with other guests.

Things got quiet for a few minutes as we hungrily sampled the bounty spread before us, interrupted only by the occasional compliments to the chef, which Marson humbly dismissed as unnecessary—he'd had lots of help, "and besides," he added, "Heather's crushed pineapple provided the crowning touch." Insipid but touching, his tribute drew a round of hear-hears.

And then, at last, when the feasting lost its frenzy, when we came up for air and sat back to enjoy each other's company while forking at our second helpings, then—inevitably—the topic turned to murder.

Marson broke the ice, telling the table, "We invited Sheriff Simms and his family, but they had plans already. I was hoping he might have a few updates on the Ellen Locke case."

With a soft laugh, Thad Manning said, "I suspect he'd rather talk about anything *else*, at least on a holiday."

Marson nodded. "You're probably right."

I said, "But there *is* some progress now. We had a productive meeting on Tuesday, at Questman Center. And Heather helped—I mean, *really* helped."

She asked, "Pineapple, anyone?" while passing the dish.

"Oh?" said Glee, on high alert. "What happened?"

Watching as she dug out her steno pad, I replied, "We have a promising new lead, but there's not much else I can say about it."

"Why not?"

Thad and Paige already knew about the developments with Zeiss Shotwell because they were both present on Tuesday. Ditto for Heather Vance. And I had already told Marson the whole story. But Yevgeny and Darnell knew nothing about the meeting with Shotwell, and for the time being, I wanted to keep them in the dark—because I was still intrigued with, and bothered by, Darnell's "thrill kill" theory. In a similar vein, I could not yet dismiss the suspicions raised by Paige's devotion to the "higher cause" of gun control. To my way of thinking, there was nothing to be gained by analyzing the possibility of Shotwell's guilt in the presence of either Paige or Darnell.

So I told Glee, "Sheriff Simms has some irons in the fire. He asked me to keep quiet."

Glee closed her notebook.

Thad said, "I *hope* he's got some irons in the fire. If he's not able to wrap this up—and fast—it's looking like *Home Sweet Humford* is toast. The city's ready to pull the filming permits."

I assured him, "This could break open sooner than you think." I could tell from Thad's relieved expression that I'd said the right thing, but truth be told, I was whistling in the wind.

Mister Puss had been making the rounds, and when he hopped into my lap again, he landed with a heavy thud. Gazing up at me, he had the woozy, drunken look of overindulgence. Then his head drooped as he slipped into a tryptophan-induced nap. His body rumbled and vibrated with something between a purr and a snore.

Glee dabbed her lips, then said wistfully, "So many lovely times—here at the loft. And this is the last of the parties. They'll be missed."

"Onward," said Marson. "Bigger and better things to come."

With a comical whimper, Glee asked, "I'll be invited?"

I told her, "Of course, doll. Wouldn't be the same without you."

Thad gestured toward the boxes piled in the corners of the room. "Looks like you're ready to go."

Marson laughed. "Hardly. Glad we have a long weekend ahead of us—we really need to make a deeper dent in the packing. Only two or three weeks till we move."

Paige said, "Then you'll be into the new place by Christmas. Nice."

I felt the drip of something acidic racing through my stomach.

Marson said to me, "The timing may be a little tight, but I think we should plan on a housewarming for Christmas."

"A *little* tight?" I asked. "But yeah, that'd be great."

Marson announced to the table, "Date and time to be determined, but I hope you'll all come."

Amid a round of assurances that everyone would attend, Yevgeny told us, "A year ago, in New York, who could guess that life would bring me here? But now I know: I love to teach. I plan to stay. For long time." Then he turned to ask Darnell, "You will go to party with me?"

"Count on it, Zhenya. I'll be here, at least till Christmas—way longer, maybe."

"Darnell?" asked Paige. "It's wonderful, being in love. But out here, you're a *long* way from the Hollywood nightlife. Don't you miss it?"

He shrugged. "A little. I miss my friends, but I've weighed all that. I'm where I want to be."

Yevgeny reminded him, "Smartphones, the internet—no one's far away anymore."

"*Tell* me." Darnell laughed. "I blab with Jane every day."

I asked, "Jane Douglas?" Darnell had earlier told me that the backstage mom of creepy little Seth Douglas had dubbed Darnell her "best friend forever."

He nodded. "She calls a lot. She worries about Seth—who wouldn't? That kid's got a screw loose."

My thoughts exactly.

Marson stood. "I don't suppose anyone has room for dessert." He was being facetious—no one declined, and there was none of that just-a-sliver nonsense.

I slid my chair back, intending to help him clear the table, but Mister Puss didn't take the hint. He was out cold in my lap.

Seeing this, Yevgeny laughed. "Stay put with *koshechka*. I help." And he got up to assist Marson with the change of courses.

While the two of them trundled back and forth to the kitchen, the rest of us gabbed and sipped wine. I watched as Marson began slicing pies. Nancy Sanderson had supplied us with pumpkin, of course, and mincemeat, which I had a hunch no one would eat. The smart money was on Glee's cherry job.

Marson brought out composed plates containing all three types of pie, centered with a scoop of ice cream. He served the ladies first.

Glee asked him, "Since you're moving, what do you plan to do with the loft?"

Sounding befuddled, Marson said, "Sell it, I suppose."

"Have you listed it?"

I sighed. "Yet another detail we haven't quite gotten around to."

Yevgeny stepped over from the kitchen with more dessert plates. "You can make this very simple. Just sell it to me."

In unison, Marson and I asked, "Really?"

"Just my style. Very New York. Perfect for two." He winked at Darnell, who flopped a hand to his chest as if he might swoon.

"Well," I said to Marson, "that would keep it in the family, so to speak." Of *course* we would sell the loft to Yevgeny.

When everyone was seated again, a spirit of merriment breezed through our conversation. And yes, Glee's pie proved to be the favorite, hands down.

Then, during a lull, I noticed that Paige was staring at her plate with a pensive frown. I asked, "Anything wrong?"

"No, sorry." She sat back, smiling weakly. "Great news—your

plans for the loft—but it makes me wonder when Thad and I will get our *own* housing needs settled." Patting her tummy, she added, "Before you-know-who comes along."

I had noticed, but of course I didn't mention, that her baby bump was now obvious.

Thad took his wife's hand. "We'll figure it out in time. We might have to just … *buy* something. Anything."

I asked, "No progress with your uncle's house?"

He shook his head. "The Gerbers won't budge."

"It's Bettina," said Paige. "She's *impossible*."

I wondered aloud, "What's that all about? She doesn't seem to have any particular *emotional* attachment to the house, and you've made offers well above market value. She strikes me as a smart cookie. Anyone with a head for numbers ought to snap at that."

Paige said, "She's an enigma—and that's putting it mildly."

I noticed that Glee had pulled out her steno pad and was jotting something.

"On a brighter note," said Paige, "I have a bit of news."

Glee was all ears. We all were.

Thad gave Paige a quizzical look. "Uh, *what?*"

"I'm nineteen weeks along now—the pregnancy—and yesterday, I had an ultrasound." Her grin assured us nothing was wrong.

"And … ?" said Thad.

Dramatic pause. "It's a boy."

Thad wrapped his arms around her; I thought he might cry. A gentle chorus of coos and awwws shared their joy.

Heather Vance asked, "Have you been thinking of names?"

"So," said Paige, "here's the deal: We agreed early on that if the baby's a girl, I'll pick her name. If it's a boy, Thad decides."

We all turned to him. "Well?" said Glee, drumming her fingers on the table. "I don't suppose you've given this any thought."

"In fact," said Thad, "I have. We'll name him Mark."

Mark Manning, I thought—this was starting to come full circle.

Glee was beaming. "I had a hunch. Do you ever hear from your uncle?"

"Sure. We talked last week. That book he meant to write before Neil died? He's finally started to noodle with it, so I'm thrilled, and I think he is, too. He had a lot of questions about Dumont—for the book, I assume. I suggested he should pay a visit, and for once, at least, he didn't say no. He knows there's a baby on the way, but he hasn't heard it's a boy. When he hears about the name, who knows? Maybe he'll hop on a plane."

Leftovers weren't an issue. We'd polished off everything except the mincemeat, which no one asked to take home. Yevgeny wanted to help clean up "his" new kitchen, but we sent him packing, along with the others, into the frigid night.

Glee had been the first to arrive, as usual, and now she was the last to leave. She crouched near the door, baby-talking Mister Puss, who had risen from his turkey coma and found his second wind. When Glee stood again, her knees crackled.

Leaning close, she told me, "I didn't want to mention this earlier, but I've been in touch with your mother."

I caught my breath. I must have looked bug-eyed. Marson hugged my shoulders.

Glee asked, "Did you know about it?"

"She called me last weekend. Said you wrote her a letter."

Glee nodded. "I heard back from her, by email. We've had some back-and-forth. Then we talked on the phone."

"Really? You and *Inez*?"

"Yes, really. And it was quite pleasant, believe it or not."

I was speechless.

"Anyway, she asked me to let you know that she's planning another visit for Christmas. She wants to arrive early enough to help you boys pack for the move." It was clear from Glee's cheery tone that she found this development heartening.

I found it stressful.

Glee lavished us with parting thanks and kisses, then reached for the door.

I picked up Mister Puss as she opened it and disappeared.

Locking up after her, Marson said, "It's official: the holidays are upon us."

I groaned as a fresh drop of something stung my stomach. Hugging Mister Puss to my shoulder, I rubbed his cheek, coaxing a purr.

"Almost forgot," said Marson. "Let's see what Thad and Paige brought us." He picked up the blue box from the hall table, where a row of pillar candles still burned. "Must be Tiffany."

I watched as he untied the ribbon and opened the lid. Removing a velvet pouch wrapped in tissue, he set the box aside. "Heavy," he said. "Must be crystal."

Whatever it was, I recalled Paige telling us, "We thought it was very 'you.'" The cat's purr burbled in my ear.

"Gosh, how sweet," said Marson, revealing a fist-sized crystal heart, deepest red, which seemed to pulse in the flicker of the candlelight.

"Lovely," I said, petting the cat, "absolutely lovely."

*It's very "you."*

Friday was a day off at the office, but not at the loft, where Marson and I spent the entire day packing and organizing, making substantial progress.

Waking up on Saturday morning, the last day of November, I looked out over the railing of the mezzanine and saw that the loft no longer looked like our home. It had been "undone." I'd experienced the same sensation three years earlier, while preparing to move from California to Wisconsin. The task, which at first seemed daunting and mind-boggling, had reached a tipping point, where the wistful inclination to hang on to the security of the past became moot. The past, having been disrupted and disassembled, no longer existed as a day-to-day continuum, but merely a memory.

Closet doors gaped behind me on the mezzanine; below, on the ground floor, cartons were stacked everywhere. The boxes were sealed and the dust of the years had been swept from under the bed, so it was time to go. I was ready. In fact, I now regretted that we would need to stay at the loft, surrounded by its disarray, until mid-December.

"Know what?" said Marson, stepping up behind me at the top of the stairs.

Mister Puss slinked between our legs and trotted down to the kitchen.

"I think," continued Marson, "we deserve to enjoy a lazy day. Maybe an afternoon at the office?"

On the surface, it seemed like a bizarre suggestion. Why would anyone want to spend the Saturday afternoon of a holiday weekend at work? But I understood Marson perfectly. We had spent Wednesday preparing for dinner guests. We had spent Thursday entertaining them. And we had spent Friday, dawn till dusk, as slaves to the arduous chore of boxing up our lives. I ached all over. Twenty-four years younger than Marson, I hated to think how *he* must have felt.

So the idea of spending a quiet afternoon at our desks was oddly appealing. With no other staff around, with the phones switched to voice mail, we could catch up on a few projects and—above all—escape the mess we had created at home.

I turned to him at the top of the stairs, held him in my arms, and delivered a deep kiss. I was still in my bathrobe, but he was already dressed nattily for the day—that's just Marson being Marson. "I think," I said, "you're a genius."

"I think," he said, "you're a little fruity."

"Correct," I said. "Fruity and frisky."

Some minutes later, we arrived downstairs to find Mister Puss waiting—not very patiently—seated on the kitchen island. He gave us a knowing, disapproving look. Had he worn glasses, he would have slid them down his nose in order to peer at us over the top of the frames.

Our tardiness was forgiven when Marson popped open a small can of tuna and forked it into one of the Puiforcat bowls that served as our guest's breakfast dish. Purring, Mister Puss danced around Marson's feet, waiting for him to top off the chunks of fish with a dollop of clotted cream.

"Really?" I asked.

"Why not?" replied Marson as he set the bowl on the floor. The cat went crazy. "Poor thing," said Marson. "You'd think he's never eaten before."

During the feeding frenzy, I started a pot of coffee and stepped outside to retrieve the morning paper.

After the heavy advertising of Thanksgiving and Black Friday, the *Register*'s Saturday edition was anemically thin, with little news, reported by a skeleton staff. I set it on the countertop so Marson could "clean" it, a daily ritual that involved folding out the creases and removing any unwanted sections and circulars. There wasn't much to dispose of that day, other than the sports section, which he barely touched, pinching a corner to set it aside.

By the time we were settled at the island with the paper, our coffee, and toast, the cat had finished eating and hopped up to join us, stretching his tongue to lick cream from his whiskers. Just as I was taking my first sip of coffee, a *ping* sounded from the iPad we kept there on the counter, signaling an arriving email. "Oh, look," I said. It was a long one.

From: Mary Questman
To: Marson Miles, Brody Norris

Good morning, dear Marson and Brody. I hope your Thanksgiving was festive. It didn't seem quite right, not spending the holiday with you boys as we have done in the past, but I did manage to celebrate a semblance of Thanksgiving with my friends down here. San Miguel has many American visitors, so we went to one of the larger hotels, which served the traditional meal. The turkey was all right. Just so-so. Perhaps it was wild. But I do know this: it was no Butterball.

That aside, I've been amazed to discover how thoroughly acclimated I've become to the pace of life here. By "here," I don't necessarily mean Mexico, or even San Miguel de Allende, which couldn't be more charming. Rather, I'm referring to life "on the run," so to speak.

This past year, we have all joked a bit regarding the travel bug that seems to have taken hold of me. At first, I attributed this to pent-up desires to expand my horizons—to stretch my mind—beyond Dumont. Acting on that instinct was long overdue.

But the result of my recent travels has been more than the satisfaction of making up for lost time. Instead, I have come to realize that, during my sojourns, I have been answering a primal call. You may be thinking, "Oh, dear, she's lost another marble." And Lord knows, you may be right! But I don't know how else to describe the transition I feel I've made.

Berta senses this, too—not only for me, but for herself. As for the circle of lady friends we have joined in these travels, they have come to feel like extended family, each of us searching for meaning … in ports beyond.

So I am writing to you with mixed emotions to let you know that another opportunity has presented itself. One of the ladies has organized accommodations on a cruise that will depart in mid-January. My emotions are mixed because the voyage sounds heavenly, but it would require some logistical adjustments at home. I have tussled with my decision to participate or not, needing to consult first with you, dear Marson and Brody, regarding an important matter.

You see, this cruise is no mere island-hopping junket in the Caribbean. Rather, it's a world cruise that will last a leisurely six months. It promises to be the adventure of a lifetime.

You can probably guess the issue I need to resolve before committing to the trip: I am worried about the future welfare of Mister Puss.

He has made such an enormous difference in my life. And it goes without saying that I love him with all my heart. But it would be impossible for him to accompany me on these extended travels (quarantines and whatnot), and it would be unfair to all concerned if he and his loving hosts adjusted to an extended "visit," only to have me waltz back into town and demand his return.

I find it so difficult to write this: Would you possibly consider making a permanent home for His Majesty? I know how much he likes both of you—he's told me so—and I can think of no one who would be better parents to him.

Brody, I know that you have come to enjoy a special rapport with Mister Puss—he's told me that as well—so perhaps you could have a word with him and sound him out. I would be so pleased to know that these suggested arrangements leave him with no hurt feelings.

Looking ahead, if you would allow me occasional visiting rights, that would make my happiness complete.

Meanwhile, I am extending my current stay in San Miguel for a couple of weeks, but will return to Dumont before Christmas, which will allow time for the rather extensive preparations that need to be made prior to departing on my cruise—*if* you decide to include Mister Puss in your family.

I shall await your decision.

All my love,
Mary

I turned to Marson, asking, "Did you see that coming?"

He smiled. "Can't say I'm surprised. I was beginning to wonder when she'd get around to asking us about it. And in fact ... I was starting to worry she might *not*."

"Then, you're good with it?"

Marson nodded.

Mister Puss cocked his head with curiosity. His eyes were following the ping-pong of our conversation.

Marson told me, "I assume you're on board with this, but you'd better have a *tête-à-tête* with you-know-who." He got up, stepped over to the sink, and began rinsing something.

I had never explicitly discussed with Marson that Mister Puss seemed to communicate with me in the same manner that Mary claimed the cat spoke to her. But Marson surely intuited that *something* was going on, and he never pressed me to explain it. How's that for a trusting spouse?

The cat sat a foot or so away from me on the countertop. When I made a kissy sound, he stood and moved close to me, bumping his head to my chin. He started to purr, sliding his snout up my cheek toward my ear.

I said quietly, "We just got a message from Mary."

*Who?*

"Now, stop that. You know she loves you very much. Right?"

His purring intensified.

"Here's the deal," I said. Then I told him about Mary's desire to take a lengthy cruise and her suggestion that Mister Puss could stay with Marson and me, not just until Mary's return, but always. "Marson and I would be happy to have you, but nothing's decided yet. It's up to you. If you don't like the idea, she won't take the cruise."

The cat's purr rumbled in my ear.

"So," I said, "what should I tell her?"

*Ahoy, matey.*

Our email response to Mary was quick and joyous, informing her that Marson and I were delighted to assume guardianship of Mister Puss. We also told her that the cat was initially reluctant, but we managed to entice him with clotted cream and lavish reassurances, securing his consent (not true, but we figured it was preferable to telling Mary that her cat had agreed on the spot).

In closing, we wrote that we looked forward to seeing Mary at Christmas before bidding her *bon voyage* to parts unknown in January.

Done. We had a cat.

That afternoon, we were aflush with parental pride as we took Mister Puss to the office with us. Good thing there was no one else on the premises over the weekend, since we doubtless would have embarrassed ourselves with nonstop bragging about "our little man."

As for our little man, he seemed unfazed by the sudden tectonic shift underlying our relationship with him. To our lofty way of thinking, we had just endowed the cat with a forever home. To his mind, most likely, he had just acquired not one, but two, forever servants.

Marson asked archly, "Would His Majesty prefer to take his afternoon nap in the north salon or the south salon?" We stood in the hall between our two offices.

"South," I said. "It's warmer." And I led the cat into my office. The thermostat had been dialed back for the long weekend, but my corner digs had south windows to blunt the chill. While stooping to unclip the cat's leash, I called to Marson, "Can you crank the heat a bit?"

"Sure, kiddo. I'll be out front, sorting mail."

Moments later, I heard the furnace click on as I sat at my desk and booted up my computer. Mister Puss sauntered over to the shaft of sunlight on the floor and plopped himself in its warmth, needing to catch up on his zees. It could be a challenge—sleeping eighteen hours a day—and the morning had been hectic.

I scrolled through my directory of incoming emails, most of which I had already dealt with on my phone. I trashed most of them, saved what I needed, and then read the ones I hadn't seen. All of these were related to business, save one, which I was surprised to see had been sent by Paige Yeats, with whom I had never previously corresponded.

From: Paige Yeats @ Questman Center
To: Brody Norris @ Miles & Norris, LLC

Hello, Brody. Thad and I had such a wonderful time at Thanksgiving dinner. Our sincere thanks to you and Marson for including us.

Our conversation at the table impressed upon me the urgency to do something about the "housing crisis" Thad and I are facing. With baby Mark on the way, we need to get out of the Manor House, but Thad is stuck on the idea of reacquiring his uncle's family home, which the current owners refuse to sell.

Please keep this under your hat, but I decided to go nuclear, so to speak—with my father. If anyone can pull strings, Glenn Yeats can. I wrote to him explaining our dilemma, and I thought you might find his response of interest:

From: Glenn Yeats @ Yeats Worldwide
To: Paige Yeats @ Questman Center

Dear Paige,
Let me see what I can do about this.
Love to you and Thad.
Dad

I wrote a quick reply to Paige, wishing her luck with this new tactic and also thanking Thad and her for the red crystal heart, "which we found not only beautiful, but thoughtful and touching." I copied the message to Marson, and just as I sent it, he walked into my office with a stack of snail mail.

"I left what I could for Gertie," he said, "but we should go through the rest of this." He set the pile on my desk, then removed about half of it from the top and carried it over to his own office.

I rattled around in my desk for a letter opener—rousing Mister Puss from his slumber—and began slitting envelopes open, saving a few larger items for last. The correspondence included city and county permits I'd been waiting for, which I promptly placed in their respective job folders, contained in steel file cabinets across the room. Mister Puss followed my actions through squinting eyelids. His scowl seemed to ask, Could you *try* to keep it down?

The larger parcels contained a few trade journals, a sweater I'd ordered (receiving deliveries was easier at the office than at the loft), and a box of new coffee mugs for the break room, each wound tightly with Bubble Wrap. After freeing all of the ceramic mugs, I stacked them on the glass desktop and then trashed all the packaging in a tall metal wastebasket. Mister Puss was now on his feet, stretching his arched back.

Which left a single item I had not yet opened. It was one of those puffy, padded yellow mailers, addressed to me by hand with a heavy black marker, including the notation PERSONAL AND CONFIDENTIAL. There was no return address. Intrigued, I checked the blurry postmark—it was from Denver. Odd, I thought. I could recall no friends or acquaintances from Colorado, and we weren't working on design projects anywhere near there. Odder still, the outer yellow paper of the mailer was covered with several layers of transparent packing tape, running in both directions. The package wasn't heavy or stiff; in fact, it didn't seem to contain anything at all.

With my curiosity piqued, I tried ripping it open, but the tape made that impossible. I then tried the letter opener, but after several futile attempts, I tossed it aside. As it landed noisily on the desktop, I opened another drawer and rummaged for a scissors. Mister Puss, with his feline curiosity now outweighing his fatigue, jumped onto the desk and sat, watching me as he yawned.

Scissors in hand, I carefully trimmed an entire edge off the mailer. The cat and I peeped inside. More packaging—an inner envelope of black plastic.

I tried slipping it out, but it was stuck. Frustrated, I grabbed the inner envelope with one fist and the outer envelope with the other fist—and yanked it hard.

A rusty-hued cloud of powder rose from the package and hung over us—time seemed to stand still—before it drifted downward, settling all over me and the cat and the desk. I noticed a slip of paper fall to the floor as I began to cough. My eyes burned. The cat was hacking fiercely. I called, "Marson!"

I heard him rushing over from his office, clearly alarmed by my tone.

"What the *hell*?" he said, standing frozen at the doorway.

I crouched to pick up the paper while he entered the room, covering his nose and mouth with one hand.

The paper was a shred from the typed screenplay of *Home Sweet Humford*. On its backside, a message was scrawled with something greasy—it appeared to be lipstick, a deep shade of lavender. As Marson stepped near, I held it for him to read: BUTT OUT!

I said weakly, "Better call nine-one-one."

Marson left the room, cell phone in hand.

Mister Puss spat up a hairball.

I reached for the desk phone, punched in a number, and asked to speak to Sheriff Thomas Simms.

PART THREE

# DECEMBER

# 16

Sunday morning, I was released from an isolation room at Dumont Memorial Hospital, where I had been kept for observation overnight. A nurse rolled me down the hall in a wheelchair—which seemed ridiculous—and deposited me at a door labeled CONFERENCE, telling me, "Hope you're feeling better, Mr. Norris."

I stood. "I'm fine."

"They're waiting for you." Then she skittered away with the wheelchair.

I stepped through the door and into a space that looked like a staff lunchroom, without a window, where Sheriff Simms was seated at a table along with Marson and our primary physician, Dr. Teresa Ortiz. They stood to greet me with warm smiles and cheery words as I hugged my husband. I'd been scrubbed and disinfected—my hair looked like hell—but Marson had delivered a clean change of clothes earlier that morning, so at least I was feeling put-together.

Once we were all seated, Simms said to me, "So here's where things stand. Most important: the powder mailed to your office was not a biohazard. Testing for that was straightforward and conclusive. But we still have samples out for qualitative analysis. Once we determine what's *in* the powder, that could help us figure out who sent it."

"It was weird," I said. "It had that rusty hue."

Dr. Ortiz said, "You were never in serious danger, Brody—

except for the scare factor. Sorry you went through this."

"Thanks, Teresa."

"Still," said Simms, "it was a threat, coupled with a demand—to butt out of the Ellen Locke investigation—and we take that very seriously."

I turned to Marson. "How's Mister Puss?"

"Resting comfortably with the vet. Jim Phelps said not to worry. His Majesty's hacking spell was just a respiratory reaction to the powder, spontaneous and passing. No harm done—and he got rid of a monster hairball."

I rolled my eyes. "I suppose *that's* being held as evidence."

With a laugh, Simms assured me, "No."

Marson asked him, "Then it's safe to return to the office?"

"Sure. You'll be back in business tomorrow. My crew is finished there, and I asked them to clean things up."

Teresa looked perplexed. She said, "This is out of my realm, but I can't help thinking: Since the package was mailed from Denver, doesn't that suggest who might've sent it?"

Simms and I looked at each other, then shrugged. He said, "Brody and Marson don't know anyone in Denver. And no connections popped up in our background checks of 'persons of interest' from the film production. Because the package was covered with plastic tape, it was loaded with fingerprints, mostly smudged, from all the handling. No clues there, I'm afraid."

Teresa tapped her chin, wondering aloud, "But why Denver...?"

"One of the oldest tricks in the book," said Simms. "Let's say you live in Los Angeles and want to mail something that can't be traced. You put plenty of postage on it, then put it in a bigger envelope and mail it to someone else, let's say in Denver. You ask them to drop it in any mailbox there. Maybe you explain it as a practical joke. Or maybe you just pay them to ask no questions. Pretty simple. And very effective."

Nodding, Teresa said, "Then it could've come from ... *anyone*."

"Exactly," said Simms. He turned to me, "And that's why I'm offering police protection at your home, Brody. That package could've originated in LA or anywhere else—like right here in Dumont."

I shook my head. "Has word gotten out that this happened? Is it news?"

"Hope not. Nothing to be served by telling the public about it."

"Then," I said, "if there's suddenly a 'police presence' at the loft, won't that raise a lot of questions?"

"Brody," he said, "I can deal with that risk. But I can't deal with the risk that *somebody* out there—somebody who's already made threatening demands—might take things to the next level."

He was right, of course. On a prior case, troubling developments had prompted Simms to post deputies outside the loft—in front on First Avenue and in the back alley where we parked—a wise precaution that required rotating shifts three times that first day. And then the days dragged on. And before long, Marson and I came to feel like prisoners in our own home. I couldn't force Marson to deal with that again—unless *he* felt there was now a danger that outweighed the intrusion.

So I asked him: "What do you think? Safe and sound? Or go it alone?"

He grinned. "You and I together—we're never 'alone,' kiddo."

I turned to the sheriff. "We appreciate your offer. But no thank you, Thomas."

Simms blew a breathy, quiet whistle. "Lay low. Okay?"

That Sunday—it was December first—we left the hospital and arrived home at the loft before noon. The first thing I did was shower and change again, cleansing myself of the antiseptic smell and turning the page on my bad-hair day.

*Grrring.*

Feeling human again, I was in the right frame of mind to trot to the door and reach to open it without even bothering to steal a peek from the nearby window—in case sinister forces lurked without.

"Special delivery," said Jim Phelps with a jolly laugh, chomping on his pipe as the smoke of cherry tobacco rose in a wispy blue cloud through the cold winter air. He handed me the leash as Mister Puss slipped indoors and rubbed against my shins.

I asked, "Care to come in, Jim? A little shot of something warm?"

"Nah, but thanks, Brody. Gotta run." With a wink of his eye and a twist of his head, he dashed to his car and then drove out of sight.

As I closed the door, Marson approached from behind. "Our little man is home?"

I unclipped the leash, and the cat trotted over to Marson, who swooped him up and gave him a vigorous petting, which surprised me—Marson was wearing a black sweater, a magnet for sheddings. While Marson welcomed Mister Puss home with soothing words, I fetched a sticky lint roller.

Back where we belonged, the three of us spent the entire remainder of the day at the loft—lying low, as Simms had suggested.

I packed and sealed a few more cartons, mostly tableware and serving pieces that we used for entertaining, which would not be needed again until after the move.

Marson busied himself in the kitchen with a stew for our Sunday supper, winging it without a recipe, which was not in his nature, but incorporating several partial bottles of opened wine, which seemed promising. It also helped clean out the refrigerator.

Mister Puss, when he wasn't napping, inspected and tested the empty boxes as I assembled them. He also made frequent detours to the kitchen with his sniffer on high alert, mooching anything Marson would allow—from beef scraps to carrots and even a pearl onion. His Majesty was not amused by the onion's flavor and put it to better use as a plaything, batting it around the house for ten minutes until Marson snatched it up and trashed it.

After dinner, after polishing off a bottle of Château Margaux that we opened for the occasion (it was extraordinary, but Marson's slapdash stew was even better), after spending a few hours of reading and gabbing and lazy rollicking with the cat, we spiraled up the stairs to the mezzanine and prepared to turn out the lights.

Mister Puss sat on the bed, waiting for us to tuck ourselves in. And after we did, after we kissed good night, the cat remained on guard, still waiting. Every time a foot or an elbow nudged beneath the covers, he played a frenzied game of whacking moles, which didn't end until, at last, our little family fell into a deep, hibernal sleep.

Monday morning, Marson went to the office, but I thought it was time to check on progress at our "perfect house." Because of Thanksgiving and packing and my brief but frightening biohazard quarantine, I hadn't seen the place in nearly a week.

It had been even longer since Mister Puss had visited the new house, and I felt he'd better get used to it, since it would soon be *his* home, too. So off we went.

The seasons had turned. With a flip of the calendar, December had brought winter to Wisconsin—no snow yet, but it was only a matter of time. The dry, freezing nights and gusty north winds had stripped the trees of the last of their leaves. The morning frost had left slick patches on the road leading out of town.

In the warm car, Mister Puss stretched his paws to the dashboard and watched the tunnel of naked branches whisk past the windshield. I switched off the radio—Schönberg wasn't right for our cozy drive through the woods. The simple, reassuring drone of the engine was far more pleasing than the music's atonal breakaway from romanticism.

Up ahead, Carter Construction's burly black-and-yellow sign loomed as big as a billboard, and I thought it was probably time to talk to Clem about removing it.

The driveway up the embankment to the house was now wide open and clean. Clem's truck was parked near the garage, but all the heavy equipment had disappeared. Construction debris had been removed, so I could soon call in the landscaper to get going with the hardscaping, although most of the plantings would need to wait until spring. Meanwhile, the half-dozen vans and pickups parked on the roadway indicated the presence of tradesmen spiffing up the interior.

Sitting in my car, taking it all in, I was startled to realize that the project looked … finished.

"Let's check it out," I told Mister Puss as I got him out of the car and led him up the driveway on his leash.

Stepping through the front door, I called, "Clem?"

"Kitchen, Brody."

I found him leading a meeting of eight or ten workers, gathered around the room's center island, reviewing plans and checklists. "Hey, Brody," he said, "full throttle now. You'll be in before you know it."

The others agreed with nods and smiles. One of them—a painter, and *really* cute, I noted—gave me a friendly little salute, saying, "Thanks for the overtime, boss."

"You're very welcome," I told him. He held my gaze longer than a straight man would. Or was I the one doing the staring?

"And, Brody," said Clem, "next couple days, I'll get that construction sign outta here. It was my job, and I'm proud of it, but it's *your* 'perfect house.'"

"Awww, Clem—I'll *miss* it."

He laughed. "Yeah, like ducks you will."

With Mister Puss in tow, I followed Clem through the house as he pointed out a few issues, made suggestions, asked for decisions.

Then we walked out to the cantilevered balcony that looked over the stream, which cascaded to the open prairie beyond. The water had already frozen by night and thawed by day, more than once, and it crackled in the sunlight now as soft strips of ice hesitated at the drop-off before falling over the edge.

Clem said quietly, "It's so damn beautiful. You're a lucky man."

Within an hour or so, my inspection was complete, and I could ogle the hot painter for only so long before getting in the way—or getting in trouble—so I said goodbye to Clem Carter and returned to my car with Mister Puss.

Heading back toward town, I arrived at the intersection where, a month earlier, my mother had told me to turn right. She then guided me north, across the county line, to an improbable old roadhouse she remembered, Polly's Palace.

I paused at the intersection with my foot on the brake, recalling an incident at Polly's, where I had noticed a black woman having a lavish steak-and-champagne lunch with a man who reminded me of Conrad Houghes, one of the main investors in Thad Manning's film. Drumming my fingers on the steering wheel, I checked my watch—not quite eleven. I didn't know if Polly's would be open at that hour, but decided to give it a try. I turned right.

A few minutes later, I watched for the dogleg—to the left, then to the right—and soon found myself approaching the ramshackle pub, still standing, against all odds, in the vast openness of barren fields. When I pulled into the gravel parking lot alongside the building and cut the engine, Mister Puss gave me an acerbic look.

Forestalling a snarky conversation, I took his leash and opened the door. "Come on," I said. But my thoughts were focused on the only other vehicle parked there—a massive Harley-Davidson, which looked like one of the two I saw during my prior visit.

Had they belonged to the lunch couple? If so, where was the other one now?

When I stepped up to the porch with Mister Puss, I stood on tiptoes to peek through the door's tiny window. Seeing a few lights, I entered. "Hello?" I called.

"Be right there," said a woman, presumably Junior, Polly's daughter. But when she appeared, it was the black woman I'd seen lunching last time.

I asked, "Too early for lunch?"

"Not at all. Bar or table?"

"Bar's fine. Okay with the cat in here?"

She tossed her hand. "Don't sweat it—code enforcement hasn't been out this way in five years. At Polly's, anything goes." Then she stepped over to take a look at the cat. "Pretty! Hi there, honey. I'm LuAnn."

I told her, "This is Mister Puss. And I'm Brody. He's crazy for your shrimp cocktail. So am I."

LuAnn raised her brows. "Lucky cat. Two orders, then."

"Just one. I'll share it."

"Can do, Brody." LuAnn stepped behind the bar.

I took a stool. Mister Puss hopped up to the one next to me.

LuAnn asked, "So you've been here before?"

"Just once—about a month ago, with my mother. *You* were having a champagne lunch that day."

"Aha"—she snapped a finger—"thought I recognized you."

"Is, uh … is Junior here?"

"Not yet. I'm her wife. Something to drink?"

I had a busy day ahead of me, so we discussed booze-free options, and I settled on a Virgin Mary, which LuAnn thought would be great with the shrimp. Then I mentioned casually, "I'll have to bring my husband out here sometime. We're building a house, just over the county line." The point, of course, was to inform her that I, too, was gay.

"Bring him in. Love to meet him." She set the drink in front of me—garnished with a whole celery stalk and assorted whatnot on skewers—then she slipped away to work on the shrimp cocktail.

I glanced at the framed photo of Liberace with the elder Polly, and it occurred to me that I now knew at least two lesbian restaurateurs—Nancy Sanderson and Junior—whose love interests were black—Nia Butler and LuAnn. Was this a Wisconsin thing?

When the shrimp arrived, looking gorgeous in their shells and tasting as fabulous as I remembered, Mister Puss was wowed and humbled by his good fortune, waiting patiently on his stool as I peeled and shared the bounty. Our clever little man.

While we ate, LuAnn busied herself behind the bar, giving us a chance to talk. She asked, "How's the shrimp?"

"None better. But I have to tell you, for sheer decadence, I've never seen a lunch quite like the one you were having last time. Those New York strips—what were they, like, two pounds each?"

"You got it."

"And washing it down with Dom Pérignon? Talk about over-the-top. You do that every day?"

She laughed. "Of *course* not."

I waited.

"That guy came in here, and he's all sorta West Coast or whatever. It was early—like today—no one else here except Junior and me. And he says, 'What's the best steak you got?' And I told him. And he's like, 'What's the best *wine* you got?' And I told him. Then he says, 'Hate to eat alone. You'll join me for lunch, right?'"

With a hoot of laughter, I asked LuAnn, "What'd you say to *that*?"

"I asked the guy, 'You're not *from* here, are ya?' And he says, 'Nope, LA, Tinseltown. So how 'bout it?' And I told him, 'Sure, if you're buyin, I'm eatin.'"

"I *love* it," I said. "So? What was he *doing* here?"

LuAnn tossed her arms in a far-flung shrug. "You tell *me*. He was all hush-hush, said something about a 'picture,' said he had to keep it under his hat or whatever. Right! I spotted a loser the minute he walked in. But he did pay for the meal. Cash."

"Do you remember his name?"

She shook her head. "Never told me."

While peeling another shrimp, I asked, "How'd he get here that day? I mean, did he drive?"

She shrugged again. "Just walked in the door. Hour later, walked out again."

Mister Puss purred loudly as I fed him a chunk of shrimp as big as my thumb. I said to LuAnn, "When I arrived with my mom that day, I noticed two motorcycles parked outside. Then, when I saw the two of you eating, I sorta figured you were a biker couple."

"You're *half* right," she told me. "One of those is mine—it's out there now. But the other belongs to Junior—she's running an errand. Never thought of us as a biker couple, but I guess the shoe fits."

"Did the guy come on to you?"

"*Course* he did! You were gone by then, but after a four-hundred-dollar lunch, he figured he had *something* coming—and he said so." She chortled at the memory of it.

"Oh, brother." I cleaned my hands with a lemony finger towel. "I assume you explained the situation."

"Told him to talk to my wife. He didn't say a word, though, cuz Junior came out from behind the bar. Had the baseball bat. We keep it back here"—LuAnn showed it to me—"just in case."

As I was driving back toward Dumont, my phone rang. The dashboard readout announced the caller as THAD MANNING.

After we greeted each other, Thad said, "This is the damnedest thing, Brody." He didn't sound upset, but excited. "Paige apparently let her father know we've been having trouble with the Gerbers, trying to buy back my uncle Mark's house—and he told her he'd try to help. Can you believe it?"

I could, actually. I said, "No kidding?"

"No kidding," he assured me. "And he's coming here to give us a hand."

"Glenn Yeats is coming *here*?" I asked, astonished. "Coming to *Dumont*? When?"

"Now. Right now. He flew to Green Bay and just got on a helicopter. He'll land in Dumont, on the commons, within a few minutes. Then he's meeting us at the house on Prairie Street. The Gerbers are waiting. Wanna join us?"

Well, duh. So I floored it.

D. Glenn Yeats (the "D" stood for Dwight) was known to be a bit of a recluse, something of an enigma. He had recently turned seventy, and his only child, Paige, was the product of his first marriage. A second marriage also failed, and he had remained single for twenty-odd years. During high school and a few unfinished years of college, he had proven himself a computer wiz—back in the early days, when it mattered. With a good idea and a keen sense of marketing, he went on to build a global business empire and amassed untold billions, which consistently landed him among a handful of the world's wealthiest men, rotating their slots near the top of the list.

As I swung into Dumont and skirted the downtown, I could hear the flutter of chopper blades. Slowing down to look up, I saw not one helicopter, but three, descending toward the commons. Mister Puss hunkered on the floor of the car as I swerved through the historic residential area, approaching the Taliesin house on Prairie Street, which was already crowded with police and security vehicles.

I parked about a block from the house and walked Mister Puss at a trot, approaching a small crowd that milled at the curb. The one-of-a-kind fuchsia hatchback was parked along the way, meaning that Glee Savage was already on hand, working on a column for tomorrow morning's *Register*. I spotted Sheriff Simms with a few of his deputies, as well as a private security detail, waiting for the arrival of Glenn Yeats, now being driven from the commons with his daughter, Paige, who had met him there.

Thad Manning stood with Harlan and Bettina Gerber, gabbing on the steps of the front porch. When he saw me, he waved me over.

Moving in his direction through the crowd, I paused to say hello to Sheriff Simms.

With a broad smile, he cuffed my shoulder, asking, "You snagged a front-row seat for this?"

"Seems so." Although we couldn't see the motorcade yet, sirens grew louder as it approached.

Simms said, "If you have a minute afterward, try to find me, okay? Got something to tell you about."

"Sure thing, Thomas." And I dashed away with Mister Puss to join Thad and the Gerbers. They greeted me absently while focusing on the commotion down the street.

With the black SUVs—with the flashers and sirens, the cop cars and motorcycle patrolmen—it was an arrival fit for a head of state. Then everything grew quiet as the huskiest of the SUVs—not pretty, but it bespoke power—slowed to a halt at the curb in front of the house. Two security people opened the back doors. Paige Yeats hopped out on the street side and moved around the back of the vehicle to wait at the other open door. And then, at the curb:

Out stepped Glenn Yeats himself.

Ummm. Given his fame, wealth, and reputation—not to mention all the hoopla—I had expected a commanding presence of heroic stature. But in spite of his designer clothing, surely custom-tailored, he looked like a bit of a dweeb, and he was shorter than his daughter by at least six inches, which could not be wholly attributed to her Miu Miu pumps.

As Paige led her father up to the house, Thad stepped down from the porch to greet them on the walkway. "Welcome to Dumont, Glenn—can't believe you're here. I'd like you to meet some people."

I assumed Thad would introduce the Gerbers to his father-in-law, and he did. But then Thad turned to *me*. I froze as he said, "Glenn, it's my pleasure to introduce Brody Norris, an architect of exceptional talent. If things move forward with the house, we want Brody to take over the restoration and renovation."

It was news to me—and welcome news, at that.

"*Hey* there, Brody," said the legendary e-titan, shaking my hand with both of his, folksy as could be. "Sounds like you've got your work cut out for you." Then he looked at my feet, chuckling. "And who's this?"

I'd forgotten that the cat was with me. Finding my voice, I explained, "That's Mister Puss. He's in Thad's movie."

Yeats hunkered down to pet the cat while asking me, "How'd you get'm to walk on a harness?"

"Oh, he just sorta ... took to it."

"My, my. What a clever little guy."

"Thank you, Mr. Yeats."

He stood, eyeing me with a friendly scowl. "Call me Glenn—everybody else does."

They most certainly did not.

And a moment later, the cat and I followed Glenn, Paige, and Thad as the Gerbers led us into the house.

"My, my," said Glenn, looking about. "Taliesin, isn't it? The real deal."

"It is indeed," said Bettina, all atwitter (an adjective that had never previously, in my experience, applied to her). "Can we offer you something to drink?"

"Nah," said Glenn, wagging a hand, "not much time. Let's do some business." Without moving farther into the house, standing there in the front hall, he said to the Gerbers, "I understand you're reluctant to sell, and I don't blame you, so let's make this simple." He made them an offer that was easily ten times the property's going value.

The Gerbers glanced at each other, poker-faced.

Glenn continued, "And I know this is sorta sudden, and you'll need somewhere to live, and I hear you've talked about Florida, so I'll throw in a place I've got there—*real* nice, plenty of room, part of a larger estate, everything included—golf, maintenance, you name it, it's yours."

"B'b'but, Mr. Yeats," said Harlan Gerber, "that's extremely generous of you, but you see, Bettina and I, we've built a business here in Dumont. We've put our whole lives into it, and it's doing well, but we're not quite ready to retire—not just yet."

"Ah," said Glenn, nodding, "the business, almost forgot. Electrical engineering, I believe. Yeats Worldwide can easily fit that into our current portfolio." He then rattled off some formula and made an acquisition offer that made the Gerbers' eyes bug. Wrapping things up, he said, "Trust me—you'll never miss the Wisconsin winters. So how 'bout it?" He checked his watch.

Harlan looked at his wife with a nervous grin.

Bettina blurted, "Yes! Oh, *thank* you, Mr. Yeats—it's a deal."

They both eagerly shook hands with Glenn, who told them, "My people will get in touch to take care of the particulars, later today or tomorrow. Happy this worked out. So if you'll excuse me, I need to be going." Not three minutes had passed since he'd entered the house.

"Dad," said Paige, "do you mind if I stay here awhile?"

"Of course not," he said, kissing her cheek. "You've got some planning to do."

"I really do," she said, patting her tummy. She turned to Mrs. Gerber. "I truly hate to rush you, Bettina, but the baby's due in April. We'd love to be in by then."

"April?" asked Bettina. "You'll be in by *New Year's*, honey."

New Year's was only four weeks off, but I could tell from Bettina's tone that she meant to start packing that very night.

Out on the street, Thad and I and Mister Puss escorted Glenn Yeats to his vehicle. We exchanged warm words of parting, and then the motorcade roared off toward the town commons, where idling choppers awaited departure. Glee Savage hopped into her vintage Gremlin and puttered away after them. The small crowd of onlookers drifted off. The excitement was over.

Sheriff Simms stepped over to Thad and me. "How'd it go?"

"Great," said Thad. "We got the house."

"Thomas," I asked, "you wanted to tell me something? Developments?"

Thad interjected, "If you think I should leave..."

Simms said, "No, that's okay, Thad. You should hear this, too." Turning to me, he said, "We got the analysis back for the powder."

"Powder?" asked Thad.

He hadn't yet heard about the envelope from Denver—with the powder, the page from the screenplay, and the threatening demand for me to "butt out" of the investigation. So Simms and I filled him in.

"Jesus," said Thad. He asked me, "But you're okay, right?"

Simms said, "Brody was never in danger—other than being terrorized, which is bad enough. The powder wasn't a biohazard, but we sent it out for further analysis, hoping for some leads. The powder had an odd hue to it, sort of rusty. Now we know why. It contained a walnut shade of foundation makeup, available only from a New York company that supplies professional theaters and movie studios. It was mixed with common talcum powder."

I didn't know what Simms made of this, but to my mind, it raised strong suspicions about Darnell Passalacqua—the makeup artist, whose tackle box might also include the lavender lipstick that was used to write the note. Plus, Darnell had mentioned that before turning to the beauty industry, he had completed a degree in biochemistry, which implies a knowledge of biotoxins—or how to fake them. I hoped I was mistaken, not only for Darnell's sake, but for Yevgeny's. They were planning a future together.

Thad was truly alarmed. "Ellen's killer *must* have been someone inside the production company. This is bound to make problems for the film project."

Just then, a fluttering of chopper blades disturbed the quiet afternoon. Looking in the direction of the commons, we saw D. Glenn Yeats ascend to the heavens and shrink to a dark speck that disappeared in the clouds.

"On a brighter note," said Thad, "Paige wanted that house for me, and she knew how to get it. Talk about 'deus ex machina.'"

"Not only that," said Simms. "Talk about 'helicopter parenting.'"

CHAPTER

# 17

Marson, who had kept his nose to the grindstone at the office that day, didn't believe me when I strolled in that afternoon and told him I'd been shooting the breeze with Glenn Yeats. "He shook my hand," I said. "He even petted Mister Puss—called him 'a clever little guy.'"

Marson gave the cat a skeptical look, as if waiting for affirmation. *Meow.*

By the next morning, Marson not only believed me, but was pumping me for details of everything that had happened. I fetched the Tuesday edition of the *Register* from outside the loft, then unfurled it on the counter as Marson was pouring coffee. I told him, "Read all about it."

### Inside Dumont

## D. Glenn Yeats 'drops' into town
## for surprise visit with family here

By Glee Savage

•

DECEMBER 3, DUMONT, WI — Travel can be *such* a drag. The lines, the crowding, the delays and cancellations. But when you're D. Glenn Yeats, things are a little different. Dumont got a glimpse of the software mogul's rarefied world yesterday when he dropped into town for a quick visit with his daughter and son-in-law, a.k.a. Paige Yeats and Thad Manning.

After arriving in Green Bay on his private Airbus ACJ,

Yeats made a quick hop by helicopter to Dumont, landing on the town commons, where he was greeted by his daughter and by Mayor Clyde Wentworth. From there, Yeats and daughter Paige were transported less than a mile by motorcade—with full security detail—to Prairie Street, where they joined Thad Manning at the historic Taliesin house once owned by Thad's uncle, Mark Manning, a noted journalist who once served as publisher of this paper.

The purpose of Yeats's visit was to facilitate the sale of the house by its current owners, Harlan and Bettina Gerber, to Thad Manning, who has wanted to raise a family there with his wife. The couple is expecting to welcome their first child in the spring.

It was a whirlwind visit, with the Yeats motorcade returning to the commons approximately five minutes after it arrived.

Speaking later by phone, Bettina Gerber revealed that an agreement for the sale was reached, but she offered no details regarding terms of the deal, which will remain private. Her tone was decidedly upbeat.

The scene outside the house was festive during the "royal visit," and among the onlookers, this reporter was able to interview a friend of Mrs. Gerber, a woman who wished to remain anonymous. She agreed, however, to share background observations.

When asked if it seemed like overkill to bring in Glenn Yeats for such a routine transaction, the woman replied, "Bettina doesn't want to sell the place, period. She has her reasons."

This reporter persisted: "What sort of reasons?"

The woman's answer was vague: "Maybe Bettina just loves that house. Wouldn't you? Or maybe she's just holding out for the right offer; she's mighty good with numbers. Or maybe it's something else completely."

Whatever the reason, it now appears that Thad Manning, along with his wife and their future child, will soon come home to the house where he spent his formative years in Dumont.

And how's that for a fairy-tale ending?

Just before I left for the office with Mister Puss—not quite nine o'clock—my phone rang. The readout informed me that my mother was calling.

After we greeted each other, she asked, "What've you been up to?"

I couldn't resist: "I spent a few minutes with D. Glenn Yeats yesterday."

"Not really." Her tone was less enthusiastic than mine.

"Yes, really. He came to help Paige and Thad with their 'housing problem.' Helicopter, motorcade—a big deal, by Dumont standards."

Silence on the line.

I asked, "What's wrong?"

"He's one of *them*," she said. "One of the megarich, the elite, the one percent of the one in a million."

Since her college years, Inez had been an activist and community organizer. While she had a taste for nice things and had enjoyed what most would describe as a privileged life, she had come of age during the hippie era and still embraced the tenets of that generation. She took unvarnished pride in her disdain for power and the men who wield it—and it was easy to equate the most powerful men with the most wealthy.

"Glenn seemed sorta nice," I told her. "Mister Puss liked him; he purred."

"That's … *something*, I guess."

Changing the topic, I asked, "And what's new with *you*?"

"Well"—her voice had taken on a playful tone—"I'm *here*."

Stupidly, I asked, "Here? Where?"

"Dumont, of course. I'm sure you and Marson can use a hand getting ready for the move. You're both busy boys, and I'm … *not*. So I'm at your service. Let me help."

She did make sense. It was a kind offer, and of course we could use the help. "But," I said, "we're really torn up at the loft."

"I'm sure you are. That's why I'm here."

"I mean, I don't know where we'd *put* you—during your stay."

"Oh, sweetie," she said, "I don't intend to *stay* with you. Far too intrusive. No, I've already made other arrangements."

"Wow, that's great, Mom. I have a busy morning at the office, but let's have lunch. Meet me at the club?"

"Delighted."

By "the club," I meant the clubhouse at Dumont Country Club, where Marson and I had a business membership. Neither of us golfed—that is, not very well—but many of our clients did, and the others simply enjoyed being entertained there.

Shortly before noon, after leaving Mister Puss in Marson's care at the office, I drove out past the edge of town to meet my mother.

In December in Wisconsin, the club's grounds were looking pale and dormant. The golf course, built in the 1920s, was designed to the natural contours of the land, punctuated by rocky outcroppings that had been left by a prehistoric glacier. The fairways, groomed but fallow, extended off toward the gentle hills as I drove along the winding entryway beneath a canopy of oaks. Sapphire splotches of the noontide sky peeked through the clinging brown leaves and dappled the windshield with dancing sunbeams.

On a Tuesday, out of season, there wouldn't be much of a lunch crowd. Pulling into the driveway that circled beneath a soaring porte cochère of fieldstone and timbers, I noted the absence of the usual eager crew of college-age parking valets at the entrance. Today, it seemed, there was only one, but he was not at the podium—off parking a car, no doubt. A few tony imports had been

parked right there near the door, but the car that caught my eye
—parked front and center, befitting the sweetest ride in all of
Dumont—was a vintage Gremlin hatchback, custom-painted a
metallic shade of fuchsia and adorned with retro whitewalls and
baby moon hubcaps, with its windows freshly spiffed.

Glee Savage was on the premises.

She wasn't a member of the club, but her work at the *Register*
often brought her here to cover meetings and events at the clubhouse. Invariably, the valets treated her like royalty—and coveted
her car as the epitome of cool.

I got out of my car and stood in a brisk breeze while the valet
sprinted up from the parking lot, hidden behind a berm. Winded,
he told me, "Sorry to keep you waiting, Mr. Norris."

"No problem, Clyde." He was the mayor's son. Well into his
thirties, he had inherited his father's people skills, but not his am-
bitions. I said, "My mother is meeting me for lunch. Do you know
if she's here yet?"

"You bet. Arrived a few minutes ago. Enjoy, Mr. Norris." He
hopped into my car and tootled away to park it with the riffraff
behind the berm.

So: Glee Savage and Inez Norris were both inside the building.
Had they spotted each other yet? Although their forty-year feud—
separated by some two thousand miles—had recently achieved a
semblance of détente, I shuddered to think of what could happen
when, rounding a corner or taking a powder, they might succumb
to the forces of chance and be brought face-to-face.

Girding myself, I stepped through the double doors and made
my way along the quiet hallways past several empty conference
rooms, then proceeded toward the rear of the clubhouse, where
the formal dining room commanded a lofty view of turf and trees
stretching out to distant knolls.

Stepping into the room, I scanned the sparse crowd of din-
ers, and there at *our* table—the table always reserved for Marson

and me at the center of the window wall—there sat Glee and my mother, gabbing their heads off, tittering over champagne cocktails. I was relieved to note they'd ordered one for me as well.

They were so engaged in their conversation, they didn't even see me till I arrived at the table. "Well, *there* you are, sweetie," said my mother. "We were worried you were stuck at the office."

I checked my watch. I wasn't late; they'd arrived early, and their drinks were nearly empty. I kissed my mother, then Glee, who said to me, "Sorry to tag along, but your mother invited me."

Inez added, "I needed a ride. Hope you don't mind."

I assured them both, "Of course not." Then I sat at the table and took a slug of the champagne cocktail. "Nice."

Inez lifted her glass, agreeing, "Nice to decompress."

"Rough flight?" I asked. "When did you arrive?"

"Last night. The flight was fine."

But she hadn't phoned until that morning. Confused, I asked, "Where did you stay?"

"At Glee's, of course."

Glee added, "Where else?"

I told Inez, "Just assumed you were back at the Manor House."

"Oh, it's lovely there, but pricey, and I'll be here at least a couple of weeks, till after your move. So Glee invited me to stay with her."

Glee said, "We were up till *all* hours, catching up—and there may have been a wee bit of drinking—so if you're wondering why I look like hell, now you know."

I laughed. "Trust me, doll—you *never* look like hell."

"Welcome, Mr. Norris," said Victor, the head waiter, who appeared out of nowhere, having approached me from behind. "Such a pleasure to meet your mother today."

Inez and Glee flashed each other girlish grins, out of character for both of them. But it was difficult not to be charmed by Victor, whose attractiveness was apparent even to my lesbian mother. I reminded myself that she and Glee had shared a similar attraction to Gordon Harper, the college sweetheart Glee had intended to marry. But then Inez, on a whim, ran off with him to California and eventually produced … *moi.* This was the reason for the forty-year feud. And this was the reason Glee had come to think of me as the son she never had.

Victor recited specials and presented menus. I tapped the rim of my champagne flute, telling him, "Better bring another round." He bobbed his head and turned away.

We all watched him leave.

Under her breath, Glee said, "*Caramba*—what a view."

I looked into Glee's eyes. Then I stared at my mother. I asked them both, "Is it truly over? The grudge?"

Inez exhaled a breathy sigh. With a weak smile, she said, "That's up to Glee. I wronged her."

"To be more accurate," I said, "you betrayed her."

Inez nodded. "We were young. I was impetuous. But that's no excuse." She turned to Glee. "I'm sorry. Can you forgive me?"

With a blank expression, Glee let the apology hang there. As the seconds passed, Inez seemed to wither before my eyes. Then Glee cracked a pensive smile. "It was the crisis of my early life. But it was also a turning point—I learned to be independent."

"For all the wrong reasons …," said Inez with a slow shake of her head.

"Plus," Glee continued, "there's a silver lining to all this that makes up for everything. And he's sitting right here."

I reached to take her hand.

She told my mother, "If none of this had happened, Brody wouldn't be around. And wouldn't *that* be a terrible tragedy?"

Inez sniffled.

With the hearts-and-flowers dispatched, the tone of our table chat became more lighthearted, even chipper. Glee had once told me that she and Inez, during their school years, were "thick as thieves." Now, it seemed, they were making up for lost time.

"Don't look now," Glee said with a wild grin, leaning over her crab cakes to tap my mother's hand, "but your sister just walked in."

Inez nearly choked on her tofu-and-kale salad.

I nearly choked on my Stroganoff.

My mother's sister, my aunt, was Prucilla Miles, née Norris, the ex-wife of my current husband. She still frequented the club, usually alone, always ready to bend anyone's ear with her stiff-upper-lip musings about being dumped by her husband for her nephew—an anguished tale that had grown stale with the passing of years.

With a blurt of laughter, Glee told us, "Made you look!"

"For Christ's *sake*, Glee," said Inez, also laughing, flopping a hand to her chest.

Later, Victor suggested cherries jubilee for dessert, a club specialty, prepared tableside. We all claimed we "couldn't possibly," but what the hell, it was a celebration—Mom's arrival and the reconciliation with Glee—so Victor went to work, dazzling everyone in the room when he ignited the kirschwasser. There was even a round of applause.

While eating the hot boozy-sweet cherries, served with ice cream that melted and puddled into a heavy sauce, we gabbed about this and that.

Inez and Glee were delighted to hear that Marson and I were "adopting" Mister Puss as a permanent addition to our home, although Glee was chagrined to learn that her friend of so many years, Mary Questman, now planned to spend much of her time away from Dumont.

Both Inez and Glee were horrified to learn about my experience with the rust-colored powder and my brief quarantine at the hospital, but I assured them I was never in danger. I did not, however, confide any theories of how the powder incident might point to Ellen Locke's killer.

While finishing dessert, Inez suggested ways she could help Marson and me prepare for our move. She made notes on her calendar, and I offered to rent a car for her so she wouldn't need to depend on Glee for rides during her stay.

A few minutes later, Glee leaned over her coffee to tap my hand. "Don't look now," she said with a grin, "but Bettina Gerber just walked in."

Tricked once, I didn't take the bait. "And let me guess," I said. "She's strolling arm in arm with D. Glenn Yeats, who's dangling the keys to the jet."

"No," Glee replied matter-of-factly, "she's with the sheriff's wife."

I turned to look. And sure enough, there was Bettina Gerber with Gloria Simms, led by Victor. If Glee hadn't announced their arrival, I might not have recognized Bettina, who had dolled herself up and, literally, let her hair down; she looked like a different woman. But Gloria Simms took the prize, as usual, for style and pizazz; she made every other woman in Dumont, with the exception of Glee Savage, look a tad dowdy.

They were walking toward their table on a path that would skirt ours. As I stood to greet them, they paused. Victor went ahead to place their menus and pull their chairs.

I introduced Bettina and Gloria to my mother. They already knew Glee, who asked, "What brings you ladies out today—anything I might share with the world?" I saw her hand digging for her steno pad in her purse.

Bettina laughed pleasantly. "I'm sure no one would find it of interest." Her tone was airy and nonchalant, a decided contrast to her brusque manner during our previous encounters. She acted as if she didn't have a care in the world—and after yesterday's jaw-dropping deal with Glenn Yeats, she probably didn't.

The sheriff's wife explained, "Bettina works with me on the library's programming committee. But she and Harlan had a sudden change of plans—as you may have read in this morning's paper." Gloria winked at Glee.

"So," said Bettina, "I need to bring Gloria up to speed on a few projects I can't finish."

I said, "You're not wasting any time—moving out of town."

Bettina shrugged. "The time is right." Then she and Gloria stepped to their table.

When I sat again, Inez leaned forward on her elbows. "Tell me *everything* about Gloria Simms." My mother had a special interest in black women.

I suggested, "You might ask Sheriff Simms about that. Word on the street is, his wife is straight."

Glee Savage was rarely at a loss for words. But she didn't have much to say as the three of us finished lunch, got up from the table, and filed out of the dining room.

When we stepped outside to the porte cochère, the valet jumped to attention and said, "You're all set, Miss Savage." Clyde handed her the keys to the Gremlin, parked a few feet away.

She passed him a five, saying, "I'll wait with Mr. Norris while you get his car." And Clyde trotted off.

Inez and I moseyed over to the fuchsia hatchback with Glee, but she didn't seem ready to leave. After she and Inez thanked me for lunch—again—and after Inez reconfirmed her plan to work on projects at the loft the next day, Glee said, "You saw my column this morning, right?"

"Of course."

"The anonymous 'background' from one of Bettina's friends—you've already read what she told me on the record. But there was more to it."

"Do tell."

"Let me back up—Thanksgiving dinner at your place. At the table that day, I got curious when you and Paige Yeats were talking about Bettina, and neither of you could make sense of her attachment to the house on Prairie Street. Paige and Thad had already offered to buy it well above market value, but Bettina was adamant: no sale. Why, we all wondered, was she holding out?"

I said, "I recall that conversation—you started taking notes."

Glee nodded. "Bettina has never been very 'social,' but this is a small town, and I was aware of several women she counted as friends. I happened to see one of them yesterday in the crowd outside the house. She's probably Bettina's *best* friend, so she knows what she's talking about."

"May I ask her name?"

"She's a source, and I agreed to confidentiality, so let's just call her Madame X."

My mother gave Glee a look. "Madame X? Isn't that a tad cloak-and-dagger?"

Ignoring Inez, I said to Glee, "Okay. Madame X gave you certain quotes on the record. But what about *off* the record?"

Glee hesitated. "I'll tell you what she said, and you can take it or leave it, but you didn't hear it from me."

"Got it."

"On Thanksgiving, you described Bettina as a 'smart cookie,' with a 'head for numbers.' Makes sense—she's an electrical engineer. So it also makes sense that Bettina might be the sort of person with an interest in gambling—cracking the odds, gaming the system, sussing out the math. Turns out, Madame X informed me that Bettina not only *loves* to gamble, but got into it *way* over her head. Indian casinos are just a short drive away, and they all know Bettina. For some reason, when she and Harlan bought the house on Prairie Street, they put it in her name—business angle, I guess. And now, with all her gambling losses, the house ended up in hock for all it's worth."

I asked, "What did Harlan think about that?"

"He didn't have a clue."

## 18

Glee's revelation felt like the discovery of a missing link.

From the outset, the circumstances of Ellen Locke's death—electrocution—had suggested that the killer might have more than a passing knowledge of how electricity works, not to mention the harm it can do. Although it wouldn't take an electrical engineer to devise what happened to Ellen Locke, I'd found it oddly coincidental that just such a degreed professional, Bettina Gerber, happened to be present at the time and place of the murder.

Obviously, then, Bettina had the means and the opportunity to kill Ellen. But she was easily dismissed for lack of a conceivable motive—until now.

Now I knew that Bettina had a serious gambling problem, amassing debts that led her to borrow against the Taliesin house, which was titled in her name alone, although it was her husband's home and investment as well. For whatever reason, they must have chosen to file their taxes separately; unsuspecting Harlan didn't have a clue that Bettina had already, in effect, sold the house out from under him—to the bank.

Had there been a history of contention between them regarding her gambling? Had she vowed to kick the habit? Had there been threats of consequences if she did not? Would she stoop to anything to prevent Harlan from learning what she had done?

If so, that explained her prior refusal to sell the house to Thad Manning. His offers had been generous, but not *astronomically* generous—they weren't high enough to disguise the debt that had eaten away most of the Gerbers' investment. Nonetheless, Thad kept persisting, and Harlan was growing more interested in selling to him, despite his wife's objections.

Had Bettina, therefore, sought to quell the pressure to sell the house? Had she reasoned that if Thad's film project were dealt a death blow, he might give up on Dumont and go away altogether? Ellen Locke's murder now seemed to be nudging things in that direction—film production unions, as well as the city of Dumont, were poised to make it impossible for the project to continue.

And then, just yesterday, deus ex machina. Glenn Yeats swooped into town and made an offer, an *astronomically* generous offer that Bettina agreed to at once. It made chump change of Bettina's debts, and even if Harlan became aware of them, he would surely concede that, in the end, his wife was one smart cookie.

If my new theory was correct, Ellen's Locke's death was ultimately pointless—the house on Prairie Street was being sold after all. But Bettina didn't care. Happy as a clam, she was off with Harlan to start a pampered new life on the beaches of Florida.

Wednesday, the day after I learned about Bettina's gambling habit, Sheriff Simms asked me to meet him at Questman Center. He wanted to review the footage from the test shoot once again, and Paige Yeats had agreed to set us up with Questman's geeky but adorable A/V guy, Laurencio, right after lunch.

After leaving Mister Puss at the office with Marson, I drove over to meet Simms. Along the way, I considered what to tell him regarding Bettina Gerber. Given that my theory regarding her gambling was highly speculative, based thinly on facts and heavily on ifs, I decided not to mention this to Simms—yet.

Pulling into the parking lot, I saw that the sheriff's unmarked cruiser was already there, so I locked up and headed indoors.

When I entered the reception room outside the executive offices, Timothy set aside his nail file, telling me, "You *just* missed them. Miss Yeats took that *dreamy* lawman down to the video studio." Timothy stood. "Shall I show you the way?"

"I know where it is," I said, "but thanks."

As I turned to leave, he asked, "Where's the furbaby today?"

"He has a busy afternoon. Hairdo. Claw job."

Timothy nodded knowingly. "And people think it just happens…"

Entering the video studio, which was empty, I crossed over to the editing suite. Through its large, thick window, I could see Simms and Paige huddled with Laurencio at the console. When I stepped through the door, they turned to greet me.

"Hey, Brody," said Simms. "Thanks for coming."

He and I shook hands. Paige and I kissed cheeks. Laurencio and I shared lingering looks—no words needed.

"What I have in mind," Simms said, "is to look over the footage again—at least some highlights. It's been three weeks since we last did this, so maybe we'll notice something we've missed."

I agreed: "Worth a try."

"I've never seen this," said Paige. "Thad told me it looks great. Mind if I stay?"

Simms said, "Good idea. Can't hurt to have a fresh pair of eyes."

So the three of us settled at the table facing the seven-foot display, and Laurencio brought over a remote. Handing it to Simms, he said, "You're an old pro with this by now."

I watched as Laurencio returned to work at his console. Before he sat, he turned to look back and saw me watching. He said to all of us, "If you need anything, you know where to find me." But he was looking squarely at me.

Simms had a notebook, in which he'd marked a list with the particular takes he wanted to review from each camera. Navigating the menu file on the screen, he brought up each of these snippets, many lasting only a few seconds, and played them several times.

Much of the commentary came from Paige, seeing all of this video for the first time.

"I must admit, he's a genius," she said of Zeiss Shotwell's cinematography.

"Thad was right. This setting couldn't be duplicated anywhere else," she said of her husband's insistence on shooting in Dumont.

"My God, what a perfect little Hollywood mug! He's a natural for the silver screen," she said of Mister Puss.

With a laugh, I retorted, "Perfect little mug? Since the filming, his head's gotten so big, he barely fits through the door."

Later, Paige simply said, "Ouch," when she saw the tilted video of Ellen Locke dropping to the ground with her toes smoking in the wet grass. I watched as Wesley Sugita, himself a professional electrician, rushed into the frame just before the picture went black.

We all sat in silence, pondering the climactic moment. Then Paige said, "I suppose you've already considered the irony."

"How so?" I asked. Although I'd caught her meaning, I wanted to hear her say it.

Paige obliged. "Ellen was a gun nut—and proud of it. Even there on the job, she was armed to the teeth, just *daring* anyone to question her so-called rights. What point was served by that? None. She was just being a jerk. And then, ironically, all that firepower couldn't protect her—the chief electrician—from a tragic accident involving electricity, of all things."

Paige had to be aware that no one else considered Ellen's death an accident. Why would she try to minimize it?

I said to her, "When Ellen was killed, Sheriff Simms was standing out of sight with his deputies and the security detail. I was near Thad and Zeiss, watching the monitors. Where were you?"

"Me? Why?"

Hearing the slightest defensiveness in her tone, I shrugged. "Just trying to collect different perspectives—visual perspectives—of what happened."

"Ah, of course. I was in the catering area, watching the shoot from one of the picnic tables. I wasn't far from the vat—but I didn't look that way till everyone else did."

Simms said, "Try placing yourself back in that instant. When you heard the sharp crack of the electricity shorting, when you turned to see what had happened, what was your first reaction?"

"I was surprised, naturally. And concerned. I mean, you could tell at a glance that something was very wrong."

Simms asked, "You thought it was an accident?"

"That was my gut reaction, and it still makes sense to me." Paige collected her thoughts. "Look, Sheriff, I know you're investigating this as a murder, and you're the expert—not me—but Ellen was killed five *weeks* ago. Maybe you haven't found a killer because there *wasn't* a killer. If there was, who is he?"

Or "she," I thought.

Simms looked demoralized. The investigation had dragged on far too long, and his reputation—as well as the future of the film project—was now in serious jeopardy. What's more, I felt that Paige was taunting him. Why would she do that?

If she sincerely believed the killing was an accident, she might have been nudging him to see the light. Less benignly, she might have simply enjoyed being bitchy. Or, if she knew that the killing was *not* an accident, she might have been trying to deflect suspicion from someone.

Someone like her.

I recalled the sinking feeling I had suppressed during my first visit to her office at Questman Center, when I learned that her "higher cause" of gun control had approached the level of zealotry. I recalled her telling me, "The world's a better place with one less gun nut."

Then I thought of the threatening rusty-hued powder that was sent to my office, which contained a particular shade of theatrical makeup not readily available outside the profession. Paige Yeats, a Hollywood star, was no outsider.

Simms was saying to her, "If I thought Ellen Locke's death was an accident, believe me, I'd be more than happy to let it go. But everything points to murder, and I've sworn an oath to uphold the law—so I can't just walk away from this. Either way, accident or murder, I'll bet the answer is right there in front of us, in the video, but I still don't have enough background to make sense of it."

I said, "In your defense, Thomas, you haven't had *access* to the background you need. Virtually everyone in that video is now in California."

Paige nodded. "Sheriff, I understand—you've been hampered by jurisdiction. You can't just 'order' people to return to Dumont, right?"

"Right."

"What's the old saying?" she asked. "Something about catching flies with honey..."

From across the room, Laurencio piped up: "You can catch more flies with honey than with vinegar."

We all turned to him.

He explained, "My mother's English wasn't so good, but she watched a lot of soap operas."

"Sure," said Simms, brightening. "Don't *order* them back. Entice them back. Send them an invitation they can't refuse."

"Like what?" I asked skeptically.

Simms turned to Paige. "I'll need Thad's help with this. Let's say he plans a 'memorial' for Ellen, combined with a preview of the test scene, and everyone who was involved is 'cordially invited to attend.' Also mention that I'll be there for an update on the investigation. Word it in such a way to leave the *impression* that not attending would look suspicious."

Paige grinned. "Thad wants this wrapped up—I'm certain he'll play along. When do you want to do this? Where?"

"Soon," said Simms, "this weekend, if possible. And right here at Questman Center, if you can work it into the schedule."

Paige asked, "Laurencio...?"

"There you go," he said as a production chart of Questman's three theaters appeared on the large video display.

"Perfect," said Paige. "We could do it in the Studio Theater on Saturday afternoon. That's our smallest venue, a 'black box' seating up to a hundred, depending on how we configure it. Plus, we can feed video there for projection."

"Sounds like a plan," said Simms.

And a few minutes later, after comparing notes and agreeing on a task list, the three of us got up from the table and prepared to leave. Paige walked Sheriff Simms out of the editing suite and through the video studio. I lingered a few seconds to check my phone, then followed.

"Mr. Norris?" said Laurencio as I stepped to the doorway.

I looked back at him.

"See you Saturday," he said.

My mother had been busy at the loft all day and had offered to prepare a simple supper that we could all share after Marson and I returned from the office. Since Inez was staying with Glee Savage, we told her she was welcome to invite Glee to join us, but Glee would be working that evening, covering a monthly meeting of the library board. So it would be just the three of us for dinner— plus Mister Puss.

While Marson had put in a productive day—on *paying* jobs—I had frittered away most of the afternoon with my sidekick duties, first at Questman Center and then, back at the office, on follow-ups from the task list, coordinating with Thad Manning for Saturday's "memorial." Although Sheriff Simms had the most at stake in solving the riddle of Ellen Locke's death, I was no less eager to wrap it up and return to my true calling.

When Marson and I arrived home with the cat on that dark December evening, it was an unusual pleasure to find the lights already on, the wholesome smells of dinner simmering in the kitchen, and my mother cheerfully welcoming us as "my boys."

Marson laughed, reminding her, "I'm only three years younger than you, Inez."

"But you have a boyish spirit."

"Aha," said Marson. "I'll buy that."

We opened a bottle of wine before dinner and shared reports of our activities that day. Shortly before we moved to the table, our landline rang. Marson got up to answer it. "Well, *hello*, Yevgeny. What can I do for you?"

Yevgeny Krymov, who was buying the loft from us—the papers were now signed—wanted to know if he could drop by later to do some measuring. Several months earlier, when he left New York to begin his teaching gig in Wisconsin, the uncertainty of his long-range plans had prompted him to put all of his furniture in storage. Now that his plans had firmed up, he needed to determine what to ship and what to sell.

Marson said into the phone, "*Mi casa es su casa.* Just give us an hour first. We'll be delighted to see you."

An hour or so later, after we finished eating, Marson was in the kitchen with Inez, fussing with cleanup. I was in the living room, going through the day's mail, tossing shredded scraps for the cat to play with.

*Grrring.*

Mister Puss shot to the door.

Swinging the door wide to greet Yevgeny, I found that he was accompanied by Darnell Passalacqua, which came as no surprise.

By now, they were known to all as a couple, and the loft would soon be their new home—their "love nest," as Darnell referred to it.

Marson and Inez came out from the kitchen to greet them amid a lavish round of hugs and kisses. Inez offered them dessert—she'd found time to whip up a cheesecake that afternoon, which the three of us had barely dented—but Yevgeny and Darnell declined, having already eaten. "In that case," said Marson, "I'll bet there's still room for an after-dinner drink."

Indeed there was. Marson poured a spot of port for Yevgeny. Darnell, already tipsy, chose cognac. I was still nursing a glass of wine from dinner. Inez, who never drank much, had switched to water. And Marson had nothing.

Marson offered to help Yevgeny with the tape measure, recording the numbers and sketching simple floor plans—he was an architect, after all. While they set to work, starting in the kitchen, I settled with Darnell, Inez, and Mister Puss in the main room, arranging ourselves on the loveseats beneath the huge Mexican chandelier of punched tin.

Although Inez had been standing beside me at the time of Ellen Locke's death, she had no direct connection to the film project, and her time in Dumont had been brief. Her knowledge of the investigation was limited to whatever Glee Savage or I might have told her.

That night at the loft, Inez sat near Darnell on an adjacent loveseat. Leaning toward each other in conversation, they were so close that their knees almost touched. Inez peppered him with questions about Hollywood and his plans with Yevgeny and his involvement with the film and his knowledge of the victim, Ellen Locke. Darnell, gabbing and tippling, answered my mother with his usual manic intensity and laughable lisp.

I patted my thigh, summoning Mister Puss to my lap. When I rubbed behind his ears, he erupted with a rumbling purr.

Watching Darnell engage with my mom—hearing his gushy,

good-natured patter—I understood why Yevgeny had so readily committed to building a life with him. Their contrasting person- alities filled a void for each other.

However, while watching Darnell's extended laugh-a-minute routine, I also contemplated—for the second time that day—the rusty-hued powder that was sent to my office, which contained a walnut shade of foundation makeup available only to professionals.

That afternoon, I had thought of this while weighing the po- tential guilt of Paige Yeats, a professional actress whose motive might have been a "higher cause."

That evening, I again considered the potential guilt of Darnell, a professional makeup artist whose motive might have been a no-motive "thrill kill."

And the day before, I had been weighing the potential guilt of Bettina Gerber, an electrical engineer with a leaden secret to protect—but no conceivable connection to the walnut shade of makeup. Was I missing something?

Mister Puss reached his paws to my shoulder and slid his snout up my cheek. His purr thundered through the soft fur of his chin.

Inez said to Darnell, "It must have been just *awful*. Everyone working on the movie must have felt the loss."

"That depends." Darnell swigged his cognac. "Ellen was *not* very popular. Slept around a *lot*. But sex is not always love. Some people, they are lovers. Others, they are friends. Others, just users."

I stroked the cat's spine as the pad of his nose touched my ear. *Others just blah, blah, blah.*

Inez said, "Friends are great. But the right lover—even better."

"So true." Darnell nodded gravely. "Had a best friend forever, my bitch princess forever, but now I have Yevgeny."

*It was ugly.*

Darnell continued, "Yevgeny—my Zhenya, my beautiful gray- eyed love."

*Virginia smokehouse.*

I asked the cat, "Huh?"

*What a ham.*

Yevgeny descended the spiral stairs from the mezzanine with Marson. "Are you ready?"

Darnell asked, "Finished already?"

Yevgeny held aloft the sheaf of notes and sketches Marson had made for him.

We stood as they strolled into our midst. Marson said to me, "Yevgeny was telling me about the furniture he has in storage. Maybe we could use some of it."

I had seen a photo feature of Yevgeny's New York co-op in *Interior Digest*. It occupied an entire floor of a vintage building with Central Park views. The globe-trotting superstar of the ballet world had modestly described it as his *pied-à-terre*. The much smaller loft in Dumont could accommodate only a fraction of his museum-worthy collection of important furnishings, antique and modern.

"Yevgeny," I said, "let's talk."

CHAPTER

# 19

By the next morning, everyone involved with shooting the test scene in Dumont received an email from the film's director.

Thursday, December 5
To: *Home Sweet Humford* cast, crew, extras, investors
From: Thad Manning, executive producer and director

My friends and fellow artists, I know that many of you have wondered if there will be a memorial for our fallen coworker, Ellen Locke, the film's gaffer, who died under suspicious circumstances during our test shoot in Dumont. I understand that Ellen's extended family, from whom she was estranged, decided on private burial arrangements, allowing none of you a sense of closure for this tragic turn of events.

I cordially invite you to a program we have organized as a tribute to Ellen, to be held this Saturday, December 7, beginning at 2:00 P.M. in the Studio Theater at Questman Center for the Performing Arts, Dumont. I know this invitation arrives with very short notice, especially for those of you now in California, but I am confident you will want to attend.

The program will include remembrances of Ellen—to which you will be welcome to contribute—as well as an unofficial "premiere" of a rough cut of the scene that was filmed on the day of Ellen's death.

Further, Dumont County's sheriff, Thomas Simms, will be with us to provide an update regarding his investigation of what happened that fateful day. Many of you, of course, have already met with Sheriff Simms, and he is now especially eager to inform you of his progress.

We assume all of you will choose to attend, so there is no need to respond. We look forward to seeing you on Saturday.

In friendship,
Thad

On Saturday, I arrived at Questman Center well before two to review the planned program with Sheriff Simms, Thad Manning, and Paige Yeats. Although Marson had not been involved in any aspect of the filming, he came along not only to offer moral support, but to satisfy his growing curiosity. Mister Puss, now a member of the family, accompanied us, looking especially handsome that afternoon in his harness of tanned leather. Marson held the matching leash.

Stepping into the empty lobby, we saw a discreet sign on a brass stanchion, stating simply ELLEN LOCKE MEMORIAL, with an arrow pointing the way to the Studio Theater.

I had been in the "black box" theater for several prior events, and other than its black walls, floor, and ceiling, it never looked the same twice. Designed to offer flexibility for smaller productions, the stage and seating could be configured for virtually any type of performance—theater, dance, music recital, or in this case, a memorial service with the ulterior purpose of unmasking a killer.

When we entered the rear of the theater, Paige was down in front, near the platform that served as a stage, going over production details with Laurencio and another tech guy, who wore a headset. To the side of the stage, Sheriff Simms huddled with Thad, comparing notes, while the guy with the headset directed someone to tweak the lighting on a photo of the deceased, displayed front and center on an easel. The life-size blowup showed Ellen Locke head-to-toe in full paramilitary regalia, including assault rifle, bandoliers, a machete hanging from her belt, and sunglasses so dark they appeared black. In a word, she looked like a terrorist.

I leaned to tell Marson, "Twenty bucks: Paige chose that picture." My husband grinned but said nothing.

We moved toward the stage, and while waiting for Paige to finish her conversation with the tech crew, I examined a few floral tributes that were clustered near the easel. The most lavish of them, all white, was from Thad and Paige, but the card bore no sentimental inscription. Smaller arrangements—some in white, others a mishmash of autumnal and holiday colors—bore cards identifying the senders as Miranda Lemarr, Wesley Sugita, and Zeiss Shotwell, as well as others whose names I didn't recognize.

A side door opened from backstage, and two deliverymen hauled in a last-minute addition to the flower arrangements—this one the biggest of all. By any measure, it was overwrought, a giant horseshoe of roses and orchids that looked more appropriate to a derby finish than a funeral. A white sash with golden letters bore the words GONE TOO SOON, REMEMBERED ALWAYS. I stepped close to read the card—the sender was Conrad Houghes.

Looking over my shoulder, Marson asked, "Wasn't he ...?"

"Right," I said, "he's that disagreeable investor who met with Thad at our loft a few weeks ago. He's also the current love interest of Miranda Lemarr—and he was trying to protect Miranda from Ellen's extortion threats."

Marson said, "Talk about over the top. That sash reads more like gloating than sympathy."

"Exactly. Know what else?"

"Hm?" asked Marson.

"Twenty bucks: Conrad Houghes won't be here."

Marson reminded me, "I'm keeping track of those twenties."

Paige Yeats joined us, checking her watch. "Won't be long. It'll be interesting to see who shows up."

"No kiddin," I said.

The three of us, plus the cat, walked over to Thad and Sheriff Simms. After a round of greetings, Simms stepped me aside.

He explained, "Thad will speak first and show the video. Folks will share their remembrances. Then it's my turn, and I'll hand it over to you. Ready?"

I was. Over the past two days, Simms and I had gone over every detail of every theory, and we were now agreed on a strategy.

Laurencio was watching me. I acknowledged him with a smile while trying to focus on my conversation with Simms. Laurencio then disappeared into the control booth.

By two-fifteen, everyone who was going to be there had arrived. With soft New Age music burbling in the background, the assembly (I could not quite describe them as "mourners") turned in their seats to gab with each other. Their tone was so lighthearted, they gave the impression that there was no other way they'd rather spend a Saturday afternoon—and some of these people had traveled two thousand miles on short notice.

Thad Manning sat on the stage with Sheriff Simms, facing the "bereaved." I was surprised when Thad invited me to sit onstage with them, but I readily agreed to do so, as it would afford me a good view of everyone else during the program. Waiting for things to begin, I did a quick head count of the crowd, which numbered forty or so.

Because no one from Ellen Locke's family was present, the front row was open to all takers, but the only taker was Marson, who sat off to one side with Mister Puss in the adjacent seat. Just before the music ended, Glee Savage skittered in, representing the

*Dumont Daily Register*. Dressed totally in black (no one else had bothered), she chose one of the many empty seats near Marson.

The second row was more popular. Wes Sugita, the assistant electrician who had replaced Ellen Locke on the film project, sat with the hair-and-makeup artist, Darnell Passalacqua, and Darnell's new love, Yevgeny Krymov; the three gay men had arrived together. Joining them and sitting next to Darnell was his gal pal, Jane Douglas, mother of child star Seth Douglas, who'd apparently been left at home in California.

Also sitting in the second row was Zeiss Shotwell, the always turtlenecked cinematographer who had been secretly married to Ellen Locke—and had benefitted from her death. And at the center of the row sat the star of *Home Sweet Humford*, lovely Miranda Lemarr. As I had guessed, she was *not* accompanied by her current love interest, Conrad Houghes, who had stayed at home, sending a big-ass floral tribute to the deceased, whom he despised.

The three remaining rows in the small theater were occupied by everyone else. Most of the local extras who appeared in the test scene were present, including electrical engineer Bettina Gerber, accompanied by her husband, Harlan, both looking dreamy-eyed as newlyweds, still pinching themselves over their newfound wealth, courtesy of D. Glenn Yeats.

In addition to the extras, most of the film's technical crew and support staff were present. I didn't know many of them, but Nancy Sanderson was there, who had catered the event on the commons, along with her inamorata, Nia Butler, the city's code-enforcement officer. I was delighted as well to spot Dr. Jim Phelps, the veterinarian.

And behind the back row, standing in the shadows, arms crossed, keeping an eye on things, was Paige Yeats.

The music stopped. The silence was sweet—my love-hate thing for oboes had reached its limit.

A cough or two. A purring cat. The wooden legs of Thad's chair screeched on the stage floor as he rose to address the gathering. He waited, heightening anticipation of his remarks—what a pro.

"It's hard to find words," he said at last, "to express our shared feelings at the loss of our colleague Ellen Locke. Like everyone in this room, she lent her skills to our film project with dedication and professionalism—high praise for anyone whose life work is devoted to this quirky and magical business."

Heads nodded their agreement. I couldn't help noticing that Thad's remarks—which were clearly not spontaneous, but pre-pared—avoided so many of the words that pepper most eulogies. He made no reference to sympathy, sorrow, or mourning. During the few minutes he continued to speak, he said nothing regard-ing the character of the deceased or her sterling qualities or the void now felt by those left behind. No mention of affections, let alone love.

"In the end," said Thad, "all of us in this business are remem-bered primarily for our work. And Ellen Locke's last job was the recent filming of the Dumont test scene for *Home Sweet Humford*. In fact, everyone here was involved. Therefore, as a tribute not only to Ellen, but to all of you, I'd now like to share a preview, a rough cut, of the work we did that day." Looking toward the window of the tech booth, he said, "Laurencio?" Then he moved away as the lights dimmed and a full-size movie screen descended from the rear of the stage.

In the darkened room, we watched the edited scene, lasting just over a minute, compiled from the hours of video, the hundreds of takes from three cameras. We saw Yevgeny on the park bench, the autograph hounds in the background, the arrival of Miran-da Lemarr and her son played by Seth Douglas, accompanied by Mister Puss as Oolong. When they joined in conversation, we saw closeups of the actors and the cat.

In the audience, Mister Puss sat transfixed by the film, on high alert as his face filled the screen. Our little ham purred loudly as the room swelled with a chorus of *Awww*. And when it was over, the assembly erupted in applause—odd for a funeral, indeed.

"And now," said Thad as the lights rose, "I'd like to invite anyone with memories of Ellen to stand and share them."

Coughing and fidgeting, but no volunteers.

Thad suggested, "Wes? You probably worked most closely with Ellen."

Wesley Sugita reluctantly stood. He wasn't an actor, and his words were halting, his voice barely heard. "My relationship with Ellen was strictly professional. As for memories, they're nothing special, I'm afraid. And my feelings about her are, well … not quite appropriate for this gathering." He sat as a wave of murmurs and soft chuckles drifted through the room.

"Well, then," said Thad, stifling a laugh of his own, "anyone else?" After an awkward silence, he added, "Guess not—so let's hear from Sheriff Thomas Simms. I'm sure you're all eager to learn about his progress with the investigation. Thomas?"

More murmurs as Thad sat and Simms stood, moving to center stage.

"Hello, everybody," said the sheriff. "It's no secret that I'm disappointed. Ellen Locke died thirty-seven days ago, and we quickly determined it was no accident. Someone killed her; it was murder. And I'm embarrassed it's taken so long to make so little progress. But now that you're all here, maybe we can nudge things forward. First—and forgive me, because you've never seen anything like this at a memorial service—I'm going to show you a short video clip of what actually happened that day." With a nod to the control booth, he said, "Okay, Laurencio."

Louder murmurs as the room darkened.

Then everyone watched as the tilted video began, captured

by accident, showing the area around the galvanized vat—and seconds later, everyone witnessed the last few seconds of Ellen Locke's life. She collapsed in the wet grass, smoke rising from her toes. Wes Sugita was seen rushing into the frame just before the screen went black.

The murmurs rose to a crossfire of agitated conversations as the house lights came up.

"Sorry you had to see that," said Simms, "but now you have a better idea of what we've been dealing with—and why it's so important to bring Ellen Locke's killer to justice. Don't get me wrong. I'm well aware that some of you—a *lot* of you—didn't much care for Ellen." He pointed to the screen: "But she didn't deserve *that*."

The nodding crowd jabbered their assent.

Simms gestured to me. "Many of you know Brody Norris." I stood. He explained, "For those of you who don't, Brody has an important connection to the movie. He and his husband are the proud parents of Mister Puss—who played Oolong."

A smattering of applause. Mister Puss turned and nodded with an attitude of *noblesse oblige*.

"But Brody is also a close friend. I like how he thinks. He's offered important insights on a couple of prior cases. And today— he wants to share a few insights with *you*." Simms stepped aside.

I moved to center stage. From the front row, Marson gave me a wink of encouragement. Mister Puss purred.

"Hi, everyone. I'm afraid I'm out of my element here—I'm an architect. In fact, so is my husband, Marson Miles, who designed Questman Center."

Oohs and ahs. The locals all knew that, but it was news to the Hollywood crowd.

"Any good architect," I continued, "needs well-honed problem-solving skills. Designing a building that artfully meets the many mundane requirements of your client—that's a far cry from crime solving, I admit—but both processes involve the weighing of many variables, a keen sense of detail, and sure, a bit of intuition. Which leaves us with the underlying question: Who killed Ellen Locke?"

A hand fluttered from the second row. I said, "Yes, Miranda?"

The starlet asked, "Are you saying you've figured this out, Brody?"

"Not sure. But let's look at a few possibilities. For starters, Sheriff Simms and I have been wondering who might *not* show up today. Failure to do so could be explained by many reasons, but staying away *might* point to guilt, or at least a guilty conscience."

Miranda heaved a big sigh, which seemed almost comical. "Oh, *that*," she said. "I assume you're talking about Connie. I *told* him those flowers weren't a good idea."

For the sake of those gathered who didn't know who Miranda was referring to, I explained, "Conrad Houghes is a financial backer of the film. He strongly disagrees with Thad Manning about doing location shooting in Dumont. He's not here today— he sent that lavish floral arrangement instead—but he *was* here at the time Ellen died." I did not explain that he and Miranda were lovers. I did not explain the extortion angle regarding Miranda's past.

But I did say to Zeiss Shotwell, who was sitting near Miranda, "The day after the murder, a Friday, you left the Manor House with Conrad Houghes, sharing a rental car down to Milwaukee to catch your flights home, correct?"

"That's right, old chap. Not a pleasant drive, I must say."

"Do you know for a fact that he got on a plane that afternoon?"

"I assume so, but couldn't swear to it. We weren't on the same flight. He dropped me at the terminal, then drove off to return the rental."

I said, "I have reason to believe Houghes didn't fly back to California that weekend." I did not explain that I'd seen Houghes that Saturday at Polly's Palace, making the huge mistake of trying to pick up a black lesbian over a four-hundred-dollar lunch.

Miranda said, "Oh, I can explain *that*. Connie phoned at the last minute. He was in the car in Milwaukee—just got a call about a deal he was trying to land, so he needed to spend the weekend in Chicago."

I had no reason to inform Miranda otherwise.

Zeiss said to me, "But I'm confused. I thought you were married to ... what's her name ... Heather?"

Hand on hip, I gave him a get-real look. He was still unaware of the ruse we'd set up, with Heather Vance, the coroner, posing as my wife. He also had no clue that Simms and I had eavesdropped on the secrets Zeiss had shared with Heather. So I turned the tables on him.

"No," I said, "I'm not married to Heather. But I understand *you* were married to Ellen Locke at the time of her death."

He froze. "That was nobody's business."

Simms stood. "In a murder investigation, it is."

"But," I said, "I have a hunch Zeiss would *never* wear a walnut shade of foundation makeup—not his coloring at all."

Peering at Shotwell, Simms rubbed his chin. "Nah ... probably not."

Miranda fluttered her hand. Speaking for many, she said, "I'm lost."

Simms told everyone about the incident: "An envelope arrived at Brody's office containing a note warning him to butt out of the investigation. It also contained a suspicious powder that sent him to an isolation unit at the hospital. Analysis of the powder revealed that it was not a biohazard, but it was partially composed of a specialty makeup used in the film industry."

Simms let the facts sink in before concluding, "Brody wasn't hurt, thank God. But it proved that someone means business. And the note—get this—was written on a page of the movie script."

The collective gasp was loud enough to drain the room of oxygen—or so it seemed.

"That's *awful*," said Miranda, standing. "The note on the script means it came from one of *us*"—she made a gesture encompassing the room.

"Probably," I said. "And there was no shortage of motives. So let's look at those."

Miranda sat again. The room got quiet.

I asked, "What might drive a person to kill someone else?" Then I ran them through the litany of motives I'd considered:

"Self-defense," I said, "which might include the suppression of a secret you don't want revealed." Miranda Lemarr, who had been blackmailed by the victim, squirmed. Bettina Gerber, who couldn't let her husband find out about her gambling woes, squirmed.

"Money," I said. "Greed, pure and simple. Avarice. Advancement." Wesley Sugita, who had been promoted to the victim's job, squirmed. Zeiss Shotwell, who'd landed a windfall as the result of his sham marriage to the victim, squirmed.

"Obsession," I said. "Dedication to a higher cause." Paige Yeats, who saw the victim as a gun nut, squirmed.

"Thrill kill," I said. "A perfect crime. A murder without a motive." Darnell Passalacqua, whose tackle box of makeup supplies probably included a walnut shade of foundation from a specialty house in New York, squirmed.

Having run through all but one of the motives on my list, I paused, making eye contact with Jim Phelps, the vet, sitting near the back of the theater. I recalled our conversation in his office the day before Thanksgiving, when he said, "Seems to me, more often than not, you've got to really *hate* a person to want to kill'm."

"Hate," I said to the crowd. "Or revenge. Or even the flipside of hate—unrequited love." No one squirmed. Instead, they all seemed to ponder the possibilities.

Once again, the fluttering hand was Miranda's. "I don't mean to trash the dead, but unrequited love? For *Ellen*? That's a stretch."

I said, "But I can think of someone who had a crush on the victim—a creepy crush, a dead-end fantasy."

Miranda laughed. "*Seth*? Sure, Seth Douglas had this 'hot mama' thing going on, and it was creepy, all right—but he's a kid. He's like, what, twelve?"

Jane Douglas, Seth's mother, blurted, "How dare you! How dare *any* of you say such hateful things about Seth?" Then she mumbled, "He's sixteen, by the way."

I looked at Sheriff Simms.

He said to Jane, "Before we continue this conversation, Mrs. Douglas, I'm wondering if you'd prefer some privacy—these matters are highly personal."

"*No*, Sheriff—if you have something to say, say it here. Seth has nothing to hide. For that matter, neither do I. Are you guessing *I* killed Ellen to protect Seth from her 'evil influence'?"

I told Jane, "No, that's not it at all. Your son strikes me as a very troubled young man, but you surely love him, and I sense how you've struggled to get him on the right track. That's highly commendable."

She squared her shoulders. "Thank you."

"What's more, your struggles with Seth have been yours alone, which is all the more heroic."

Jane Douglas, a plain-looking woman working in a world of glamour, a single mother trying to build a career for her pampered son, a shit of a kid adored by the box office—Jane Douglas, the self-professed "best friend forever" of Darnell Passalacqua, who had abandoned her for a Russian dancer in central Wisconsin, of all places—Jane Douglas then closed her eyes.

I said, "Why have you struggled alone, Jane? What happened to Seth's father? His name was Nate, right?"

She inhaled deeply and held her breath. Then it drained from her, but her eyes remained closed.

I said, "About two weeks after the murder, Miranda Lemarr came back to Dumont to pose for publicity photos for the movie. Mister Puss was in them, too, so I was there. During setup, folks were talking, and your name came up. A guy mentioned that you'd been through some rough times, that your husband died a few years ago. I was curious about the circumstances, but all he would tell me was: 'It was ugly.'"

I was quoting Darnell, which Jane didn't need to know.

"I forgot about that," I said. "But three weeks later, last Wednesday night, you popped up in a conversation again, and someone *else* reminded me of those exact words: 'It was ugly.'"

I was quoting Mister Puss, which *no one* needed to know.

Darnell, sitting next to Jane, wrapped an arm around her shoulders. "It's okay, bitch princess."

Jane sniffled. "'Ugly' doesn't begin to describe it. Nate was the love of my life, the father of my only child. Where do you think Seth got his good looks? Nate was a studio electrician. He sometimes worked with Ellen. Sure, they were friendly. But then they got *too* friendly. And for some reason—I'll *never* figure it out—Nate was just infatuated by Ellen's interest in guns. I mean, he wasn't *like* that, but it must've been a turn-on. Weird, huh? So they were having a fling, and he went off with her one weekend to a survivalist retreat—whatever the hell *that* is—and he was killed. A self-inflicted gun accident, they say. But the details don't matter. Fact is, Nate died because of Ellen. Of *course* I hated her."

Jane took a deep breath, calming herself. "When Ellen stuck her hand in that vat, she got what she deserved. Wish I'd thought of it, but the simple truth is, I didn't. Anyone there could've done it. The setup was easy."

I reminded her, "*You* were there. *You* could've done it. And you had good reason to do it. Plus, as you say, the setup was easy."

"You're guessing, Brody, and guessing is cheap. But you can't prove a thing."

Stepping within inches of Jane, I looked her in the eye. "What would you say if I told you that your friend in Denver got in touch with me? My address was on the envelope—no problem reaching me. Seems there was some concern about this strange 'favor' you'd asked. Your friend wanted to make sure nothing was wrong."

There was no mistaking the terror, the defeat, in Jane's eyes.

Slumping next to Darnell, she muttered, "Oh, Christ…"

Sheriff Simms stepped forward. "Mrs. Douglas?"

At the back of the dead-quiet theater, Paige Yeats signaled for Laurencio to cue up some music.

An oboe wept.

CHAPTER

20

The mystery of Ellen Locke's murder had been solved, but two Saturdays later, in Dumont, news of it was still the talk of the town.

**Inside Dumont**

*Thad Manning's film back on track*
*for spring production here*

By Glee Savage

•

DECEMBER 21, DUMONT, WI—When Dumont County sheriff Thomas Simms arrested Jane Douglas for the murder of Ellen Locke two weeks ago, justice was served. The rule of law was restored.

At a less lofty level, however, the arrest also set into motion a sequence of events that now assures Thad Manning that his film project, titled *Home Sweet Humford*, will be produced on schedule, with location shooting to begin in Dumont this coming spring. Both the city and the film's governing unions are now satisfied that the circumstances of Locke's death present no future danger to the production company or the community.

Thad Manning told us, "We're so grateful to Sheriff Simms for resolving this tragedy. He deserves to be written into the script. In fact, I suggested it, but he just wasn't interested."

Even before tragedy struck, one of the film's principal investors, Conrad Houghes, had been lobbying Manning to move the on-location shooting closer to Hollywood. At the time, Houghes objected to the cost and inconvenience of filming in Dumont. Not any more, though.

When reached by phone, Houghes explained, "That murder had *everything*—hate, passion, sizzle. Then, nailing the killer at the victim's funeral—you can't *buy* publicity like that. This'll be box-office gold. So, Dumont, here we come."

Meanwhile, gentle reader, things are back to normal in our fair city, just in time for peaceful holidays.

B ack to normal? Easy for Glee to say. But for Marson and me, things were hectic, making our move from the loft on First Avenue to the "perfect house" on the outskirts of town, where a wooded ravine opened to virgin prairie.

We had finished the move on Wednesday and had now spent three nights under our new roof. Mister Puss adapted to the change more easily than we did—all he had to do was find a shaft of sunlight on the floor and plop into it, while Marson and I tended to the minutiae of feathering a new nest.

On the first morning we woke up there, Thursday, Marson told me over coffee, "I think we should invite a few friends over—not really a housewarming, just a casual get-together, an afternoon open house. I want them to see what you've done."

With a tinge of wariness, I asked, "When?"

"Well, it ought to be before Christmas. How about Saturday?"

"That's two days away," I reminded him. "Know what, though? Let's do it."

So we spread the word.

O n that Saturday before Christmas, we awoke to the season's first significant snowfall—not the messy kind that melts, but the *real* kind that sticks. It was a morning of dazzling whiteness.

My mother let herself in before we were finished with coffee

and the paper. She'd been a godsend. Having arrived in town nearly three weeks earlier, Inez had rolled up her sleeves and helped us
every step of the way. And now, here she was, back again, ready to
pitch in for the party. "Whew!" she said, thumping the door closed
behind her. "It's winter in Wisconsin."

"Right on schedule," said Marson. Ever the precisionist, he reminded us, "December twenty-first, the solstice."

Wearing a heavy coat she'd borrowed from Glee, Inez carried
a box into the kitchen, telling us, "There's a couple more outside
the door."

I got off my duff and retrieved them.

While Inez unloaded things—cleaning supplies and assorted
kitchen whatnot—I moseyed out to the living room, where I stood
motionless, taking it all in. The spectacular prairie view beyond the
wall of windows was the room's main feature, but Mother Nature's
splendor now had some man-made competition.

The day before, late afternoon, a truck rumbled up our driveway with an express delivery from Yevgeny's storage facility in
New York. We had gone over his inventory list, cherry-picking a
few items before he sent the remainder to auction. Our purchases
were jaw-droppers, and now, there they were, residing under our
own roof.

A pair of English Regency daybeds from the early 1800s faced
each other in the living room's main seating area; their steel-gray
suede upholstery lent a contemporary note to the fanciful antiques.
Mister Puss sprawled on one of them, looking convincingly regal.
Perpendicular to the daybeds sat a pair of vellum-covered Art
Deco armchairs from the 1930s; designed by Jean-Michel Frank,
they anchored the entire grouping with their cubist heft. The far
side of the room was dominated by a monumental French dining
table designed by Gilbert Poillerat in the 1940s; its massive glass
top sat on a wrought-iron base with silver-leafed details. No din-

ing chairs yet, but the table itself would provide the perfect grazing area for today's guests.

"Brody, my *gosh*," said Inez, stepping out of the kitchen and getting her first look at the furniture. "I've never seen such a stunning room."

"It still needs some tweaking," I said.

It wasn't finished, but it was home. And with Christmas coming, all it needed was a few friends to warm it up.

Nancy Sanderson was not only a guest, but our caterer, so she arrived first with Nia Butler and went to work. Nia wore her perpetual outfit, resembling an improvised cop uniform, but she'd spruced it up with a sprig of holly pinned to her collar.

The guest list had grown beyond the "few friends" suggested by Marson and now included our office staff, some local clients, and several lesser acquaintances—about thirty in all. They were invited to arrive anytime after two, allowing them to see the place first in daylight and, later, in the early dusk of the solstice.

Glee Savage was never shy about being first to arrive, and true to form, she rang the bell on the stroke of two. After greeting Marson and me with lavish kisses and profuse praise for the house, she leaned to tell me, "Don't forget, Brody love: I've got first dibs on a photo feature."

I assured her, "First you and the *Register*—then *ArchitecAmerica*."

Satisfied, she disappeared into the kitchen to hobnob with my mother and Nancy Sanderson.

Next to arrive were Sheriff Simms, with his wife, Gloria, and their son, Tommy. I hadn't seen the boy in six months. Now in third grade, he seemed to have grown an inch—each month. He was cute as ever, but losing that look of childish innocence. He went over to pet Mister Puss on one of the daybeds.

When Gloria ambled away to admire the view from the wall

of glass, Sheriff Simms took me aside. "Brody," he said, "I've gotta hand it to you—once again. You keep making a hero out of me."

"Nonsense, Thomas. Everything I know about sidekicking, I learned from you."

"Oh, yeah?" Simms laughed. "I couldn't believe it, at that so-called memorial service, when you asked Jane Douglas, 'What would you say if I told you that your friend in Denver got in touch with me?'"

I had never, of course, heard from anyone in Denver.

Simms continued, "I never taught you *that* technique. Where'd you pick it up—*Perry Mason* reruns?"

I admitted nothing.

Soon after, our builder, Clem Carter, arrived with his wife and was eager to give her the backstage tour of the perfect house. Gertie, our receptionist, arrived with most of our other office staff. Then came the three doctors in our lives: Dr. Teresa Ortiz, our physician; Dr. Jim Phelps, the veterinarian to His Royal Highness; and finally, Dr. Heather Vance, the county coroner (and my occasional decoy "wife").

When the bell rang again, Marson answered the door, feigning surprise. "Well, *whom* do we have here?"

"Hello, Mr. Miles. Thanks for inviting me back. Hello, Mr. Norris."

It was none other than Laurencio, the techie from Questman Center. He had seemed so set on getting to know us, we obliged by befriending him—plus, he'd been an absolute wiz with all the electronics lurking in the new house.

Next time we answered the door, it was Yevgeny Krymov and Darnell Passalacqua, who had already moved into the loft on First Avenue. Spotting his old furniture in our new living room, Yevgeny gave me a knowing nod. "You have exquisite taste, yes?"

Then, after a considerable lapse of arrivals, the bell rang again. I checked my watch; the afternoon was sliding away. I had no doubt who was waiting outside the door.

"Paige and Thad!" I welcomed them inside with hugs. The Hollywood couple was always last to arrive, a surefire guarantee they would wow a full house with their entrance.

"Congratulations," said Thad. "It's gorgeous," said Paige.

I asked, "And how about you two? Have you moved out of the Manor House yet?"

Paige Yeats grinned, looking happy—and plenty pregnant.

Thad Manning explained, "The Gerbers could hardly wait to get out of town and head to Florida. Yesterday, Paige and I spent our first night in the house on Prairie Street—what a blast from the past. But the place needs some work, some sensitive updating. Can we ask you to help us?"

I assured them, "I'd be offended if you didn't."

Paige said, "Getting into that house, with baby Mark on the way, what a huge relief. Plus, guess what."

I obliged: "What?"

"Yesterday," she said, "I heard from none other than Basil Hutchins."

I asked, "Is he *okay*?" No one had been able to reach Questman Center's previous executive director since his departure for the Canary Islands ten weeks earlier.

"Perfectly fine." Paige tossed her arms. "He never *left*. Decided to spend a while up in Door County—said he needed some 're-covery time' from his 'arduous labors' at Questman Center." Paige snorted a derisive laugh. "My guess—up there in the sticks, he was probably shacked up with some chippy—till she couldn't *stand* him any longer."

"Well," I noted, "at least he's all right."

Coyly, Thad said to me, "One more thing. Just a minor item."

"You've captured my interest. What's up?"

Thad shared a warm smile with Paige, then told me, "My uncle's coming back from Molokai for a visit. Mark's been hinting about this. Book research, whatever. But then, when I told him the news about the house—and baby Mark—well, that did it. He booked the trip. Landed in Chicago around noon. Driving up to Dumont as we speak. He'll meet us here, if that's okay."

"Of *course*," I said.

The doorbell rang. Mister Puss shot across the room to wait at the threshold, flicking his tail. When we lived at the loft, he had responded this way to every *grrring* of the rusty old twist bell. But this was the first time he'd shown interest in the more melodious chime at the new house.

When Marson answered the door, Mister Puss jumped into Mary Questman's arms. Marson announced to the room, "Look who's back!"

As Mary and her faithful companion, Berta, stepped inside, our little crowd erupted with applause and joyous greetings.

I leaned to Thad and Paige, telling them, "Seems you've been upstaged."

Though Mary and Berta had been away just over two months, they appeared to have gone through a lifetime of changes. They were both deeply tanned—not surprising—but they also seemed to glow with a new spirit, a spirit of adventure. They were dressed much differently than before, having acquired new wardrobes while away. Not to say that Mary had lost her sense of style—not at all—but there was something more earthy and vital about her look. And Berta, I noted, now dressed more like Mary herself; gone were any clues that Berta was a servant.

While holding Mister Puss, Mary gave me a big kiss. "I think His Majesty will be perfectly happy in his new home." The cat purred loudly.

"And we're happy to have him," I said. "How long will you be in town?"

"Just a couple of weeks—then off we go again."

Within an hour, with the party in full swing, dusk was descending upon the prairie beyond the windows. Marson glided about the room, ever the consummate host, tending to our guests' needs while keeping the conversation lively. Mister Puss had also been gliding about the room, mooching the bounty of Nancy's table from anyone who would offer a handout—and they all did—until the cat, sated, came over to nudge against my shins.

"Need some air?" I asked, needing some myself.

So I got the cat into his harness and leash. I shrugged into the Loro Piana topcoat I had brought from California three years earlier. I told Marson, "Taking the cat out for a few minutes."

"Sure, kiddo."

We kissed. Then I walked Mister Puss out the door.

A soft snow had begun falling, adding to that from the night before. In the cold, still air, we crossed the entry terrace and moved toward the rear of the house, where the little stream, icy but not yet frozen, rippled through the contours of the moraine, heading for the drop to the prairie. A blurry cascade of snowflakes drifted from the indigo sky.

Mister Puss pranced delicately through the snow, pausing to sniff this and that. We climbed a gentle knoll, a clearing in the trees that looked back upon the angular forms of the house and the warm glow of its lights.

I heard a car approach on the road below, come to a stop on the frosty pavement, and honk. Seconds later, the door to the house opened, and Glee Savage stepped out, looking down the embankment. After a breathless silence, she let out a loud squeal and returned to the open door, calling inside, "Thad! Your uncle Mark is here."

Thad Manning, Paige, and Marson came out the door and rushed with Glee down the stairs to the driveway.

A car door closed with a thud, and voices rose with excitement as everyone returned, surrounding a handsome man in his mid-sixties, bombarding him with a wild chorus of greetings and laughter and questions.

Glee remained on the terrace as the others stepped inside. She looked back into the falling night, calling, "*Brody?*"

I waved my arm overhead, catching her eye.

She smiled. "Come *on*." Her bracelets jangled as she summoned me. "Come and meet Mark Manning." And she went indoors.

I was eager to meet him. But at the moment, I was enjoying some quiet time among the white-dusted birches with Mister Puss. In that hushed setting, I pondered the last couple of months—darkened by the murder of Ellen Locke, but also brightened by a convergence of events with a common thread, the happier theme of homecomings.

Mark Manning had just reappeared in Dumont, where his family had roots. After so many years, he had now come home.

Mark's nephew, Thad Manning, had also returned to Dumont, where he and his wife would start a family in the same house that Thad once called home.

Inez, my mother, had come home, at least for a while—back in the good graces of Glee Savage, thick as thieves again—back in Dumont, where they both grew up.

Mary Questman had come home with Berta, if only long enough to pack for their next journey.

Yevgeny Krymov and Darnell Passalacqua had recently settled in the loft where Marson and I began our shared life—the loft where, tonight, they would go home together.

Marson and I, of course, were enjoying a homecoming of our own, moving into the "perfect house" that he had challenged me to design for us. Just us. Except—now—we were three.

There in the snow, Mister Puss looked up at me, wanting to be held.

I lifted him from the ground and warmed him in my arms. He rested his chin on my shoulder and broke into a purr.

"Ready?" I asked as his purr grew louder in my ear.

*Let's go home.*

And home we went.

•

## ACKNOWLEDGMENTS

Once again, I first want to acknowledge and thank *you*, my readers, for supplying the enthusiasm that has propelled this unlikely series. Because of it, you now find in your hands the third Mister Puss mystery, *HomeComing*.

I could not have brought this book to publication without the help of many friends and associates, including attorney David Grey, who guided me with various plot details. For their keen attention to the words on the page, I thank Amy Knupp, Barbara McReal, and Larry Warnock. A special note of gratitude goes to Lynn DeTurk, who contributed her evocative poem "Home" as the epigraph to this volume.

As always, my agent, Mitchell Waters, has been generous with his encouragement and wise counsel. And my husband, Leon Pascucci, has been a steady font of patience, support, and good cheer. My sincere thanks to all.

— *Michael Craft*

Readers who know me primarily for my seven
Mark Manning mysteries, published between 1997
and 2004, are well acquainted with the fictitious
town of Dumont, Wisconsin, which served as the
setting for the last five installments of the series, beginning with *Body Language* in 1999; that novel also
introduced the character Glee Savage. Because my
recent fiction, beginning with the 2016 story collection *Inside Dumont*, returned to that setting with
Glee still present, many longtime readers have wondered: What happened to Mark Manning?

*HomeComing* provides some answers. It also offers
a tantalizing glimpse backwards to the origins of a
distinctive Taliesin house on Prairie Street and the
tragic events that unfolded there. If you're curious
to know more about the house—and its significance
to Mark Manning and his nephew, Thad—you'll
find the whole story in *Body Language*, Mark Manning mystery #3. The original print editions from
Kensington Books can be hard to find, but the 2013
digital edition from Open Road Media is readily
available from online booksellers.

Michael Craft is the author of seventeen novels, four of which have been honored as finalists for Lambda Literary Awards. His second Mister Puss mystery, *ChoirMaster*, was a 2020 Gold Winner of the IBPA Benjamin Franklin Award, and his prize-winning short fiction has appeared in British as well as American literary journals.

Craft grew up in Illinois and spent his middle years in Wisconsin, which inspired the fictitious setting of this book. He holds an MFA in creative writing from Antioch University, Los Angeles, and now lives in Rancho Mirage, California.

In 2017, Michael Craft's professional papers were acquired by the Special Collections Department of the Rivera Library at the University of California, Riverside. A comprehensive archive of his manuscripts, working notes, correspondence, and other relevant documents, along with every edition of his completed works, is now cataloged and available for both scholarly research and public enjoyment.

Visit the author's website at www.michaelcraft.com.

The text of this book was set in Adobe Caslon Pro, a 1990 digital revival designed by Carol Twombly, based on the original specimen pages produced by William Caslon between 1734 and 1770 in London. Caslon is a serif typeface classified as "old style."

William Caslon's enduring typefaces spread throughout the British Empire, including British North America, where the family of fonts was favored above all others by printer Benjamin Franklin. Early printings of the Declaration of Independence and the Constitution were set in Caslon. After a brief period of decline in the early nineteenth century, Caslon returned to popularity, particularly for setting body text and books.

Numerous redesigns of Caslon have reliably transitioned the face from hot type to phototypesetting to digital. Among its many conspicuous uses today, Adobe Caslon is the text face of *The New Yorker*.

Made in the USA
Las Vegas, NV
16 November 2020